That's
What
Friends
Are For

That's What Friends Are For

MEL SHERRATT writing as
MARCIE STEELE

bookouture

Published by Bookouture

An imprint of StoryFire Ltd.
23 Sussex Road, Ickenham, UB10 8PN
United Kingdom

www.bookouture.com

ISBN: 978-1-910751-63-3
eBook ISBN: 978-1-910751-62-6

For Alison, Talli and Sharon – the best friends I am so lucky to have.

PROLOGUE – 1995

'Did you see the way Matt kept staring at you, Lou?' Sam Wheldon asked her best friend as they walked home from the school disco.

Louise Pellington turned to her with a grimace. 'Euw, he's our Ryan's mate, I don't fancy him in the slightest. What about you, though? I saw you looking at Reece.'

'I know, but I'm not sure if he's my type. I like my men mean and moody. Reece is too goody-goody for me.'

'I thought it would be me who would want a bad boy,' teased Louise.

'Neither of us would know what to do with one,' Sam pointed out.

'Agreed. I can't wait to get married though. I want a huge wedding with lots of guests, no expense spared, and a three week honeymoon afterwards.' Louise broke free and ran in front of Sam pretending to waltz with a partner. 'My first dance will be to something really smoochy, like The Pretender's 'I'll Stand by You'. Everyone will be crying because they will be so happy for me. I'll have four children and a big house and a dog and—'

'Four!' exclaimed Sam. 'I'm not sure I could cope with one!'

'But you do want kids?'

'Yes! I'm tired of just me and dad.'

'That's why you're an honorary member of the Pellington's.' Louise danced a little more before stopping while Sam caught up with her. 'I have enough family for the both of us. Wait until we all start having children – we'll have to start our own nursery!'

'I don't want any until I'm at least twenty,' said Sam.

'Oh, me too.' Louise linked her arm back through Sam's. 'I want to leave Hedworth and go to London, travel the world, see some life, before being tied down with a baby. And I need to find a decent man first, and I won't find him here. What about your wedding?'

'Me?' Sam paused while she thought – what did she want?

'I'd like my wedding to be a small affair,' she told her, 'surrounded by my close friends, and my dad can walk me down the aisle. I might not even have a church service, just a registry do. I'll look beautiful in a long white dress and flowers in my hair. And you can be my chief bridesmaid and wear a dress that makes you look like a fairy.'

'Thanks a lot.' Louise nudged her gently. 'And will you stay in Hedworth or come to London with me?'

'I'm not sure. It's okay in Hedworth but it's not very exciting is it?'

'No, I can't wait to leave school and move out.'

'Me too,' said Sam. 'And if my dad thinks I'll be working on the fruit and veg stall for the rest of my life, he's got another think coming. Saturdays are enough for me.'

'We should make a pact,' Louise spoke excitedly. 'We shouldn't marry anyone, or have children, until we are at least twenty-one. And we should have a double wedding.'

Sam nodded. 'Of course, because we're best friends forever.'

CHAPTER ONE

Sam Wheldon turned over in bed and faced her sleeping husband. Hands tucked under her chin, she stared at his familiar face. It wasn't as if she didn't love Reece any more. She did, there was no doubt about that. But lately something wasn't working. She didn't know whether it was because he worked away during the week and she'd got too used to a single life or if it was something deeper than that. Reece was a steady, reliable guy and not everyone could keep the passion alive for so many years, surely?

Watching someone sleep should be so romantic, she thought, holding in a sigh in case she woke him. In his day, he'd been the proverbial tall, dark and handsome man that everyone wanted but age had taken away most of his hair and added a few weather worn lines. Even so, he kept himself fit, not looking a day over twenty-eight when in reality he was pushing thirty-six.

Reece had been the school heart throb. Sam had thought he was cool from the minute she'd noticed him hanging around with her friend Louise's brother, Ryan. One night, the two of them had sneaked into the local pub, all eyeliner and lip gloss to make them look eighteen, even though they'd barely reached sweet sixteen, and Sam got chatting to him. She'd seen him around for as long as she could remember, but hadn't really spoken to him until then.

They'd been together for two years before marrying when she was twenty. Now, she couldn't remember a time when Reece hadn't been in her life. Yet …

She closed her eyes, trying not to liken him to Dan Wilshaw, the man who could make her knees quiver with one smile. On Friday morning, he'd stopped at her market stall to talk to her again and she'd been so tongue tied she'd had to resort to a nod, feeling the mortification as her cheeks reddened. Dan had noticed too and had flirted with her, making her blush even more.

She thought back to when she had first noticed him a few weeks ago. Sam sold fruit and veg at the local indoor market, having inherited the business when she was just eighteen, after her dad had died. Dan had called at one of the stalls opposite hers and bought a mobile phone. Surreptitiously, Sam watched him from a distance. He caught her looking a couple of times but she'd been quick to hide behind her own customers. Moments later, he'd walked across to her stall and bought an apple. Sam was sure it had been meant as a symbol. It was the forbidden fruit: he obviously knew she was married. Well, that and the fact she was wearing a wedding ring.

It had been a one off meeting, or so she thought. Dan had called at the stall the next day, and the next, so much so that Louise, and her sister, Nicci, who worked on the stall too, had started to rib her about him, and she'd been mortified.

Yet, when he'd caught her away from the stall and asked her to join him for coffee at the café on the next aisle, she'd found herself saying yes. Even though she knew they shouldn't, they'd swapped phone numbers and so the texting had begun.

Dan had made it perfectly clear from the moment they'd shared that first coffee that he wanted her. There was something that she wanted from him too, but she was married. Good girls didn't have affairs, did they? But the more she thought of him, the more she wanted a little excitement in her life. It was sorely missing right now.

Reece stirred, stretching his arms above his head. Sam felt guilty almost immediately.

'Morning,' he smiled.

'Morning.' She stayed huddled under the covers, hoping her body language would be enough to stop him reaching over to her.

They lay in silence for a moment before Reece threw back the duvet. He kissed her lightly on the forehead before jumping out of the bed.

'I'd better get up. I'm meeting Matt for a run before I head back to Sheffield. I reckon a ten-miler is on the cards today.'

It took all of Sam's strength to smile. But she needn't have bothered, because Reece wouldn't have noticed anyway. It had been a long time since Reece had noticed anything that Sam did – or said, for that matter.

She pulled the duvet over her head to block out the day. Already, she was counting down the hours until Reece would be leaving. After lunch, he'd pick up his bag full of freshly washed clothes that she'd ironed while catching up on Saturday night television after their customary takeaway.

Where were they heading, her and Reece? They'd been married for the past fourteen years, would be for the next fifty or so, she presumed. She wondered if he felt as bored as she was. They were definitely stuck in a rut but they had once been happy. It was just that things had gone stale. Sam craved excitement, passion, all the things that she should have been getting from Reece. And, even if she wasn't sure that she loved him any more, she wouldn't cheat on him. Would she?

She let out another big sigh. No wonder Dan Wilshaw was filling her thoughts.

Louise Pellington lifted her head from the pillow, slowly opened one eye and promptly closed it as memories of what she had done came flooding back. She turned onto her side, pushed her hair away from her face and huddled in the foetal position. Hadn't she made a New Year's resolution only ten days ago not to go off with Rob Masters *again*? She felt a tear trickle down her cheek and onto her nose.

She'd known Rob since high school and had lost count of the many times they'd hooked up over the years. After every drunken episode she'd be remorseful, adamant that this would be the last time. But when the slow, lovey-dovey records came on, she and Rob would end up on the dance floor, bodies moulded together with practiced precision, arms entwined around each other, lips locked. It was depressing really, the way they clung to each other.

Friends with extras, she'd read somewhere in her daughter's teenage magazine. Charley Pellington was fifteen and the old head of the family, as she often told her mother when Louise wasn't keen to act her age of thirty-four. According to the magazine, a friend with extras was someone there for whenever the need arose – or maybe that should be aroused? Louise couldn't even bring herself to laugh at that last thought.

Now, lying alone in her bed, she felt the shame wash over her as it always did. She knew what Rob Masters and the rest of his mates thought of her. *Loose Louise*, they called her. And they were right. It wasn't a secret; they often said it to her face. But at the time, she didn't care. Not until she sobered up and realised she'd done what she'd promised herself she wouldn't do ever again.

It all boiled down to loneliness. Louise tried to assuage some of the guilt that she felt. Rob used her. Sure, he was always there for her when she needed him. What man in their right mind would turn down sex on a plate? But in the back of *her* mind, Louise knew she used him too, and it wasn't what she wanted. She wanted someone who would love her in return for all the love she had to give.

Yet when would she ever find someone like that? She felt past her sell-by date already. All those dreams of big weddings and happy-ever-afters that she'd dreamed about as a child had accounted to nothing. Marriage had left her a lonely divorcee who couldn't get a decent man, whatever she tried. And Louise knew that if she carried on like this, by the time she found anyone half decent she'd be too old to enjoy him.

Why couldn't her marriage have survived the early years? If she hadn't caught her husband, Brian, with another woman, maybe they'd have been able to work at things.

But then again, despite his shenanigans, he'd never really accepted Charley. Charley had only been a toddler when they'd met and he'd been fine with her at first. He'd take her out to the park, showing her off as if she were his own flesh and blood, and buy her presents, spoil her at Christmas and birthdays. But the more she grew up, the more he said she reminded him that she wasn't his daughter. And the fact that she wouldn't tell him who Charley's father was became another bone of contention.

Come off it, she scolded herself inwardly. Brian leaving hadn't been anything to do with Charley. Louise had thought that by marrying him and providing Charley with a father it would be the fairytale life she'd dreamt of as a child. She'd got her man, and she had her daughter, but she wasn't at all happy. So, in true Louise style, she'd began to nag at him, constantly winding him up. It didn't take long for them to start living separate lives before eventually he left altogether.

And now it seemed she was set for a lonely life forever if she couldn't find a decent enough man. She wished she could find someone reliable, someone like her friend, Matt, who would put up with her and her ways. Someone who would love Charley as he did. It wasn't for want of not trying enough. She hit the pubs and clubs of Hedworth every weekend seeking that someone special.

How had everything gone so wrong? Was it life that had got in the way, or was it something to do with her? Because right now, Louise wasn't feeling particularly proud of herself.

After Reece returned from his run, he and Sam had wrapped up warmly and decided to go for roast beef with all the trimmings at the local pub. It had been quite pleasant, and they'd bumped into a few friends who had popped in too. It meant that Sam didn't get to chat to Reece much, which was good and bad because sharing a lunch would have given them a break from the norm. Pretty soon it was time for him to get back to his digs in Sheffield.

Their house was a small semi-detached in a quiet, leafy street only five miles from the city centre of Hedworth, where Sam's market stall was located. Martin Wheldon, Sam's dad, had died of a heart attack when he was just thirty-six. It had been sudden and brutal and she would never forget the horrifying image of him collapsed on the kitchen floor right in front of her. A post mortem had revealed a faulty valve in his heart. It had also left her an orphan, as Sam's mum, Angela, had died of a brain tumour when Sam was four.

Both Martin and Angela had been only children, so Sam had grown up very much the centre of their world. There

were no aunties, uncles and cousins, and both sets of grand-
parents had gone by the time she was fifteen. So it had been
the two of them for years, and one of the reasons why she had
only a few close friends. She didn't let people in easily.

During her teens, she'd become really close to her dad.
He'd been there for everything: laughing with her as he'd
tried to help out with her maths homework, watching over
her when she was sick, looking out for her when she was
upset about something. Before his death, Martin had worked
hard to improve the house over the years, which Sam inherited, so she was in a more fortunate position than her friends.
Having added her individual style to it for the past sixteen
years, their house now had a modern feel: all wooden floors,
chromes and bright colours. It was also her sanctuary at the
end of a day spent on her feet.

After they returned back from lunch, Reece dropped his
bombshell a few minutes before he was due to leave. Sam noticed he'd been a bit quiet on the way back from the pub and
had put it down to his usual tiredness after his long week at
work. But even back at the house, she'd seen him glancing at
her a few times, studying her, as if he wanted to speak to her
but didn't know how to start.

The conversation came when they were both in the living
room sorting out his things. Sam was squashing rolled-up
socks down one side of his holdall. She could feel the tense
atmosphere around them. It was a relief when he spoke, until
she heard what he had to say.

'Sam.' Reece shoved in another pair of jeans, studiously not looking at her as he spoke. 'Would it bother you if I didn't come home for the next few weeks?'

Oh.

Well, would it?

A sense of dread rippled through her. If she was honest, she knew how she *should* feel but it wasn't necessarily how she *did* feel. But that was more of a problem than she would care to admit.

'Why?' She laughed, a little awkwardly. 'You're not planning on doing a runner, are you?'

Reece's laugh was a little awkward too. 'Some of the lads have been offered a job in Germany,' he told her, whilst avoiding answering her question. 'It's only for four weeks, five at tops. I thought—'

'Five weeks!' Sam put down a box of mince pies left over from Christmas. Her shoulders dropped.

'It's good money,' Reece added. 'I could make double what I do on the site now.'

'Money's not everything. It's not as if we need it.' Sam glanced around their impressive living room with the best of everything in it – leather settees, a few expensive figurines and photographs, all the latest gadgets for cinema-style television viewing.

'I know but …well …'

Sam sighed, realising that was why he was packing more than he normally would. It was obvious he'd already made up his mind and she definitely didn't know what to think about that!

'If you want to go, I'm not going to stop you,' she said. 'But five weeks?'

Reece shrugged. 'It's probably going to be no more than four. And it's not as if we see that much of each other anyway. I'll be back before you know it.'

Sam's mouth hung agape. He didn't seem bothered at all. But, she told herself – part of her didn't really care either way. She *was* used to not having him around. Yet the other part of her wanted to scream out to him. *Don't leave me, not for that long. I'm lonely and I can't trust myself. I need you to stay. I want you to love me. I want to feel like you still need me.*

'You'd better bring me back something nice,' she told him instead with a wag of her index finger.

As Reece moved towards her and kissed her on the cheek before giving her a token hug, Sam pondered on this new revelation. Looking on the bright side of things, five weeks wouldn't be that long without him. He was right; they didn't see that much of each other now so it wouldn't seem too different.

Besides, all of this fantasy thinking of Dan Wilshaw could be harmful to her marriage. She owed it to them both to give the relationship the go it needed. After sixteen years together, all the ups and downs, they had to try to get their marriage back on track.

Five weeks would give them a good break, get them out the rut.

CHAPTER TWO

'CHARLEY! Are you getting out of that bed or do I have to come and drag you out of it? It's half past seven. Get a move on!'

Charley Pellington pulled her pink duvet over her head and snuggled into her comfort zone. She didn't care what time it was. She wasn't going anywhere today, despite it being a school day.

She listened to her mum going about her usual three minute dash into the bathroom before running downstairs like an Olympic athlete in training for the one hundred metre final. Moments later, the familiar sounds of *Good Morning Britain* burst forth into the silence, water gushed from the tap and she heard the kettle warming up.

More silence for a while. Then clatter, clatter, clatter. Charley checked her clock again. Only five minutes to go and she would be able to relax.

'CHARLEY! I won't tell you again! Sam's waiting for me. I have to go!'

'Then go!' Charley shouted, rolling her eyes.

'Not until I see that you're up!'

'Okay, okay!' Knowing that Louise wouldn't leave until she saw her only daughter on her feet, Charley flounced out and across the landing. She hung her head over the balcony, blonde hair hanging down as she continued. 'I'm up.'

Louise nodded. She grabbed first her keys and then her handbag, flinging it over her shoulder. 'Now, have you got what you need for today?'

'Yes.'

'Homework done?'

Another sigh. 'Yes, Mum. I'm fifteen, not five. You're going to be late, aren't you?'

'Oh, ha bloody ha. Are you calling into the market after school?'

'If I can have some money off you.'

A horn beeped. Louise reached for her purse quickly, searched about inside it. 'I've only got a fiver.' She held the note in the air.

'Cool!' Charley smiled for the first time that morning. 'I could get some new lippy from Melissa's stall.'

'I didn't say you could have it all,' Louise sniped, knowing full well that she wouldn't see any of it again once it left her hand. 'Just make sure you buy me a Crunchie for tonight.'

Another beep came from outside. 'I'm coming!' Louise blew a kiss and smiled at Charley before she left.

As soon as she heard the front door close behind her, Charley dived back into bed.

'Come on,' Sam cried through the half-open window of her car door as Louise finally emerged and ran down the path towards her. 'I'm going to get caught in traffic if you don't buck yourself up.'

'Sorry, sorry. Charley's just conned another fiver off me. Honestly, that girl thinks I'm made of money.'

'Money might make the world go round but it isn't everything,' she snapped, recalling her conversation yesterday with Reece. Almost immediately, she hoped Louise hadn't noticed her sharp tone.

She indicated right, checked over her shoulder to see that the road was clear and pulled away from the kerb. Minutes later, they were stuck in traffic.

Sam banged her hand on the steering wheel. 'Why can't you ever be ready?' she moaned. 'We'd have missed all this if you'd come out when I beeped the first time.'

Louise was busy applying her mascara, pumping the wand brutally into the container. She always added layers of the stuff, anything to accentuate her deep-set eyes. 'Ah, come on,' she said. 'I'm always late on Mondays. Anyway, who's going to sack us? You're the boss.'

'You had me fooled on that one.'

Louise licked her tongue across her bare lips and took out her lippy. 'So what did you get up to yesterday? Anything interesting?'

'Nope. Just the usual. What about you?'

Louise felt a blush slowly rising up from her neck. 'Same old, same old,' she replied, not wanting to admit what had happened.

'Club on Saturday night, pissed, hangover … Rob Masters?' Sam raised her eyebrows questioningly.

'Yes, Rob Masters,' she admitted.

'Oh, Lou!' Sam moved the car forward a few feet. 'You have no respect for yourself.'

'You don't have to remind me. Listen, is Reece home next weekend? Because if he isn't, do you fancy a night out on the town? I could do with a chaperone, someone to keep me from his clutches.'

Sam sighed. 'More like the other way round, if you ask me.'

Louise laughed. 'You sound like my mother. Come on, how about it?'

'What about Charley?'

'She'll probably be staying over at Sophie's and if she isn't, Matt will look after her.'

'Have you asked him?'

'There's no need. He's always around for Charley.'

Sam looked at her pointedly. 'You take him for granted, you know.'

'I do know, yes. But he's a darling and he adores her.'

'Actually, it's you that he really adores but I'm not going to labour that point again.'

'That's because it isn't true. Matt is just a friend.'

Louise and Matt's relationship – if you could call it that – was complicated. They'd dated during their last year at high school but things had fizzled out within a matter of weeks. Afterwards, they'd kept in touch as friends, even when Louise had found herself pregnant with Charley when she was only eighteen. But things had petered off slightly when Louise had met and fallen in love with Brian Thompson.

There had been no double wedding as they had dreamed about when they were teenagers. Louise's wedded bliss had lasted five years, followed by a messy divorce. Matt went on to have two long term relationships but, Sam suspected, he'd always have a soft spot for their friend. Even his latest relationship was off more than it was on. Matt was always there for Louise and she didn't appreciate just how much. He spent most of his free time with her and Charley. Charley got on really well with him and loved it when her mum went out and Matt came round to babysit.

'So what do you think?' Louise pressed her.

'It's Monday morning,' she stressed, 'and you're already thinking about Saturday?'

'What else is there to think about – or do around here? Live for the weekend, you know that's my motto.'

Both Sam and Louise had lived in Hedworth all their lives. It was a medium-sized city with, according to the last census, a population of around 165,000. It was well-known for a good night out if you were in your early twenties, with Sampson Street being the place to be seen, and had a few bars that catered for the older clientele. But it didn't offer that much of a difference if visited on a regular basis. Louise wasn't put off by this, though.

'And I bet you wish you had the odd weekend to yourself every now and then, hmm?' she added.

Sam didn't want to tell Louise that Reece had headed off to Germany just yet because she was still reeling from the revelation. Okay, admittedly she'd been thinking of Dan Wilshaw, but that was more because she knew that fluttering-in-her-tummy feeling when she saw him was what she really wanted back with Reece.

She sighed, wishing there was a way that she could get things re-ignited with Reece again. She shouldn't even be thinking of anyone else. Infidelity wasn't something she wanted in her vocabulary.

Louise wasn't giving up on her night out that easily. 'I suppose Reece could come too, if he's around. At a push, I could deal with that.' She twirled up a lipstick and moved it onto her lips.

Sam nudged the car forward a few lengths and decided to change the subject. 'I'll think about it. How is my god-daughter, by the way? Still being hormonal?'

'As ever.' Louise flicked up the mirror on the windscreen visor and turned back to Sam with a pout. 'I can't believe how she's changed over the past couple of years. The minute she turned into a teenager, she's been nothing but moody and stroppy. I wish I knew what she was getting up to. I've been looking for her diary but she must take it with her. I haven't been able to—'

'You've looked for Charley's diary!' said Sam, shocked.

'Of course I have. I had one at that age.'

'Yes, but Sandra didn't read it!'

'My mum would never have found it, the amount of times I had to hide it because of Ryan.' Ryan was Louise's older brother by two years. 'I also know that she'd have killed me if she *had* read it. I know what I got up to at that age, so I worry about Charl.'

'You did alright.' Sam wouldn't let Louise become the martyr, as she was prone to doing.

'Yeah, sure,' Louise scoffed. 'Single mum at eighteen. That's a fine example to set. I don't want her getting caught like I did.'

Sam fiddled with the radio while she waited for the traffic lights to change. Two more sets of lights and they'd be there.

'Oh, I know she added a lot to my life,' Louise continued, 'but you know what I mean. If I hadn't had her when I was so young—'

'Oh, stop moaning. Charley's a good kid. She won't make the same mistakes as you.'

Louise's head turned ninety degrees sharply. 'Well, thanks for the vote of confidence,' she snapped.

'Well, thanks for confiding in me,' Sam snapped back.

'Oh, don't start that again.'

Louise and Sam had been friends since their first day at nursery school. By the time Louise had hung her coat up on the peg with the white star sticker next to Sam's green pear, they'd already formed a friendship that would take them through the next thirty years. But there was one secret between them. When Louise became pregnant not long after her eighteenth birthday, Sam supported her through antenatal classes, labour pains, Charley's terrible twos and beyond. But Louise never told anyone who Charley's father was. Over the years, Sam got used to not knowing but still she didn't like it.

'Anyway,' Louise added. 'I feel like I'm seventy-four not thirty-four. I'm just so bored. A good lashing in the pub will do me the world of good.'

'You do that every week!' Sam lowered her voice. 'Look, I don't mean to be all preachy, but I worry about you.'

'I know, and I love you for it, but really, I'm okay.' Louise nodded her head vehememtly. 'So, how about it?'

Arriving at the market, Sam drove into the car park, thankful there were a few spaces left for the traders. She switched off the engine and pulled up the handbrake.

'I don't know if I'm up to it,' she replied. Glancing in the mirror before she got out, Sam noticed how pale she looked. It was only her short, red hair flicked under at the ends and framing her face that gave her some much needed colour. She wore neutral-coloured makeup, the heavy lids above blue eyes denoting her lack of sleep. She hoped she wouldn't wear her heart on her sleeve, worrying about Reece's sudden need to leave her for longer than a week.

'What's the matter?' Louise's seatbelt flew back as she unbuckled it. 'You're not coming down with anything, are you? You do look a little peaky.'

'Actually,' Sam fibbed, seeing this as a way out of a long and lengthy marriage guidance session if she did spill the beans. 'I do feel faint, if you must know.'

'Don't worry. You'll be fine by Friday.' Louise opened her door and then turned back to her friend. 'Even more so once you've got a few vodkas down your neck and finished them off with a kebab supper. Shall I book the taxi for eight?'

Sam sighed as she locked the car door. Sometimes she wished that Louise would grow up and think about someone else for a change. Charley was far more well-behaved for her fifteen years.

But then again, perhaps it was time to worry about herself more. The fact that she was starting to preach to her best friend about her going out too much made her own life seem boring in comparison.

As soon as the door shut behind her mum, Charley dived back into bed. She reached for her phone to text her friend, Sophie, but there was already a message waiting from her.

'What were you up to on Sat night? You never told me what you did when I saw you yest.'

Charley sighed. That was all she needed, rumours going around the school that she was frigid. On Saturday evening, Matt had called round to look after her because her mum was going to be out late. Charley didn't need a babysitter as such but Matt was a family friend and her mum preferred someone to be around if she was going to get home later than midnight. Besides, Charley adored Matt. He was part of the furniture at their house. Often he'd take time out to chat with her about school and TV programs. She could ask him advice about most things too.

Charley had told him she and Sophie were going to the shops and she'd be home by ten. Well, she wasn't lying about the shops. But she didn't tell him they were meeting up with some of the lads from school. She'd hooked up with Aaron Smithson. Nothing had happened though, apart from a snogging session. But Aaron had been really annoyed when she'd stopped his wandering hands, and then he'd gone off in a strop. It was one thing to try it on, but to persistently continue when she'd said no, and sulk when he didn't get his own way? She'd decided yesterday she would finish things when she saw him next. There was no way she was putting out to someone who didn't care about her.

She texted Sophie back.

'Didn't do anything. Come round. Tell you then. Coast clear.'

Ten minutes later, the two of them were in the kitchen. Charley made coffee for them both. Even though she was still in her dressing gown and pyjamas, her hair had been straightened and she had added a bit of make-up, lippy, eye shadow and mascara. If she had been ready for school, she would have looked like a mirror image of her friend, with their slight frames and long legs that were perfect for the short skirts that were rolled up at the waist. When they were out together, they looked more like twins than friends.

With a sigh, she flopped down at the tiny kitchen table, shoved into a corner that was barely big enough for it. Although Mum tried her best to keep on top of everything, and the house was always spotless, the kitchen in the terraced house was in need of a good lick of paint, the years-old lino flooring in bad need of replacement. Money was tight with just Louise working but she made it as homely as possible. And there was always food on the table, so Charley couldn't complain.

Sophie was dressed in school uniform, a striped tie hung down in front of a v-necked maroon jumper, short navy skirt and thick black tights worn with Doctor Martens. She shrugged off her coat and turned towards her friend. 'So tell me, Charley the tease. Did you or didn't you?'

Charley looked on in disinterest. 'Did I or didn't I what?'

'You haven't got a clue, have you?' Sophie gasped, covering her mouth with a hand. 'I thought you'd have had at least one text message from someone other than me.'

'Sophie,' Charley sighed in exasperation, 'what is it I'm supposed to have done this time?'

Sophie didn't hold anything back. 'Aaron's telling everyone he shagged you on Saturday night, that you also gave him a blowjob and that you *swallowed*.'

Charley nearly fell off her chair. 'He said what! When? But … how do you know all this? I only saw you last night and—'

'Never mind that.' Sophie pulled out a chair. 'Why didn't you tell me? I was –'

'I didn't tell you because nothing happened!'

Sophie looked up to see Charley's distraught expression.

'I know!' she said quickly. 'It was a joke. Sorry.'

'I would have told you,' said Charley. 'Especially if I had done *that*, you know I would. I mean come on, you think I'd put my mouth around Aaron's … yuck. I would never. Not yet, anyway.'

Sophie and Charley had set themselves a moral code of sexual conduct. As soon as they reached their teens, they'd made a pact not to sleep with anyone until they were absolutely sure that it was right for them. They didn't want to be called slags, slappers, or whatever else the boys at school would come up with before dumping them to move on to the next conquest. And both of them had been scared when one of their school friends, Chloe Whitaker, became pregnant at fourteen. As for the thought of anything oral? Charley was saving that for when she was more grown up. Besides, she didn't want to end up like her mum, pregnant with her at eighteen. It was her worst fear.

'Aaron Smithson is an idiot.' Sophie reached for the biscuit tin, opened it and sighed when she saw it was empty. 'Anyway, don't worry. It'll all blow over soon.'

Both girls burst into laughter at Sophie's unfortunate choice of words.

Charley folded her arms. 'I was thinking of skipping school anyway. Fancy it?'

Sophie nodded. 'You can tell me about Alex too. I want to know all of the gossip.'

Charley beamed then. Alex was a boy she'd met online about a month ago. They'd started chatting quite often and last week they'd exchanged WhatsApp messages. Charley looked forward to every one of them.

'Okay.' She nodded in agreement. 'But let's hit the shops first, see what's going down.'

Sophie giggled. 'Well, it sure as hell wasn't you!'

CHAPTER THREE

Hedworth Shopping Centre was a tiny place in comparison to some, more the size of a large department store in a major city. Over its two floors, there were a few high street stores to tempt the serious city shoppers, as well as a few of the local suppliers. A high street to its right and a few smaller streets behind it made up the bulk of the shops.

Long before Sam was born – even before her parents, too – the indoor market used to be situated next to the town hall and was the cornerstone of Hedworth. When the new shopping centre had been built in the late eighties, the market had been relocated. This latest place was perfect for browsing trade or for people who knew exactly what they were after. Good quality, locally produced food and fresh items were all found there.

In front of the modern red brick building a pedestrianised cobblestone walkway ran its length, large stone plant pots dotted here and there for extra colour. In summer, when the flowers were in bloom it was a beautiful place to relax and have a sandwich at lunchtime. In winter, its shadows were long but it never looked dull in the dim light.

Monday mornings were always manic in Hedworth. The doors to the market were only closed at five thirty on a Saturday evening but by the time Monday came around, it was as if they'd been shut for a month.

Sam loved the hustle and bustle of the place. Bang on the dot of eight, her delivery would arrive and they'd start to stock the stall. She had a walk-in booth, twice the size of the original one that she'd inherited from her dad. Back then, the stall had been one tiny table in the far corner. Over the years, she had expanded and now stocked organic food and exotic fruit as well as her normal range. A framed photo of her parents took pride of place on the back wall, moving with her several times as she had relocated to larger stalls. Now, this one was in the middle of an aisle, in prime position, and she had two full-time staff, Louise, and Louise's younger sister, Nicci.

'Morning, Sam. Grand day again,' Duncan Tamworth greeted her, as he carried in trays full of bananas. He placed them carefully on the floor before standing up and rubbing his back. His small and portly frame wasn't really meant for lugging heavy items around.

'You need to get that seen to, Duncan,' Sam told him as she pulled back the tissue paper to inspect her merchandise. 'It'll only get worse lugging all this about. Louise, give Duncan a hand, will you?'

Louise, who was making a hot drink, put down the coffee jar with a sigh. 'I'm coming, Mrs slave driver. Since when did anyone start the day before drinking at least three mugs of coffee?'

Sam ignored the comment. Louise always had some excuse not to start the minute she walked through the door. Even though she'd been working on the stall for the past seven years, she never failed to realise that if she got all the sorting finished for eight thirty, they could sit down for a coffee in peace. Sam needed everything shipshape for when the first customer was let in. From nine a.m. every Monday morning, it would be manic until around two o'clock when it would start to die down a little. At least, she reminded herself now, the morning rush gave her no time to think about Reece – or Dan Wilshaw.

Once Duncan had gone and apples and oranges and bananas were on the shelves, along with sacks of potatoes and carrots, and every imaginable salad vegetable had been placed in their baskets, Sam finally felt herself relax. She checked her watch. Now it was time for coffee.

'Tell me more about Saturday night,' she encouraged Louise, as she flicked on the kettle and grabbed three mugs from the wooden rack Reece had put up in the tiny partitioned room he'd created at the back of the unit. 'Why get down and dirty with Rob again?'

Louise pulled her hair into a ponytail and fastened it back with a covered elastic band. 'Oh, I don't know.' She sighed dramatically. 'It must be the booze. I always feel like that when I go on the vodka.'

'Then stay on lager.' Sam passed a coffee to her.

'Good morning, lovelies.' Nicci Pellington beamed as she squeezed herself into the room. 'How goes it on this fine day?'

'At least I see one of us had a good weekend,' Louise muttered.

After she'd taken off her coat, Sam passed Nicci a mug too.

'Yes, I did.' Nicci grinned. 'We had a cosy night in on Saturday, if you catch my drift. Then a long lie-in on Sunday morning—'

'Oh please,' Louise complained with a grimace. 'You're my baby sister. That's too much information.'

'Jealousy will get you nowhere.' Nicci wagged a finger at her. 'Anyway, I'm not sad and single, nor married, so I get lots of loving.'

'Well, that puts me in my place, too,' Sam laughed. She picked up her drink and moved past her, leaving the sisters to it. For all their bantering, they got on really well most of the time. Louise was the middle child of three. Her brother, Ryan, was thirty-six. Nicci was twenty-seven and often told everyone that her mum said she was the best mistake she'd ever made. Louise had been seven when Nicci was born and her status of youngest child disappeared overnight. She couldn't even say that she was the only girl. From the first day Nicola Pellington arrived home from the hospital, Louise seemed to develop middle child syndrome. To this day, Sam didn't think it had ever left her.

Nicci was practically a double of her older sister, which unfortunately for Louise was a nightmare. The years between them only showed up her wrinkles. Both women naturally had dirty brown hair like their dad: both of them had it dyed chocolate brown every few weeks. They were the same height at five foot six apiece and apart from a stone in weight could hardly be told apart when seen from the back view. Many customers mixed their names up – much to Louise's delight, and Nicci's dismay, over the years.

While Nicci checked her make-up in the small mirror above the sink, Sam pulled the final few boxes out into the aisle.

'Morning, Sam. Good weekend?' Melissa Harper shouted across to her. A small and curvy brunette in her early forties, Melissa sold make-up and accessories. Her stall was always a riot of colour. She was busy at the front of it, throwing items into the bargain basket.

'Good, thanks,' Sam fibbed and feigned a smile. 'You?'

'Not too bad, but it's all over so quickly, isn't it? One minute we're leaving here, the next it's Monday morning again. It's like groundhog day.'

'Tell me about it.' Sam waved to Clara over on the shoe stall at the end of the aisle. She was hauling a trolley piled high with boxes, no doubt full of the latest designs in footwear. Clara sold cheap and cheerful shoes but she always went to great lengths to give the women of Hedworth something good for their money. For Sam's mind, Hedworth was definitely short on good shoe shops. There was Chandlers on the high street but they weren't as fashionable, and only a few collections could be found upstairs in the larger shops.

Sam threw out her hand and caught an apple as it tried to escape her stall. She carefully put it back in its place before glancing around at the place she knew so well that it could be her second home. Sam had grown up with most of the stall holders. Many of them had known her since she'd been born and had tales to tell of how she'd sat in her pushchair while her parents worked around her. How her mum worked part-time until Sam started school. How shocked they were when Angela passed away so young. How devastated they were when Martin died suddenly.

There were twenty-eight stalls in total, fourteen stalls in their aisle, seven each side. Along with Melissa selling make-up and Clara selling shoes, there were stalls for most occasions and needs. Haberdashery, knitting, clothing, underwear and car accessories. Cupcake Delights sold the most heavenly cakes that none of them could resist come three p.m.

Geoff Adams sold the best home baked scones and flat breads she'd ever tasted. Then there were greetings cards, a fancy dress stall and a T-shirt printing stand. At the back of the market were all the meat and cheese counters. Across the way, Ryan and Matt sold mobile phone accessories. Ryan was Louise and Nicci's brother and they all knew Matt as a friend from school.

Just to her right, Sam caught Malcolm Worthington out of the corner of her eye. A tall and thin man with short grey hair, Malcolm and his wife, Maureen, sold sweets. Sam knew that Nicci hoped that some day in the future they'd be her in-laws when she married their son, Jay.

Today there was some kind of commotion going on in front of the stall. Louise noticed it too when she joined Sam a few moments later.

'Who's that?' Sam asked, spotting Ryan and Matt talking to a young woman. 'Does she look familiar to you?'

Sam turned to look again. She did recognise her vaguely but she couldn't think who she was.

'Oh, no. Please tell me it isn't.'

Both Sam and Louise turned as Nicci joined them with a groan. 'It's Jay's sister, Jess,' she explained. 'She must be back from London.'

'Ah, the prodigal one,' said Sam, understanding the groan immediately.

'Yes, she's a bit of a black sheep,' said Nicci. 'She moved to London a few years ago after being caught having an affair with a man she was working for.'

'Didn't you know she was here?' Louise asked.

Nicci shook her head. 'Jay told me she was thinking of coming back, but we had nothing more concrete than that.'

All three women stood in a line watching Jess Worthington busy flirting and pouting at Ryan and Matt.

Jess was tall like her father, and skinny like her mother. Her dark hair hung down in waves, the expensive cut of her jeans accentuating her long legs. Above them, a thick Aran jumper and a multi-coloured scarf with fingerless gloves to keep her hands warm and her fingers free to work.

Louise puffed and folded her arms to show her disgust. 'If she pushes her chest out any further, we'll be able to have a feel from here.'

'She's really pretty, though, isn't she?' said Sam, still looking over at them.

'Well, she looks pretty desperate, if you ask me.'

Sam laughed and nudged her friend playfully. 'Like you, you mean?'

Louise grinned back at her, realising how patronising she sounded.

Nicci frowned before catching the gist of the conversation. 'Oh, Louise.' She shook her head. 'Please don't tell me that you ended up with Rob Masters again!'

Although Jess loved all the attention she was getting that morning at the market, she would much rather have been in London. At eight forty-five, she would just be coming up from the tube at Paddington station and grabbing her daily coffee and blueberry muffin. She would be making her way to the offices she worked at, to the desk where she would open her emails and check Laurie Porter's appointments for the day.

Well, she would have been doing all that – if Laurie hadn't decided to finish things with her the minute she told him her news.

Jess had worked at Porter's Finance as Laurie's personal assistant for the past four years; and for three and a half of those years, she'd been sleeping with the boss. It was the reason she'd wanted to stay in the job for so long. The pay wasn't much but the joy she received as his bit on the side had been worth it. She'd played the game well, or so she'd thought.

Now she found herself back in the godforsaken place of Hedworth, although she was trying to keep a low profile this morning. Attention to the stall would bring Nicci across to question her and that was another thing she was dreading. Nicci and Jess had been in the same year at high school. They hadn't liked each other then and the bad feelings had escalated even more since Nicci became an item with her brother, Jay.

She lifted her head as she heard laughter. Although she hadn't seen either of her brother's friends, Ryan Pellington or Matt Goodridge in a while, Jess knew them well. They had often been round her house when she was younger. Now they reminded her of the Mitchell brothers from *Eastenders* – all clean shaven and muscly, with hardly a hair on their heads between them. Ryan oozed a raw sex appeal like Ross Kemp. Matt wasn't too far behind either.

'Hiya, Jess.' Sam came up behind her, closely followed by Louise.

Jess smiled widely at her, ignoring Louise. She'd always got on well with Sam when she'd seen her out with her husband. But she had never been much for Louise, and she was glad that Nicci hadn't come across too.

'Hi, Sam,' she said. 'How are you?'

'Good, thanks. What brings you back to Hedworth? I thought you were settled in London?'

'Got another guilty secret?' Louise asked snidely, before Jess could reply.

'Wouldn't you like to know?' Jess chided. 'Actually, I needed a bit of space so I thought I'd help out on the stall. Besides, it gives Mum and Dad some spare time if I'm here, doesn't it, Dad?'

Malcolm Worthington beamed at his daughter. 'It certainly does, love. We could always do with an extra pair of hands.'

'If you need any help,' Sam pointed down the aisle, 'we're not far away. You know us all, and I'm sure Nicci will be across to say hello soon.'

'Oh, I doubt that very much.' Jess pulled her face at the impending argument. Later that morning she was going to ask her dad if he would speak to her brother and see if she could stay with him and Nicci for a while. For the past few nights, she'd been at her parents, but just recently, they'd downsized to a bungalow and there was hardly room for the two of them, never mind Jess and all her belongings.

Sam had seen the same expression on Nicci's face when she'd suggested that she said hello to Jess. But before she could question Jess any further, Louise butted in.

'Why's that then?' she asked. 'Got something to hide?'

'Mind your own business.' Jess gave her a filthy look. 'You're only after finding the gossip and I'm not going to give it to you.'

Louise shrugged her shoulders. 'It'll all come out in the wash. Nothing stays secret around here for long. You should know that after the last time you left.'

'That has nothing to do –'

'Blimey, is that the time?' Malcolm Worthington pushed past them with an armful of boxes. 'Don't you lot have anything to do before we open? Come on, away with you.'

* * *

Once the morning rush was underway, by ten thirty all thoughts of the weekend had long since been forgotten. Sam waited for a lull in trade before heading out to pick up a few items they had run short of.

'We need some plastic bags,' she said, ticking off things with her fingers. 'And some yellow stickers. Oh, and a roll of Sellotape. Anything else while I'm there?'

Louise and Nicci couldn't think of anything, so she set off for the stock room at the bottom of the market.

Sam located the items she required, plonked one box on top of the other and headed back. She was nearly at the door when she spotted Dan Wilshaw walking right towards her. She felt her heart quickening at the sight of him. He wore a long black coat over tailored, pin-striped trousers, slick square-toe boots and a pale blue shirt, open at the neck to reveal a few black hairs curled tightly on his chest. Immediately Sam cursed the fact she hadn't made more of an effort to conceal her lack of sleep. But with no mirror she didn't have time to check her appearance. Deliberately, she pushed the boxes further up so that he couldn't see too much of her face.

'Hi,' she managed to say, feeling the heat of an emerging blush. 'This is staff only. You really shoudn't be in here.'

Dan smiled warmly. 'I was just passing …' He removed the top box and placed it on the window ledge next to them. Then he grabbed the other box but, instead of taking it from her, pushed Sam gently back until she felt the wall behind her. His face was inches away from hers, only the box now separating them, he gazed into her eyes.

'I want to be with you, Sam Wheldon,' he spoke softly.

Sam gulped. It was hard to do anything else in close proximity to the man of her fantasies when he was staring at her intensely.

'I'm married, Dan,' she stuttered a few moments later.

'But we shouldn't let that stop us.'

'St— stop us?'

Before she could protest, he leaned closer and kissed her. Afterwards he pulled away, gazed into her eyes for a long second. Then he kissed her again, just enough for her lips to ache for more.

'Dan, stop,' she whispered without meaning. 'Someone might see.'

But Dan just pushed his chest forward. The flimsy cardboard box between them began to shudder. At least it was covering her breasts, thought Sam, feeling no less safe as the box began to collapse in on itself.

She prayed that the exit door leading to the public would stay closed for ever as Dan kissed her again. This time he kissed her properly. Tenderly, he nibbled her bottom lip before easing her mouth open again with his tongue.

Eventually they broke free.

'You are one sexy woman, Sam Wheldon,' he told her, looking from her eyes to her chest and back to her eyes again. 'What's a man got to do to get some time with you?'

'I can't be with you. You know that I'm –'

'I have to see you.' Dan's hand moved to cup her chin and he gazed into her eyes again. She swallowed down the feelings erupting inside her. She hadn't felt this way in a long time with Reece. This was so wrong, yet … so right.

Suddenly, the door crashed open and Mike Sharpe pushed a trolley full of rubbish through it, cursing loudly. As if burned, Dan moved away and Sam stooped to pick up the box and its contents strewn across the floor.

'Bleeding trolley,' Mike grimaced as he walked past them. 'Wonky wheel, if you ask me but will the council shell out for a new one? I don't think so. Oh, Sam, Louise told me to tell you to hurry up and get your arse back to the stall.'

'I'm on my way.' Sam reached up for the box on the window ledge and piled it on top of the other one, hoping to hide her blushes. Once Mike had disappeared, she looked at Dan. They burst out laughing, Sam with relief that they hadn't been caught.

'I feel like a love struck teenager,' Dan said, grabbing Sam's bottom as they walked back towards the door.

Sam took a step away from him. 'Don't do that.'

Dan raised his hands in mock surrender. 'I can't help it.'

'Well you'd better stop because that will have to be your lot.' Sam tried to talk with her head and not her heart. 'I've told you, I'm married. You shouldn't have kissed me and I shouldn't have kissed you back. I don't think we—'

Dan pressed her up against the wall.

'No, this is wrong!' She pushed him away, grabbed the boxes and began to walk quickly away.

Cheeks burning, she made her way back to the safety of the stall. She was married. Good girls don't say yes, do they?

CHAPTER FOUR

'About time,' Louise cried, as Sam arrived back at the stall feeling all hot and flustered. 'We've been rushed off our feet. Where have you been?'

'Sorry!' Sam practically shouted. 'I couldn't find what I was looking for.'

'Dan came by about ten minutes ago asking after you.' Louise lowered her voice as she weighed out a kilo of apples for a young woman.

'I never saw him!' Sam practically shouted.

Louise quickly finished serving and turned back to her with a frown. 'What's going on?'

'Nothing!' She handed a box of bags to Louise. 'Pop these behind the counter, will you?'

Sam sought refuge in the staff room while she tried desperately to control her reddening skin. But every time she thought about what she'd done, it caused her to blush even more. Had she really kissed another man? She ran a fingertip over her lips. At first, Dan's lips had barely touched hers, as if he knew how anxious she was at the thought of what it might lead to. Then she remembered his lips moving lower, his tongue…she fanned her face with her hand. She was blushing again!

'Coffee?' She held the kettle in front of her face as Louise walked in, hoping she wouldn't notice her rosy cheeks.

'Yes, thanks, I could murder one.' Louise nodded gratefully. 'There's no one waiting to be served at the moment, and Nicci's out there anyway. I'll watch through the door while the kettle boils.'

Sam turned her back and busied herself adding coffee to their favourite mugs.

'Come on, spit it out,' Louise said eventually when Sam wasn't forthcoming with any chat. 'What's happened?'

'What?'

'You're blushing the colour of a tomato.'

'It's just hot in here.' Sam turned to her and rolled her eyes.

But Louise wasn't giving in. She folded her arms and stared at Sam.

Sam bit her lip before speaking again. 'Dan Wilshaw came to find me in the store room and he— he kissed me.'

'No!' Louise covered her mouth with her hand. 'What did you do?'

Sam grimaced. 'I kind of kissed him back.'

Louise gasped this time.

'Don't make a big fuss about it,' Sam begged her. 'It was only a kiss.'

'Only a kiss?' Louise glanced to see if Nicci needed any help and turned back to Sam when she didn't. 'Don't you realise that kissing a man can be more intimate than sleeping with him?'

'You must have read that somewhere.' Sam batted the comment away with her hand. 'It was just a kiss and it won't happen again. I told him to—'

'Sa-am,' said Louise. 'Sam! Look at me. No, actually, look at *you*! Your eyes are shining and you're virtually hyperventilating. Tell me what happened.'

'I don't really remember,' Sam said truthfully. 'One minute I was talking to him and the next he had me pushed up against the wall kissing me with a passion. Honestly, Louise, he's made me feel better than I remember feeling for a long time.'

The look on Louise's face was comical. Her best friend seemed as if she didn't know whether to shout at her or give her a high five.

'What happened after he kissed you?' Louise asked, pushing the door shut when she saw Nicci approaching.

'He kissed me again and I was all in the moment. If Mike hadn't interrupted us, I don't know what would have happened.'

'Where's my coffee?' Nicci asked as she pushed open the door and joined them. 'I'm gagging for a brew.' She looked at the glances shooting between Sam and Louise. 'What have I missed?'

'Dan Wilshaw just kissed Sam!'

'Louise!' Sam sounded distraught.

'Well, that's what happened, isn't it?'

'Yes, but I don't want everyone to know.'

'I don't know how you can take the moral high ground after you slept with Rob Masters again,' Nicci remarked in Sam's defence.

'Thanks, Nicci,' said Sam, 'but Louise is right. I shouldn't have kissed him back.'

'No, you shouldn't have.' Louise paused. 'But spill the beans. Was he good?'

'Jeez, I'm in the middle of a crisis and all you want to know is if he's a good kisser?'

'Well—'

Sam handed a mug to Nicci who took it gratefully. 'It was exciting and dangerous ... unlike everything else in my life,' she sighed. 'But it was so wrong. I shouldn't have done it.'

'I thought things were all right between you and Reece,' said Louise.

Sam still hadn't told anyone that Reece had left for Germany, and there was obviously no point in saying it right then either. Somehow she thought they might not believe her, that she might just be saying it as an excuse.

Instead, she just babbled, 'I don't know what came over me, okay? Dan just appeared out of nowhere and the next minute he pushed me up against the wall and kissed me. I didn't know he was going to show up. It wasn't as if I planned it to happen.'

Nicci headed back into the stall when she saw two women with full baskets.

'But you wanted it to?' probed Louise.

Her words hung in the air for a few moments. Sam could hardly breathe, let alone speak.

Louise stared at her before following Nicci, as several customers approached the store at once.

Sam grabbed her elbow. 'This goes no further than the three of us,' she pleaded with her friend. 'I don't know what to do right now, okay?'

Louise shrugged. 'Not my place to say anything.'

'You told Nicci!'

'That was different.'

Left with her thoughts as they went back to work, Sam struggled to think about anything but the touch of Dan's lips to her own. Feelings of guilt, exhilaration and yes, a little bit of lust, combined to make her feel utterly confused.

What was happening to her? And more to the point, what would happen to her and Reece if she let it continue?

That evening, Charley Pellington couldn't get Sex off her mind. Yes, sex with a capital S. Her iPod playing One Direction, she lay on her bed, swinging her feet backwards and forwards, trying to concentrate on the magazine article she was reading.

After bunking off today, she wondered whether it would be wise to stay off tomorrow as well, following the numerous texts and direct messages she'd received. She knew that she'd be taunted by everyone, but most of the time it didn't last long. In her school, there would always be something more scandalous happening that everyone would turn their attention to.

But Charley hated being the source of a rumour. Her Facebook account had a stream of comments on it. Some of her friends wanted to know if what Aaron was talking about was true. Some of them – especially the boys – wanted more details of what had happened. Some of the girls she didn't know so well took the opportunity to call her names.

She wrote a message on Aaron's wall, asking why he had lied, knowing that everyone would see his reply. But, so far, he hadn't answered it.

Maybe it would be worse because she hadn't gone to school today. By this time, the rumour mill would be that she'd more than likely had sex with Aaron five times, given him oral sex twice, hung from the living room lights and been taken over the kitchen table afterwards before jumping into her mum's bed for a final fling.

One thing was certain though. Aaron Smithson was the same as the rest of them. Charley cursed Sophie - she'd felt the need to broadcast their pact to the world, so that every boy in the school now wanted to try their luck with the two of them. It wasn't as if they were the only female virgins in their year. If truth be known, Charley reckoned most of the girls were all talk. There were the odd ones who she was sure were working their way through the boy's surnames in alphabetical order, so frequent were their escapades, but really they were far and few between.

Charley's feet stopped swinging for a moment as she was paralysed with fear. That would be her worst nightmare. There was no way she wanted to end up like her mum, pregnant with her at eighteen. Still, there was no chance of that – unless you listened to Aaron's side of things.

It wasn't just her feeling the pressure. Sophie had been getting her fair share of groping too. But no one had started a rumour about her. Charley knew it was because Sophie's mum wasn't like hers. *Loose Louise*, that's what everyone called her at school. That's what the nasty texts said.

'Like motha, like dghtr.'

'Fancy repeating it with me?'

'I ear u giv head now. Want 2 do it 2 me?'

'You're just like your mum, Loose Louise.'

She wasn't like her mum at all, but no one now would think that.

Most of the text messages had stopped now, but the WhatsApp messages had started instead. Longer messages, disgusting messages. Charley deleted them as they came in. Mum would go mad if she saw any of them. They were hurtful and spiteful but, in a way she wanted her to see them too. It was all Louise's fault that she got teased.

A message came in from Aaron. She opened that one. It read:

'Soz, Charl, didn't no it wud get this bad for u but can't bak down now.'

Charley deleted that one too. As if that would make things better. Aaron didn't have to live with all the name calling. She bet his mates probably thought he was a super stud. Idiot.

She flipped open her laptop and logged into Facebook to see if Alex was online. Over the past few weeks, she'd found she could always talk things through with him, even though she wouldn't talk about this in detail. But then again, he would see all the comments left about her.

CP: Hey.

AL: Hey, I've just come online. How are you?

CP: Not good. I've had a rumour started about me today
    and I wanted to let you know that it isn't true.

AL: Oh? What about?

Charley paused for a moment. If he saw her page, he
would know, so she might as well be honest.

CP: Some boy at school says that I did stuff with him, but I
    didn't. He sent messages to a few kids in my year and
    they've been calling me names.

AL: Idiot! What did he do that for?

CP: I don't know – attention, I guess?

AL: I wish I was there. I'd be able to reassure you.

CP: Thanks, but I'm okay. Just wanted to tell you, that's all.

They moved on to general chit-chat for a few minutes and
then said goodbye. Charley checked out her page again and
sighed. She logged off after reading a few more comments.

She wished she had Sophie to talk to but she'd gone off
in a huff because, according to her, all Charley wanted to do
was sit and mope rather than get out there and face it head
on. The more she hid away, Sophie argued, the more people
would believe Aaron. Charley knew she was right, but instead
she'd given her the silent treatment and Sophie had eventually stormed off, saying she'd be round in the morning to drag
her through the school gates if she had to.

Her eyes filled with tears. Why did it have to be her that
everyone was talking about?

'Charley!'

Charley pulled her earphones out as her mother nudged her.

'I've been shouting you for ages!' Louise put a mug of tea down onto the bedside cabinet. 'Do you want some toast?'

'No thanks.' Charley pretended to flick through her magazine, hoping that she'd go away.

But Louise sat down beside her. 'Are you okay, Charl? You seem pretty quiet tonight. Have you fallen out with Sophie?'

There was no way Charley would share what was happening with her mother. So she nodded. In a way it was true.

'What was it about this time?'

Charley flicked another page of her magazine over. 'Nothing, really.'

Louise sighed. 'Well, that's alright then,' she said. 'You'll be friends again tomorrow, knowing you two. Especially if it's over nothing. You'll see.'

Charley turned another page, praying that her mum wouldn't see the tears running down her cheeks. She tried to wipe at them discreetly.

But Louise did notice. 'What's the matter? I don't like to see you like this.'

Charley said nothing. Maybe if she didn't look at her, she would go away and leave her alone.

'Charl?' Louise rested her hand tentatively on her daughter's shoulder.

'Leave me alone.' Charley pushed it away. 'I'm okay.'

'I'm only trying to help!' Louise sounded hurt. 'Why won't you talk to me?'

'Because I don't want to.'

'But—'

'Can't I have any peace?' Charley pushed herself up and ran from the room. She found sanctuary in the bathroom and sat down on the side of the bath. As she looked around at the peeling wallpaper above the white tiles and the make-up and body lotions lined up untidily on the rickety shelf, she wished she didn't have to go to school any more. If she didn't have to face all those losers, everything would be much better.

Not for the first time, Charley wished her life away. She couldn't wait until she was older and could fend for herself, earning her own money. Then she'd move out and get her own place. Somewhere she could be by herself whenever she felt the need. Somewhere she could cry in peace and not have to explain how she was feeling. Somewhere she could be whoever she wanted to be.

She heard her mum shout her name again and decided to run a bath. She'd stay in here all night if she had to, rather than discuss it with Loose Louise.

Nicci was sitting in the kitchen with Jay, eating dinner. Jay had been working overtime and had called at the chippie for speed.

'Dad rang me this afternoon,' he said, after the food had been dished out and they were sitting at the table. 'He says they're struggling for room now that Jess is staying over. I said she could stay here for a while. That's okay, isn't it?'

Nicci turned to him with wide eyes that showed it clearly wasn't. 'What?'

'It's only for a few weeks.'

Nicci watched as he fidgeted uncomfortably in his chair, purposely not catching her eye. She waited until he looked up. 'For God's sake, Jay, we're a team! You should have discussed this with me before saying yes.'

'But you would have said no.'

'Too damn right. Jess is nothing but trouble.'

'She's not that bad.'

'Well.' Nicci scraped her chair on the floor in her haste to get up. She shoved it noisily back under the table and leaned on it. 'You can bloody well tell her that she can't stay here.'

'I only did it to help Mum and Dad out,' Jay protested.

'I don't want her here. She'll cause an atmosphere.'

'Don't be so dramatic, Nic. She's my little sister. I can't turn her away.'

Nicci sighed. If she didn't love him so much, she would murder him on the spot. Jason Worthington was a gullible fool but he only did things like that because he had a heart of gold. They'd been a couple for three years now and had lived together for the last twelve months. They'd bought a town house just around the corner from her parents and a few streets away from Louise. For Nicci it was the closest she could get to wedded bliss – but she still wanted the marriage ceremony. She'd been waiting ages for Jay to pop the question but so far, all her hinting had been in vain.

She watched as he finished his meal. There was a nine year age gap between them but you wouldn't think it. Jay looked quite a few years younger than his age of thirty-six. An old rocker at heart, so far he'd aged with distinction. His skin tone was rich, his eyes dark, his nose prominent. Brown, layered hair hung down to his shoulders with a longish fringe that she loved to push away from his eyes. Playing football twice a week and cycling at weekends ensured he'd kept the same trim shape he'd had when she'd first started to date him.

Jay gazed back with a puppy-dog expression. 'I'm sorry. I didn't think it would be such a big issue. I'll ring her and let her know.'

'Why do you have to be such a nice guy?' Nicci shook her head. 'Okay, she can come and stay,' she relented. 'But I'm doing it for you – and not your sister.'

Louise sat on the edge of Charley's bed, wondering what to do. She tried to put herself in her daughter's position. Could she remember what it was like at fifteen with hormones determining your every move? She knew she'd been a handful for her parents, and although Ryan had often taken advantage of this by getting away with murder while she took up their attention, poor Nicci had always got the full edge of their wrath.

CHAPTER FOUR 57

It wasn't unusual for Charley to stay in but usually Sophie
would be here too. Louise hoped they'd make up tomorrow.
In so many ways, they reminded her of when she and Sam
were younger and thick as thieves. When they had shared
dreams of double weddings and having babies at the same
time. How far from the dream were they now?

But she knew that if she hadn't had Sam to confide in,
things could have been much worse for her. Sam had been
her saviour throughout her life. She'd got her through a bad
marriage, a divorce, and she was always there to look out for
her and Charley. Yet even their strong friendship had been
threatened by her secrecy. She remembered the accusations
when she'd found out she was pregnant and refused to tell
anyone the father's name.

She recalled the tears when Charley had been born. Sam
had been there at the birth, holding her hand, tears pouring
down her face as she watched Charley emerge into the world.
In a way, they were just kids themselves, yet Sam had been
her rock, stepping into the role of big sister as well as best
friend.

But, even though Sam had been hurt, and angry, when
she'd refused to tell her who Charley's father was, how could
she have shared that information? She would have lost Sam's
friendship, and she wasn't sure she would have coped without her.

Louise shook her head in disgust. She was doing it again.
Why did she always think of herself when she should be

thinking of Charley? This wasn't about *her* ideas and dreams going wrong. This was about her daughter trying to find her way in an often lonely and cruel world. Charley and Sophie falling out would hopefully only be a tiff; they fell out more than once a day and stormed off in opposite directions. But a text message would always have them running back. They were good friends, just like she and Sam were at that age. Sam and Louise: Louise and Sam. They came as a pair, sharing everything.

Maybe she should talk to Sophie; see if she would tell her what was wrong with Charley.

No, Louise decided, standing up now. *She* should at least try and talk to Charley again. If she could just get her to open up with a few simple questions, then she might confide in her mum without feeling that she'd been badgered into anything.

She walked across to the bathroom door and knocked gently. 'Charl?'

'Go away!'

'Just let me in. I only want to talk.'

'No.'

'I know there are some things that you can't chat about with Sophie. But maybe I can help. I've been your age once, remember. I know what it's like to—'

'No, you don't. You haven't got a clue how I'm feeling.'

'But I might be able to—'

And what do you care about me anyway? All you care about is yourself.'

'Charley! I—'

'Just leave me alone, will you? I don't want to talk to you, can't you understand!'

Louise snapped. 'Fine. Have it your way,' she spoke through the bathroom door. 'But when you finally do show your face, you can tidy that room of yours. It's like a pigsty in there!'

Marching off, Louise groaned. Why had she ended the conversation like that? If there was something seriously wrong, Charley would never open up to her if she didn't show any sympathy.

She stormed downstairs in a mood with herself. Not only did she feel that she had to be mum to Charley but she had to be dad too. And it didn't seem that she was any good at either.

CHAPTER FIVE

It was Thursday evening, closing time for Hedworth market, and it was minus two outside. Sam had no intention of going anywhere fast and Nicci was rinsing out the coffee mugs before she headed off for the evening. But Louise wanted to get home as quickly as possible and close the curtains on the dark and cold night. It wasn't fit for anything else.

'Come on, you two,' she cried impatiently as she wrapped herself up to brave the elements. 'I have a date with my settee, my jimjams and a bottle of wine.'

'I'm not bothered about rushing home now that Jess will be there,' Nicci moaned, wiping her hands on a tea towel. 'Still, *Wedding Belles* is on tonight so I do have something to look forward to.'

'I don't how you can watch that program,' Louise remarked. 'Love's dream never runs its full course.'

'It will for me and Jay,' Nicci nodded vehemently. 'Not all marriages end up in divorce like yours.'

'Not all marriages end up like you think they will, either.' Louise sighed. Nicci was always going on about weddings. It drove her mad, each mention reminding her of her own failing.

'You need to find the right man,' Nicci responded, not put off by her sister's exasperated tone.

'I've got nothing to rush home for either,' added Sam, as always the peacemaker.

'Oh, hark at you two. Aren't I supposed to be the one who's got a boring life?' I'm not in a relationship, yet I have a smile on my face.'

'That's because you have a bottle of wine,' Nicci chided, pulling on her coat.

'Precisely.' Louise ignored her sarcasm. 'Which is why I'm inviting you both back to mine for a drink right now.'

'I've got work to do here first,' said Sam. 'I'll probably leave when Mike does.' Mike didn't finish until six o'clock. It was his job to check everything was secure before locking up the building.

'You work too much.' Louise wouldn't let it drop.

'Well, count me in,' said Nicci. 'I really don't want to go home to another argument.'

'Will Jess be here long, do you think?' Sam asked, remembering how angry Nicci had been when she'd told them her news.

'A few weeks, Jay says.'

Louise laughed. 'She'll be there for ages now she has her feet under the table.'

'I hope not.' Nicci lowered her voice, even though no one else would be able to hear her speak. 'I can't have sex knowing that she's in the next room.'

'Euw, you're at it again.' Louise wrinkled her nose in disgust before turning to Sam. 'Anyway, what's it to be then?'

'What's what to be?'

Louise sighed dramatically. 'Tonight. Drink. My place. I'll even cook you something, if you like?'

'I'll take a rain check, if you don't mind.' Sam shook her head.

Louise threw her hands up in exasperation. 'See you to-morrow then.'

'Night.'

Once she was alone on the stall, Sam's shoulders drooped in relief. After the hustle and bustle of the day, she loved to sit in the silence when most of the stall holders had left for home. It wasn't as if she had anything to be there for right now, and even an evening with Louise, which she usually enjoyed, wasn't exactly appealing either. She just hadn't told anyone about Reece yet and she didn't want to slip up.

She wasn't sure why she didn't want to say anything just yet about him being in Germany. It wouldn't make any difference, she supposed. But Sam kept a lot of things to herself. Louise was the outgoing, loud one of the two of them. Sam preferred to stay in the background as much as possible.

Half an hour later, she heard the jangle of keys as Mike came to lock up. She grabbed her bag and threw on her coat before he came to check their aisle. She liked Mike but she wasn't in the mood for small talk. Half wishing she had taken Louise up on her offer now, she let herself out into the chilly evening.

As she stepped into the car park, she heard someone shout her name. Busy with her hand in her bag, searching out her car keys, she looked up to see Dan in the distance. Her heart lurched when he started to slip and slide towards her across the icy car park. He looked totally different wearing chunky beige work boots, jeans and a black parka coat, with a multi-coloured striped scarf knotted at the neck, but, she had to admit, he looked as sexy as hell.

She hadn't seen him since their illicit rendezvous three days ago. But she hadn't stopped thinking about him, nor the kisses they'd shared either, and it frightened her.

'Hey there.' Dan's smile widened as he drew level with her. 'I thought you might like to grab a hot toddy somewhere before you leave? I could do with something to warm me up in this weather.'

'I'm just on my way home,' Sam told him, trying hard not to get caught up in the lust she could see in his eyes. 'I've got so much paperwork to do.'

'That's a pity.' Dan grinned at her cheekily. 'Maybe I could join you?'

'Maybe you couldn't!'

As he laughed, Sam blushed. When Louise had asked her about Dan again, after what had happened on Monday morning, she'd told her it would remain a one off. She couldn't have an affair. And she wasn't about to chuck everything away for a quick grope with a man she hardly knew, no matter how much her feet were telling her to run to him. Louise's reply had shocked her. 'Any fool can see that things have gone stale between you and Reece,' she'd told Sam with real concern. 'Maybe you need to get Dan out of your system.'

Dan held up his index finger. 'Just one drink. Where's the harm in that?'

Sam laughed inwardly. Really? He could see no harm in one drink?

Or was he, like her, wondering what it might lead to? And was he, like her, wanting it to lead there? She made her mind up in a split second.

'Oh, go on, then,' she smiled. 'Just the one.'

Jess sat on the sofa, staring at the television but not actually watching it. Before flicking over to another channel, she glanced around the room. Her brother had done well for himself by meeting Nicci. A woman's touch was evident by the faux leather cushions on the Caramac coloured three piece suite, the fluffy scatter rugs that warmed up the polished wooden flooring. Five church candles stood in a row on the top of an Adams style fireplace, the marble hearth holding bowls of fragranced balls and petals, their faint aroma mixing gently with the scents of the plug-in air fresheners.

Nicci was certainly a stickler for cleanliness, not like Jess. Jess was a slob. Perfectly turned out from the outside, but wherever she laid her hat was her hovel. Strangely enough, she found the room calming, homely and extremely welcoming. Alas, she knew *she* wasn't welcome.

There was a whole world out there for the taking but she was stuck in Hedworth. Jay and Nicci had gone to the pub.

Although Jay invited her along, Jess knew by the look on Nicci's face that it was a no-no. So she'd changed into her sweats and slouched on the settee as soon as they had gone, the weather outside completely matching her icy mood.

She was trying desperately hard not to think that she could have been having dinner at an exclusive restaurant with Laurie before they'd go off to have sex in a hotel nearby. Even though he was fifteen years her senior, Laurie had been an exceptional lover, thinking of her pleasure just as much as his own. What had started as a fling had grown into something much more for her, even though when he had ended it, she hadn't shown him her true feelings.

Jess missed him so much and not being able to talk about him to anyone made her sad. Although he technically wasn't her man, she missed the intimacy; the feeling of belonging to someone, yet still being her own person. Even now, she kept wondering if she'd done the right thing by leaving London so quickly. Maybe she should have stayed and fought for him, even though he'd made it obvious that would have been tough.

She flicked her legs up onto the settee and reached for the remote again. There must be something decent on to watch. A few minutes later, bored of channel hopping, she moved to the window. Staring out through open curtains into the dark night, the cul-de-sac outside was quiet. There were only a few houses, gardens all covered in snow that had yet to melt from two weeks ago. Not for the first time, she wished she was married and living in suburbia with two point four children.

Involuntarily, she hugged herself, wondering what Ryan would be doing right now. From the moment she'd started to work on the stall again, he'd taken a personal interest in her welfare. He'd bought her a bacon buttie on Monday morning, coffee the next, a Danish pastry yesterday and coffee again today. And he was buying lots from the stall. One hundred grams of aniseed balls, two twenty pence mixtures for his twin five-year-old girls, cola bottles and humbugs for him and Matt.

Today he had bought two sherbet dib-dabs, given one back to her and they'd dunked in their lollipops as they'd laughed together about Jay in his younger days. All the same age and inseparable unless there was a girl involved, Ryan, Jay and Matt had been known as the Three Amigos at school.

Jess already had a feeling that Ryan would be up for more if she was interested. Anyone could tell that he was game even though he was married. She had never cared about being the other woman until she'd missed her period and done a pregnancy test.

As it was prone to doing, her mind slipped back to that fateful night. It had been late, about nine thirty. They'd been out for a drink and decided to get a takeaway and go back to the office. All evening Jess had been priming herself, knowing she should tell him her news but she couldn't get the words out. In the end, he'd asked her what was wrong. And when she did tell him she was pregnant, he'd flipped. It was one thing to have a bit on the side, he told her cruelly, but he would not have a woman with a child. He accused her of sleeping around, refusing to believe it was his, saying that she was trying to trap him. She'd rushed out of the building in floods of tears after he'd hurled more abuse at her.

Back at her flat, she sat and cried, unsure what to do next. She received her answer the following morning, by text message. Laurie told her, in no uncertain terms, that she wasn't welcome back at the office.

Not one to give up without a fight, Jess went in to face the music. It was then that he'd given her a cheque for £5,000 to move on and forget. She took it, and, once she'd ensured that it had cleared, she'd booked a ticket back to Hedworth to stay with her parents. No amount of pleading with Laurie would change his mind. The money would help until she found her feet again and decided what she was going to do next.

She'd only been at her parent's home for a few hours before she realised it wasn't the right place to be. Jess had left home at nineteen and hadn't ever intended to come back. The first night there reminded her why. Her mum, a natural fusspot, followed her around like she would a toddler taking its first steps.

'Are you sure you're okay? You do look a little peaky. Shall I get you an aspirin?'

'Do you need anything washing or ironing? Shall I hang your clothes for you?'

'Did you sleep well? The room wasn't too hot – or too cold?'

To save herself from explanations, Jess told her that she'd been dumped. It had backfired hugely as Mum then had to do what mothers do best. She mothered her – or was that smothered her?

Maureen had always been over-protective toward her but it was too much for Jess. The last straw had been when she'd waited for Jess on the landing before she went to have a shower and pulled her into her arms. 'We'll spend the day together, just you and me. We'll go shopping, have coffee and cake in Somerley at the Coffee Stop.'

It had been seven thirty in the morning. Unable to stand the thought of what lay ahead, she'd struck a deal with her father to help out on the stall and was on her way to work with him by eight. And then she badgered her dad to ask Jay, if she could come and stay with him and Nicci for a few weeks. It was far from an ideal situation, however. It was one thing to have her mother looking out for her every need but it was another to be ignored and spoken to only when absolutely necessary by her brother's girlfriend. From the minute she'd arrived, Nicci had made it perfectly clear that the stay was to be a short one. She'd also taken a great interest in helping Jess look for a flat share.

But much worse than that was, being at their home she could see just how much they loved each other. And it hurt. Over the past couple of nights, she'd walk in the room and they'd be kissing or groping each other. Sometimes they'd stop what they were doing; sometimes Jess would leave the room. How long had they been together now? Three years? How did they manage to keep the passion alive?

Her thoughts turned back to Ryan. Maybe it was time to find out how far he really would go. She knew he would be hers if she played her cards right. He'd made enough remarks and instigated enough chats for her to know.

She hugged a cushion into her chest. If she couldn't find a man of her own, she'd settle for someone to pamper her, make her feel special. It was the way she was, finding comfort in being told she was beautiful and feeling desired. It was what she needed. Where was the harm in it?

Besides, if it stopped her worrying about her future, then that was good too. Because right now, she had a potentially heartbreaking decision to make. One she wished she didn't have to make by herself.

CHAPTER SIX

The drink with Dan turned into two, albeit soft ones, as they were both driving. At first they stood up at the bar. Then they ordered chips and a burger apiece and found a quieter spot to eat.

'I love this,' Dan said, once they'd eaten and the plates had been taken away. 'You and me.' His voice was so low it came out as a whisper.

Sam looked away as his gaze made her insides flip again. She pretended to be more interested in the chalk menu behind the bar. Why was this so wrong if she felt like this?

Dan reached across the table for her hand and gave it a squeeze. Sam checked her watch and gasped.

'Crikey, it's nearly nine o clock. Where did that time go?'

'Time always goes quickly when you're having fun.' Dan rubbed his thumb back and forth across the top of her wrist. 'We could always grab a coffee at mine, if you like?'

Sam gulped. She knew she'd walked right into that. Dan was fabulous company. He laughed in the right places, never mentioning Reece, only to figure out the minor details. He'd even kept his lips to himself. She hoped she hadn't led him on, just because *she* wanted to be with him.

'I can't,' she replied, regret clear in her tone.

'I know,' he realised. 'It's just that it's so hard to leave you. I've ached to kiss you again. I've thought about you constantly since Monday. You have too, haven't you? Thought about me?'

Sam nodded.

'There's a spark between us.'

'We barely know each other.'

'That's true, but you can't deny it.'

'But there shouldn't be!' Sam pulled her hand away. 'Can't you see what you do to me?'

'If you were happily married, you wouldn't be here.'

'You're right.' Sam stood up then. 'But it's because I'm married that I can't see you again. I'm sorry.'

They were silent for a moment amidst the general noise from the pub.

'You do understand why?' she asked.

Dan sighed. 'Unfortunately, I do. But it only makes me want you more – because you're so warm-hearted.'

Sam couldn't help but grin.

As they made their way back to their cars, Dan grabbed her scarf, pulled her towards him and kissed her briefly on the lips. The lightness of his touch made her cheeks burn.

'Go,' he said, 'before I change my mind.'

Sam's feet refused to move for a few seconds before her brain engaged. With reluctance, she got into her car and drove away.

Once back in the safety of her home, Sam raced up to have a shower. Unable to wash away the feel of Dan's hand on hers, his lips on her cheek, she stayed under the water for a long time. Tears of frustration stung her eyes and she squeezed them shut to stop them falling. Spending time with him made her realise what a sham her marriage was. No wonder Reece worked away; wanted to spend time in Germany, under the guise of earning some extra cash. It shocked her to think how easily she could have been led astray. She knew as much as Dan that the invitation wasn't just for coffee. If she'd gone home with him, she wouldn't have been able to resist him.

Was her relationship – her marriage – to Reece in that much of a mess? Maybe she needed to spend her time thinking about that rather than Dan Wilshaw.

Changed into pyjamas, hair still wet, it was ten thirty when there was a knock on the front door. She peered through the living room window to see Dan on her doorstep.

Shit!

She let him in. Without a word, he pulled her into his arms.

'I can't help myself,' he whispered before his lips were on hers.

Sam found herself responding before she had time to think. Dan's hands inside her top, she gasped at the touch of his fingers on her bare skin. His lips moved over her neck and down towards her chest. Her hands found their way into his shirt.

Dan stepped away then and she realised he was giving her the space to change her mind.

You have to stop said the voice within her head, but she ignored it. Right now, Sam didn't care about Reece. It was all about her and Dan.

She bit down hard on her lip as his hands explored her body. Dan Wilshaw was making her moan in ecstasy … ohhh.

'No, please!' She pushed him away.

Dan paused with a look of concern. 'Are you okay?'

She shook her head. 'I'm sorry,' she said. 'I can't. I just can't.'

'But I thought you wanted to.'

'I do – I did! Oh, I don't know. I feel so mixed up.'

Ten minutes later, Sam sat alone in the living room. She'd switched off the main light, the glow of the gas fire the only light she needed. It made her feel scared, vulnerable. But more than that, she was scared by the intensity of her feelings.

What the hell had gone on back then? It was one thing to want to be kissed by someone else, to want a show of affection, but to let another man touch her, make love to her? No, that was wrong. How could she have done that to Reece? She'd always prided herself in being a good girl and had laughed along with Louise – not at Louise – about her colourful antics since her marriage collapsed. But she had never, ever – even in her wildest dreams when she was so pissed off with Reece that she didn't want to be in the same room as him – thought that she would come so close to sleeping with another man while she was with him.

And what would have happened afterwards? There would have been no going back. Things like that couldn't just be swept under the carpet. It wasn't a mistake. It would have been a decision that had consequences.

Sam pulled her knees up to her chest and hugged herself as the tears fell. She had never felt so lonely in her life.

Louise and Nicci were on the stall before Sam the next morning. As was usual some mornings, Sam was coming in late after catching up on paperwork back at the house. Louise, spotting her chance to skive after the morning rush had gone, was moaning to Nicci about Charley's recent behaviour. Since they'd fallen out, Charley had spent every spare minute she was at home upstairs in her room.

'Maybe you need to be more forceful with her,' Nicci said, grabbing the opportunity to dunk a chocolate biscuit in her coffee while there was a lull in customers. 'Charley needs boundaries. You let her get away with murder at times.'

'She's fifteen!' Louise retorted. 'You should try setting boundaries with someone that age. She has a mind of her own. I tell her to do one thing and she goes and does another.'

'Hmm,' smiled Nicci. 'Sounds like someone else I know. Like mother, like daughter, obviously.'

'That's precisely the reason I'm worried about her,' Louise agreed, grabbing a chocolate bar and tearing off its wrapper. 'She seems really upset about something. The other night, I sat outside the bathroom door for fifteen minutes after she'd stormed off in a huff but she still wouldn't come out and talk to me.'

'I don't see why you think she would. You wouldn't have said anything to Mum when you were fifteen.'

'But it's different nowadays, isn't it?' She bit into the chocolate bar before replying. 'Daughters trust their mums with more information. They go shopping together, they lunch together. They—'

'Since when have you two ever lunched together?' Nicci raised her eyebrows. 'Or shopped together for that matter? You and Charley are like chalk and cheese.'

Louise shrugged. 'I really want us to be friends. It would be nice to go home and have a chat with her, rather than hear her music in the distance because she's shut herself in her room. It's like living with a stranger at times. I'm sure she tries to make things awkward between us.'

'I could talk to her?' Nicci suggested, aware of how much it was bothering her sister that Charley wouldn't confide in her. 'You remember what we were like when Mum asked us any kind of question.' She rolled her eyes.

'Don't I just!' Louise laughed. 'It's a good job I had you as a sister to look out for me. You got me out of lots of tellings off. Speaking of sisters,' she pointed along the aisle to where Jess was serving on the sweet stall. 'How are you getting on with the prodigal one?'

It was Nicci's turn to look exasperated. 'She's really getting my back up, if you must know, with all her sarcastic remarks and all her bragging about her life in London. And she's so untidy. I end up clearing up after her all the time.'

'She can't be that bad.' Louise hurled a full sack of potatoes to one side and sat awkwardly on it.

'But we can't get any privacy.'

'So that's what's eating you up? Haven't you had a cuddle since baby sis turned up?'

Nicci tutted at the insinuation. 'Of course we have. But she always seems to come in at such inappropriate moments. Take last night. We'd come back from the pub and were getting down and dirty in the kitchen when she walked in and interrupted us. She said she wanted a glass of water. Can you believe that?'

'Yes,' said Louise.

Nicci ignored her and continued. 'Imagine if she'd come in two minutes later. You never know –'

'You mean Jay lasts longer than two minutes?' Louise laughed. 'You jammy sod. You should think yourself lucky he lasts that long. You don't have anything to moan about.'

'Talking of men, has Sam mentioned anything else to you about Dan?' Nicci asked, keeping her voice low. 'I haven't seen him around since *the kiss* happened and I'm dying to know. Has she mentioned anything to you?'

'I have asked but she says she hasn't seen him. She said she'd sent him a message asking him not to visit the stall.'

'Oh, so that's why he's kept away.' Nicci nodded. 'I suppose it's for the best.'

'Morning. Is that kettle still warm?' Sam appeared on the stall a few minutes later as Nicci and Louise were working. 'It's so cold out there. I'm freezing.'

'Morning,' said Louise. 'Get warmed up last night, did you?'

Sam froze. 'What do you mean?'

'Knowing you, you went home and got into a hot bath. Am I right?'

'Oh. Yes,' she replied. 'It was Heaven.'

Sam rushed into the staff room before her reddening cheeks gave her away again. Friends or not, there was no way she was telling Louise and Nicci anything about what had happened last night. The guilt she was feeling wasn't for sharing. Besides, it wouldn't be a case of problem shared, problem halved for her. Louise had known Reece for as long as she had. It didn't seem fair to talk about Dan as if Reece no longer existed.

And it had made Sam wonder, through the long and lonely hours of the early morning, as she'd tried desperately to drift off to sleep, if Reece had stayed faithful to her, why he'd been working away. It would have been far easier for him to do the dirty because he was away from anyone who would see him.

Sam had sat up in bed at that point, suddenly panicking in case she had been seen by anyone she knew. She and Dan hadn't done anything untoward in the pub. But had anyone been able to tell what they had really wanted to do, had in fact gone on partly to do? And what happened if any of the neighbours had seen her invite him into the house?

Even now, she was wondering how the hell she was going to face Reece when he finally came home. What a bitch she was for allowing herself to fall under Dan's spell. She should have been stronger; strong enough to knock away his advances and talk to Reece about their ailing marriage first.

This wasn't like her, not at all. In fact, right now, Sam didn't know what to think of herself. She was so embarrassed by her antics. But she had enjoyed them. Was that so wrong?

'Something up?'

Sam came out of her trance to find Louise standing in front of her. She shook her head. 'No, I'm fine,' she replied.

'No, you're not. I know when there is something on your mind. Is it Dan?'

Sam tried to keep her face straight as she shook her head. 'I told you, I haven't seen him since Monday.'

'He hasn't rung you – or texted you?' Louise probed.

'No – I –'

'Sam doesn't have to tell you everything, Lou,' said Nicci, walking across to join them.

Louise swung round to face her. 'I *know*. I was only trying to help.'

The conversation was dropped as several customers trooped in one after the other. But Sam's mind wouldn't settle. Twice she gave out the wrong orders before heading for their staff room with her paperwork.

'Be gentle,' Nicci said, nudging Louise when Sam was out of earshot. 'You don't know what it's like for her.'

Louise sounded appalled. 'What do you mean? I've been on my own for years now.'

'Not through choice.'

'No, it's not. It's because I can't find a decent man. I'd love to be in a relationship again but who'd have me, with another man's child?'

'Everyone has excess baggage nowadays. That shouldn't stop you. But Sam's had no choice but to be by herself while Reece worked away.'

'He didn't have to leave her alone for so long,' Louise protested.

'His trade doesn't pay much around here though. And Sam says that it's not forever. He'll be home for good in a couple of years.'

'I have a feeling she won't be sitting around waiting for him then. Don't you?'

'Maybe,' Nicci agreed.

'I'll take her for a coffee, see if she'll open up to me. Will you be okay if we go to the café?'

Nicci nodded. 'Just go easy on her. She's been a real good friend to you over the years. And whether you think what she did with Dan was right or wrong, it's really none of your business.' She held up a hand as Louise went to protest. 'Nor mine. I don't like what she's doing either but it might not evolve into anything more than a few sexy feelings coming through.' She turned to the elderly woman standing in front of her with a cabbage. 'Seventy-five pence to you, my love.'

Louise stood in silence for a moment. Nicci had always been the level headed one of the Pellington kids. Even now she spoke oodles of common sense. She wondered if that was who Charley took after.

Sam came out onto the stall again.

'Fancy grabbing a break at the café?' Louise suggested.

But Sam shook her head. 'I'm okay, Lou, thanks.'

Louise glanced surreptitiously at Nicci, raising her eyebrows this time. 'Are you still coming out with me tomorrow night?' she turned back to Sam.

'Why? So I can stop you from throwing yourself at Rob Masters again?'

Louise grinned. 'What about Reece? Is he coming home this weekend?'

'No,' said Sam truthfully.

'So it's a date then?'

Sam nodded. She hadn't got anything else to do and she'd only spend the evening worrying about everything. About how she had to end this fling before it became more serious. That was, if she *could* end it. If her feelings for Dan would let her.

'At last,' said Louise. 'I can't believe how many times you've stood me up lately, so I'm holding you to this one. Nothing will stop us going out tomorrow night. Shall I come around to yours and get ready there?'

'As long as you bring a bottle of something cool and delicious with you. What are you wearing?'

Sam relaxed as Louise went though the clothes in her wardrobe, ticking off on her fingers her many outfits. At least for now she'd managed to keep things to herself. But she knew she wouldn't be able to hold out on Louise for long.

CHAPTER SEVEN

Charley and Sophie arrived at the market after finishing school for the weekend. Sophie was staying for tea at Charley's that night. Matt was going to be chaperoning them, so they were getting a lift home.

'If I hear one more person calling me Charley Cockhead, I swear I'm going to break their head in two,' she moaned as she and Sophie walked down the aisle towards the fruit and veg stall.

Sophie stifled a giggle but it was too late.

'Oi, you!' Charley nudged her.

Sophie burst out laughing then. 'I'm sorry.' She linked her arm through her friend's. 'It's just got such a ring to it. Charley the Cock –'

Charley put her hand across Sophie's mouth. 'That includes you. If you say that word, I won't be responsible for my actions. Friend or no friend.'

'Hey, ladies,' Ryan greeted them as they got to his stall. He came round to the front. 'What do you know?'

Charley shrugged. 'Nothing much.'

'School okay?'

'Fine.'

'Love lives?'

'Fine.' Ryan always teased Charley about boys but she never revealed anything. It didn't stop Sophie giggling though.

'Hi, Matt,' Charley said as she saw him approaching the stall with two cakes from Cupcake Delights.

Ryan whizzed round to face him. 'Do you fancy a quick jar in the Crown after work, mate?' he asked.

Matt shook his head. 'No can do. Got to take these two home and then we're having a curry, aren't we, girls?'

'Yes, because you burn everything when you cook.'

'I do not! Well, not everything.'

'He even burns pizza and all you have to do is shove it in the oven,' Charley told Ryan.

But Ryan wasn't interested in food talk. He pressed together his thumb and index finger. 'Just a small one?' he pleaded with Matt.

'I'll come.' Jess sidled across to join them. She'd been ear-wigging on their conversation, looking for an excuse to talk to Ryan again. This seemed a perfect opportunity to get him alone. 'I could murder a drink rather than go home with the loved-ups.'

'The loved-ups?' questioned Sophie.

'My brother and his girlfriend. They can't keep their hands off each other.'

'Jay and Nicci,' explained Charley, although she was more intrigued by the looks passing from Ryan to Jess. 'This is Jess, Jay's sister. She's just got back from London.'

'Cool,' said Sophie. 'What was it like?'

'What was what like?' said Jess.

'London!' Charley answered for Sophie. 'What was it like living there?'

Jess shrugged, only glancing at the two younger girls before returning her full attention to Ryan. He was definitely the type of man she was after. His intense blue eyes bewitched her more with every look he threw in her direction – and there had been plenty of them throughout the week. She let her eyes wander lazily down the length of his body, which left her mind wondering just exactly what was in store for her if she managed to get underneath those clothes.

Matt had noticed the looks passing between Jess and Ryan too and frowned as he heard them both laugh at some joke they'd shared. He hoped Ryan could keep his old fella in his trousers this time.

'Sam?' Ryan shouted across the aisle. 'Are you coming to the pub for a quick one or are you going back to Louise's?'

Jess sighed. That wasn't the plan she had in mind. How would she get Ryan's undivided attention if anyone else was there?

Sam appeared from the back of her stall and joined them in the aisle. 'No, I've got things to finish off first but I'll try and catch you later. Charley, why don't you go and find your mum and tell her that she can knock off, if she likes? She's away in the stock room.'

'I'd rather you came with us too.'

'I have paperwork to catch up on.' Just saying that made Sam think of the night before, after she'd said the same thing to Louise. She felt herself blushing at the thought of what she'd done with Dan.

'But you're always telling me that I'm only young once,' moaned Charley. 'Please! Come and have some fun.'

Sam was shocked to hear that. Louise was right: Charley was so level headed at times. She always seemed to be looking out for everyone else. She checked her watch: it was nearly five o'clock. The market closed at five thirty and if she locked up on her own it would only take another half hour. She nodded to Charley.

'I'll try and make it in an hour, okay?'

Louise appeared then and Charley told her of Sam's plans to join them.

'I bet you won't come,' Louise sulked.

'I'll try my best,' said Sam.

That brought a smile to Louise's face. 'Can you finish now, Matt? I've been given half an hour!'

Matt nodded and grabbed his keys and jacket. 'I'm sure you can manage without me,' he told Ryan quietly. 'It'll do you good to focus on your priorities for a while.'

Ryan threw him a sly look. 'I don't know what you mean.'

'Yes, you do. I've seen the way you're looking at Jess and I'm not covering for you again. I told you after the last time, enough was enough.'

'It's just a bit of harmless flirting, mate.' Ryan glanced over at Jess who had gone back to her stall. She was pretending not to look at him but every now and then he caught her eye momentarily.

'Just as long as it stays that way.'

Ryan saluted, stamping his feet together like a soldier on parade. 'I give you my word, partner. I'll behave myself.'

Matt shook his head in despair. He knew he was taking the mickey. Although Ryan was his best mate, sometimes he wished he wasn't. From their schooldays, he'd been one for the women, sometimes not content with just one at a time. Now he was older and married, things hadn't changed much. He wished he'd grow up and act his age.

When half past five came and she'd locked up the stall, Sam decided she would go to Louise's after all.

'Impeccable timing, as ever,' said Louise as she let Sam in. 'We're just dishing out the food. Come on through to the kitchen.'

Sam shimmied out of her coat and threw it over the banister before following the sound of laughter. Matt was having his usual banter with Charley and Sophie as he spooned rice on to several plates.

'You cheated!' Sam cried, pointing at the takeaway cartons strewn over the table.

'You didn't think we were really going to eat a curry Matt had made, did you?' Louise joked.

'Hey!' Matt slapped Louise's bottom as she sidled past him. 'I'll have you know I am a man of many talents. It's just that cooking isn't one of them.'

'I've not seen many of your talents!' Louise laughed. 'Someone's been winding you up.'

Matt feigned a hurt expression, his bottom lip protruding like a scolded child.

Charley gave him an impromptu hug. 'You're lovely, though,' she smiled up at him. 'I want to marry someone like you when I grow up.'

Matt hugged her back, raising his eyebrows at Louise. 'See, someone loves me.'

Sam was surprised when Louise came over to hug Matt too.

'*I* love you, you great big idiot,' she said, but she wouldn't look at him.

'Stop it,' said Sam. 'Or me and Sophie will join in. Group hug!'

'Hugs are only for my special ladies,' Matt explained. Then he pushed them both away gently. 'Food! Come on, I'm starving.'

After the meal, Sam insisted on doing the dishes and shooed them all into the living room. She hadn't even finished running the hot water before a word came to mind.

Adultery.

She had as much as committed adultery last night. It brought tears to her eyes. Reece had always been there for her and she'd let him down. When her dad died, it had been Reece who had held her together through it all while she'd been afraid for her future. She remembered how well he'd got on with her dad. Often, she'd left the two of them watching football or some violent action film while she and Louise went out shopping. Often, she'd come home to see them fast asleep in the living room after it had finished, no matter what time of day or night.

Even before Martin died, Reece had been part of the furniture. He'd been there to step in and become her family when she was left with no one, and for that she would always be grateful. No one except Reece really knew how close she and her dad had been. When Martin died, it was as if Sam had had her heart ripped out and he'd taken it with him. She couldn't ever explain how she felt to anyone else, not even Louise. Losing her mum at such a young age had made her more dependent on her dad. They'd been a team. Even when he'd moved Shelly Williams in for six months until their relationship had burnt to a frazzle, she'd still been close to him.

For years, Sam had thought Reece was her soulmate. After they married, their relationship went from strength to strength for the first few years but then they'd started to take each other for granted. And when they found it impossible to conceive a child, they'd drifted apart a little. Sam had fought hard to find the closeness they once shared. But when Reece had decided to work away for the best part of each week, well, that had been the final nail in the coffin.

After she'd left the kitchen spotless, Sam made her excuses and left. She had only been home from Louise's for a few minutes when the doorbell rang. She went to open the door to find Reece standing on the step.

'Hi, what are you doing back so soon? Are you okay?'

Reece looked a little nervous as he stayed outside in the porch. 'I'm not entirely sure,' he said.

'But I thought you were supposed to be in Germany.' Sam closed the door behind him when he finally came inside. The phone calls and texts she'd received from him had made her think that too. 'And why didn't you just come in? Have you lost your keys?'

'I've come to hand them back to you.'

'What?'

Sam followed him through to the living room, staying in the doorway as he perched on the edge of the settee.

'I can't do this any more,' he said.

'Do what?' For a selfish moment, she thought Reece had found out about her and Dan. He could have, couldn't he? Her heart started to beat fast in her chest.

'You and me,' he continued, looking distraught. 'The marriage thing. It's not working.'

'But it was your idea to go away for a few weeks. I thought you were happy to leave me behind.'

'Really?' He looked up at her with a pained expression.

'Well, you haven't exactly rushed home lately. You've stayed away more than you've been here. I thought you needed a complete break from me.'

'No! What I wanted was for you to fight, argue, scream and shout, beg me not to go to Germany. But you didn't.'

Sam almost laughed at the irony. It was exactly how she had felt about Reece. She wanted him to fight for *her*.

'We've practically lived apart for the past few years.' She sat down beside him on the settee. 'I thought you didn't want to be with me any more.'

'Then why didn't you say that you wanted me to stay?'

Sam paused to collect her thoughts. 'Do you mean that this was some kind of *test*?'

Reece nodded, looking sad. 'I'm not going to Germany. I just thought I'd see if you cared enough to stop me.'

'That's really sneaky.' Sam gasped at the unfairness of the situation. Why would he do that to her? More to the point, it showed that both of them were lying to each other about various things. They couldn't even communicate properly anymore. How the hell had it come to this?

'Is it?' Reece ran a hand through his hair. 'It told me what I needed to know.'

'No, it didn't!'

'Then tell me that you want me to come back home on a permanent basis and I will.'

'You mean back to working in Hedworth?'

Reece nodded. 'There are a few apartment blocks being built. I've been offered a twelve month contract.'

Sam gnawed at her bottom lip. What a mess. Reece must feel like he didn't belong here anymore. She cursed herself inwardly. Had she been inattentive to him when he came home at the weekends? Not making him feel welcome so that he'd gone to seek solace elsewhere, treating his work colleagues as his family and following them around the country?

Reece stood up, and for a second she thought he might leave.

'I'll make coffee,' he spoke softly. 'Would you like some?'

Sam nodded slightly. She watched him walk through to the kitchen and then flopped back onto the settee. If her mind had been in turmoil about kissing Dan Wilshaw earlier, it was in a complete state now.

Reece had tricked her? Really? Had he been so miserable that he'd felt the need to test her? Maybe it was sneaky but if it was the only way he could get her to admit her feelings for him, then that was wrong.

She had to tell him how she felt about them being stuck in a rut, see if the situation could be sorted. Perhaps if they got back onto some sort of even keel, things could turn around.

The doorbell rang again.

'I'll get it,' Reece shouted through.

Sam hardly ever had visitors, unless it was Louise – and she knew it wouldn't be her as she had just left her. All of a sudden, she sat up. No, it couldn't be...

She heard the door open – and then everything switched to slow motion.

'Hey, there, gorg –'

Sam ran through to the hall to see Dan standing on the doorstep, holding a bouquet of the most beautiful flowers in his hand.

'So he's the reason why you didn't care if I went to Germany or not?' Reece seethed.

'No, Reece… I. No.'

Sam looked from Reece to Dan and back to Reece. She wanted the floor to open up; she would have preferred to be anywhere else than here. As her heart reached out to the man she'd betrayed, she tried to find the right words to explain her actions. She said the best two she could think of.

'I'm sorry.'

'I take it this is a bad time,' said Dan, with a grimace.

'Piss off before I punch your lights out.' Reece kicked the door shut in Dan's face before turning to Sam. 'You bitch! No wonder you didn't want to fight for me.'

'It's not like that!' Sam cried. 'I would never do anything to hurt you.'

'And you expect me to believe that?'

'You have to. I never meant for it to happen.'

Reece's shoulders rose, as if he was ready to take whatever she said with dignity. 'Never meant for what to happen?' he asked.

Sam faltered. What the hell was she going to say to that? 'It's not what you think.'

'You have no idea what I'm thinking. No idea what I'm imagining.' Reece went to speak again but changed his mind.

Sam would never know what he was about to say because he opened the door.

'Reece, wait!' She grabbed his arm. 'Please don't go.'

But Reece pushed her hand away.

'Reece!' Sam followed him a few steps down the driveway before stopping. She stood in the cold and dark of the night as she watched him disappear. Tears poured down her cheeks. She wished she had the courage to go after him. But it was too late to make amends now, even if that had been remotely possible in the first place.

CHAPTER EIGHT

'Sam's not coming in today,' Louise told Nicci the following morning as she pushed up the metal shutters on the stall. 'I've had a text from her to say she's been throwing up. I hope she's feeling better later, because she's coming out with me tonight.'

Nicci fastened the straps on her overall and began to fill the till with coins. 'You can't expect her to go out if she's ill.'

'But she can't let me down now.'

'She isn't letting you down. She's *ill*.'

'She isn't ill. She's just moping about Dan because she doesn't know what to do.'

'How do you know that?' Nicci frowned. 'Did she say something to you last night?'

'No, but he hasn't been around, has he?'

'So you can't just jump to that conclusion!'

'Well, I—'

'Just text her to see if she's okay.'

Louise nodded but didn't reach for her phone. 'I'll do it later, when I get a minute.'

Nicci reached for hers instead. 'She might need you to fetch something for her. She doesn't have anyone else to run around for her like we do.'

'I know that.'

'Well, the least you can do is ring to see if she needs anything.' Nicci tutted. 'You're so selfish at times!'

'I will ring her!' Louise snapped, thankful for once that the front doors had opened and the Saturday morning rush to the stall had started. She wasn't feeling too well herself, if truth be known, after too much wine the night before. After Sam left, and the girls had gone up to Charley's room, she and Matt had shared a bottle of red. When he'd fallen asleep on the sofa around ten o'clock, she'd opened another bottle, only now regretting it.

Louise rang Sam and when she didn't reply, sent her a text message asking if she needed anything. When a message came back after ten minutes to say she was fine and would call her later, she sighed, hoping she wasn't going to let her down at the last minute.

As the morning wore on, regardless of her message, Louise's thoughts turned to the night out and what she'd wear. When she went out with Sam, she tended to dress more conservatively now. On one occasion, she'd worn a really short skirt, low cut top and the highest strappy sandals she could find while Sam had worn jeans and a simple white top. Sam looked like she was going out for a meal rather than a good drink and dance session and it made Louise feel rather tarty.

But no matter what, she always had a laugh with Sam and she was desperate for a good night out with her again. It had been an age since the last time, just the two of them. Even so, Sam probably wouldn't go to a club if she was well and that frustrated her. Louise wanted to stay out as late as possible.

She was so bored with her days that she wanted her nights to be lively, exciting; as well as give her the opportunity to meet someone nice. Of course she could get casual sex from Rob Masters but what she wanted was a man to call her own, to meet someone that she had actual feelings for. Someone who would treat her like a real lady, who she could treat nicely back, and who wanted her for her mind as well as her body. Someone to help keep Charley in order now she'd morphed into a stroppy teenager.

Louise wanted someone to love her too. Sam had that. Why couldn't she?

It was lunchtime and Sam still hadn't changed out of her pyjamas. Her hair flicked up in places that it shouldn't and as she'd downed most of a bottle of red before collapsing on the sofa late last night, what was left of yesterday's make-up was still caked underneath her eyes.

What a disaster last night had been. The look on Reece's face kept flashing in front of her eyes. She could almost put words to it. Hurt and humiliation, mistrust and rejection. She knew if she ever had the chance to explain, he'd never believe she and Dan weren't an item – although Dan had certainly got under her skin in the few hours she'd shared with him.

If only he hadn't turned up unannounced. She could have talked things through with Reece and decided where they were going first. Then she could have dealt with Dan, either telling him not to pursue things, or giving him the go ahead. Or indeed, waiting because she was so unsure about either.

She cursed out loud. How could she feel sorry for herself? She'd let Dan smooth talk her and had turned into a tart without a second thought for her marriage. Okay, she could blame some of it on loneliness but that didn't mean she should have acted inappropriately with another man to make herself feel better. What she'd done was unthinkable and no matter how much she cried, it wouldn't change the past. She'd let Reece down. Their marriage was over, even if she didn't want it to be.

And Dan, what was she going to do about him after sending him away? At least he'd taken his flowers with him so that she hadn't got a constant reminder of how everything had gone wrong in a matter of minutes.

The tears started again. What was she going to do? She needed to talk to Reece, explain what had really happened. She reached for her phone and dialled his number, but there was no reply.

'It's ringing but she's still not answering,' Louise told Nicci two hours later. Her fingers and thumbs flicked over the keypad of her phone. 'I'll text her, see if she'll call me later.'

'I wouldn't hold out much hope of her going out then,' Nicci warned as she weighed out two kilos of potatoes for an elderly gentleman and popped them into the carrier bag he was holding out. 'You'll have to rethink your plans.'

'I'm not going out on my own again.' Louise sighed. 'It's like being Belinda no-mates. And even I know I need to keep myself away from Rob Masters this week. It's just not healthy.'

'And you don't exactly set a good example for Charley now, do you?'

Louise looked on in horror. 'Charley doesn't know about him! I'd die with embarrassment if she did.'

Nicci placed half a white cabbage on top of the potatoes in the carrier bag. 'You'd be surprised how much Charley does know. She's not a child any more.'

'I know, but even so …'

'You need to be careful that she doesn't get the idea that it's okay going around doing that, because it isn't. Especially at her age. That's £1.72, Mr Austin. Ta very much.'

'You make it sound much worse than it is!' Louise protested, but her younger sister just shook her head.

While she served the next customer, Louise mulled over what Nicci had said. Was she a bad influence on her daughter? Would Charley grow up to think that love was hard to find and that it was okay to have casual drunken sex nearly every weekend on a night out? If she did, then yes, it would be her fault.

She stared ahead, noticing that Jess was chatting to Ryan, over on his stall again, whispering together like a pair of kids. Matt was showing a customer a few phone covers, but looked like he was trying to listen in on their conversation too; Louise saw him glancing over whilst trying to keep his customer interested in a sale. Even when he'd popped one of the covers in a bag and rung it up on the till, Ryan and Jess were still talking.

'Matt!' Louise shouted over. 'You going out tonight?'

'Yeah,' he shouted back. 'I told you I'm meeting a few mates in 'The Duck'. Do you want to come along too?'

Louise kept her sigh to herself. Even though she'd asked him once already, she'd hoped that he'd change his mind and be around to keep an eye on Charley while she went out with Sam. Although Charley was nearly sixteen, Louise hated the thought of her being alone until the early hours of the morning, and she couldn't sleep over at Sophie's every weekend. Her night out definitely looked doomed now.

'I think I'll stay in and grab another takeaway,' she shouted back.

'I can share it with you, if you like?'

'No, you go out. It'll do me good to stay in for once.'

'Okay. But let me know if you change your mind.'

Louise turned back to see Nicci shaking her head again.

'What now!'

'You shouldn't take him for granted.'

'What do you mean?'

'I know you wanted him to look after Charley.'

'No, I did not!'

'Then who was going to look after her while you went out gallivanting with Sam?'

Louise didn't have a lie ready and was annoyed that her little sister could read her so easily.

'Stop going on at me,' she snapped. 'Anyone would imagine I only think of myself. I happen to care about other people too.'

'Only when it suits,' said Nicci. 'I know you too well. You'll wear Sam down by ringing her all afternoon until she gives in, no matter how poorly she is. And Matt will do anything for you and Charley. He's already said he'd drop his plans to stay in for you. He's a really good friend but you treat him like a hired help.'

'I paid for the curry last night and all the drink to go with it!' Louise retorted.

'That was only to butter him up so that he would help you out tonight. Why didn't you ask him then if he'd watch over Charley, before he'd made plans?'

'He told me he'd already arranged to go out last night.'

Nicci tutted. 'You're trying to make him feel guilty, aren't you? You selfish cow! You'll do anything to get your own way. Honestly, Louise, sometimes I'm embarrassed to call you my sister.'

'Thanks a lot, Nicci!'

As Nicci marched over to a woman holding a bunch of bananas aloft, Louise heard her mobile phone beep. She read the text message that had arrived and huffed loudly. It was from Sam. She wasn't going to make it tonight.

After hearing the conversation shouted across between Matt and Louise, Jess sidled over to the boys' stall. Maybe she could use this news to her advantage.

'So, you're off out tonight then, Matt?' Jess queried, wrapping her hair playfully round and round her index finger as she stood talking to him and Ryan.

Matt nodded. 'Yep, you can join us if you like. I think Nicci and Jay are coming out too.'

'I'd rather eat my own vomit,' she muttered.

'Pardon?'

Jess stifled a giggle. 'I said I might just do that.' She turned back to Ryan. 'Will you be there?'

Ryan huffed. 'Me? Naw.'

'Why not?'

'Because he stays in with his *wife*,' said Matt pointedly.

Jess knew he was trying to warn her off, but she ignored him.

'Why don't you come out on your own?' she asked Ryan. 'Are you under the thumb?'

'No!' said Ryan, a little offended. 'I do go out some weekends, but not all of them. The twins take up a lot of our money.'

'I might have to babysit for you one night,' she whispered to him. 'Then you could give me a lift home. I've seen the films; the babysitter always gets the husband.'

Ryan nearly choked with laughter. He spluttered, patting himself on the chest.

'Something stuck.' He glanced at Matt, who looked nonplussed. He'd missed the comment again but realised that had been intentional. Jess didn't want him to hear what she had said to Ryan.

The tension on the stall when the two of them were together was more than electric. It was primal. Matt frowned as their heads bowed together again and Jess began to giggle. He had to do something to split them up.

'Ryan, we need some batteries fetching from the stock room,' he said. 'Size AA and AAA. I'll watch the stall while you fetch them, if you like.'

'There's enough under the counter for now,' said Ryan, never taking his eyes from Jess.

'Jess!' Malcolm shouted over. 'I need a hand over here!'

Jess sighed. 'Another day, another dollar. I'll catch up with you later.'

Ryan grinned. 'You can count on it, my lovely.'

Matt shook his head in annoyance. Ryan was such a snake at times. He wished he would realise how lucky he was to have a wife like Sarah, and two lovely little girls. The fact that Ryan seemed willing to throw it all away for some young tramp – again – was beyond his comprehension.

Well, he had covered for him before and felt bad about it. He wasn't going to do it again.

When they finally finished for that evening, Louise went home in a strop. All week she'd had a feeling that Sam would let her down at the last minute. She seemed completely out of sorts but didn't want to talk about it, even when pushed. Louise had even suggested she call round to see her but Sam had declined company altogether. Which meant either Louise went to the pub with Matt and his mates and came back early because of Charley, or she stayed in and moped alone. Choices, choices, she thought wryly. So many of them.

Charley was in the living room when she went in and if Louise wasn't mistaken, she had actually run the hoover over the carpet. She eyed her daughter suspiciously, wondering what she was after.

'You okay?' She asked as she shrugged off her thick fleece. 'Thanks for tidying up.'

'Well, you work hard, so I should do my bit every now and again.'

Louise paused, momentarily lost for words. She wanted to ask if her daughter had been abducted by aliens and replaced by a goody two-shoes clone while she'd been at work.

'Have you eaten?' she asked instead.

'No, but Sophie is coming around later. We could nip to the chippie, if you like? Oh, you're going out, aren't you?'

Ah, that explained everything. Louise assumed she and Sophie wanted some time to themselves. At least they were back on speaking terms again. She sat down beside her on the settee.

'Well, I *was* going out.' She sighed loudly. 'But Sam is poorly.'

'Oh.' The look of disappointment on Charley's face was clear.

'What are you up to, Charley Pellington?'

'Nothing!' Charley answered quickly. 'We were going to watch a DVD, that's all.'

'Sounds like a good idea.' Louise thought a little teasing was in order first. 'If I stay in with you, we could order in pizza and make it a real girlie night, if you like.'

'Cool,' said Charley. Her pout said anything but.

Louise laughed as she stood up. 'I suppose I'll crash Matt's night out and give you some peace. I'm only going to the local, mind. I'll be back around eleven so you won't be on your own for too long. Would Sophie like to sleep over?'

Charley tried to hide the grin spreading across her face. Perfect. She reached for her phone to text Sophie the good news.

'Good to go! It was a piece of cake!'

CHAPTER NINE

Charley took an age to get ready that evening. She couldn't wait for her mum to go out so that she could give Sophie the all clear. Sophie was meeting up with Connor Blackstock and Owen Machin before they all came over to her house. They were bringing vodka with them. Let the fun begin!

Dressed in a T-shirt and leggings, she applied a bit of foundation. She didn't want it to look too obvious that she was preparing for a good night in. Once Louise had gone out, Charley could add the rest quite quickly – layers of thick, black mascara like she'd seen her mum doing, a deep red lipstick and that skimpy dress she'd worn only once because Sophie said it made her look fat. Well, admittedly it did, but it also showed off her boobs.

Tonight, she was determined to go just that bit further with Connor. Despite the pact she and Sophie had made, she wanted to experience a few things for herself. And she did like Connor, even if she was going to use him to clear her name.

After the week she'd had, she knew how she could get her own back on Aaron. He and Connor were big friends and if she did things with Connor, because she hadn't done anything with Aaron, then the joke would be on him. It was a perfect plan really. And Connor Blackstock was so good-looking, with thick black hair, dark skin and eyes that did something to her when he looked her way. His body was toned, legs muscly, because he played football. She and Sophie had watched him in the park only the other day.

Charley had been surprised when he'd started showing an interest in her at school yesterday. She'd always secretly liked him but as most of the girls in their year at school fancied him too, she thought he was out of her league. Connor told her that Aaron was a fool and that he didn't know how to treat a girl. He said he wouldn't treat Charley that way if she went out with him.

As his best friend, Owen, had made it totally clear that he fancied Sophie, they'd arranged a double date tonight. Thank goodness her mum had decided to go out with Matt. She would have hated to cancel it.

'You sure you'll be okay, Charl?' Louise popped her head around the bedroom door.

Charley nodded, trying not to look as if she'd blow a gasket with excitement. 'Have a good time.'

'I'm only down the road if you need me.'

'Mum, I'll be fine! I'm not a kid any more.'

'I still worry, Charley.' Louise sighed.

Once she heard the front door close, Charley watched from behind the bedroom curtain until her mum disappeared out of sight. Then she texted Sophie to say that her mum had left. Quickly, she shimmied into the dress, found her favourite black wedge heels and applied the rest of the make-up.

With butterflies in her tummy, who would need chips! She wouldn't be able to eat.

Louise arrived at the pub to find Matt and his friends already over in the far corner. She waved as his eyes caught hers, and he held up a glass of wine she realised would be for her. Easing her way through the crowd, she said hello and sat down beside him.

The Fox and Duck public house – known locally as 'The Duck' – was a warm country style pub in the middle of the suburbs. Thankfully forgotten by the brewery, it hadn't recently undergone any of those gimmicky makeovers that could sometimes sink a pub before the first opening night was over. It had typical velvet-backed seating around the edge of the room, and light wooden tables, the stools topped to match the seating. Swirls of burgundy and cream on the heavy-duty carpet matched the colours in the curtains and for all its old clutter, the place was inviting, and full of regulars that were always up for a laugh. At least here she didn't have to queue to use the loos – unless it was New Year's Eve – she could get served at the bar after only a couple of minutes and it was a place where she'd often be bought drinks without feeling the need to return the favour – not that she ever took advantage.

The place as usual was packed, the regular disc jockey shoved into the corner and playing the same records as the last time she'd been in. DJ Dave was big into Northern soul and Motown, which meant that everyone else had to be too. Fortunately for Louise, she was quite partial to most of the tracks that he played. 'I Get My Kicks Out On The Floor' was a particular favourite, as was 'Ghost In My House'.

'Have you heard from Sam?' Matt asked.

'No,' Louise replied, immediately feeling guilty that she hadn't bothered to contact her after she'd sent the last text message. She was supposed to be her best friend. 'Anyway, what's up with you, out on your own on a Saturday? Had a row with the Mrs?'

Matt had been seeing a woman called Lorraine for about four months now. Not that Louise was counting or anything but after a while, she'd started to panic at the length of this latest relationship. Their friendship hardly ever got questioned, unless Matt went out with someone for more than three months. It wasn't as if Louise was involved with him romantically but because he spent so much time around at her home, some of his girlfriends over the years had ended up giving him grief. On the odd occasion, he'd told her he'd had to choose between her and them. She'd laughed it off, but secretly felt delighted when he'd told her she had won the toss up and no woman was going to come between him and his mates. She glanced over at him now as she settled in and took off her coat. He winked and she winked back with a grin. She was so lucky to have him as her friend.

'So?' she said, after taking a large gulp of wine. 'You haven't answered my question.'

'Night off,' said Matt.

Louise nodded slightly. She knew enough to know when Matt didn't want to talk about something. Instead she turned to Amy, who had slipped in beside her after arriving with her husband, Dave.

The next couple of hours went quickly as Louise chatted with Matt and his friends. Besides Amy and Dave, there were two more men, Harry and someone called Griff, and another couple, Sally and Chris.

Sally had recently given birth to a daughter and this was their first time out since Sophia had been born eight weeks before. Already, Sally was looking at her watch and fidgeting in her seat.

'She'll be fine.' Louise saw Amy place a comforting hand on her arm.

'Course she will,' said Louise. 'I remember when I first left Charley with my parents. I was so pleased that I could go off and dance all night without worrying about her. As if I didn't have a care in the world.'

'But you were only eighteen yourself, weren't you?' Sally said, a little too sharply for Louise's taste. 'I suppose you would feel like dancing the night away at that age. But now,' she caught her breath and tears welled up in her eyes. 'Now, I feel like I've lost my right arm.'

'I feel like I've been using my right hand a lot, lately,' Chris sniggered, noticing she was upset and trying to lighten up the conversation. Sally punched him lightly on the shoulder.

'How old is Charley, now?' Amy asked.

'Fifteen going on eighty,' replied Louise.

'When Sophia is fifteen, I'm not letting her out of my sight,' said Dave. 'I remember what I used to get up to at that age.'

'Louise still does that now, don't you?' Matt looked over his pint glass at her.

'What is it? Pick on Louise night!' she cried.

But everyone laughed it off with cries of, *at least someone is still getting some.*

'I'll have you know that my daughter is at home right now,' Louise continued haughtily. 'She's staying in with her best friend and they're watching a DVD.' Her eyes dropped. One thing was for certain, she knew that Charley and Sophie wouldn't be getting up to what she would have at that age – or rather, what she was still getting up to now …

'What kind of DVD?' asked Griff.

Louise glared at him as Matt came to her defence.

'Charley's a good girl,' he told the group. 'I wish she was my daughter.'

Louise smiled, feeling all warm inside. He really did care for her that much.

'You should've had kids of your by own now,' said Dave. 'You don't want to get involved with anyone else's.'

'Oi,' snapped Louise. 'There's nothing wrong in this day and age with bringing up someone else's children as part of your own family. If it was a problem, the world would be full of single parent families.'

'Look around you. The world already is.'

'Do you want a family, then, Matt?' Sally butted in.

'Yeah, course.' Matt laughed. 'I just need to find me a decent woman first.'

'What about Lorraine? I think you make a lovely couple.'

Yes, what about Lorraine? Louise held her breath as she waited for his reply.

As all eyes fell on Matt, he sat back in his seat. 'What's with the Spanish inquisition all of a sudden?' he cried. Then, 'stop looking at me! I'm not going to comment!'

Saved by the sounds of DJ Dave as he started on his second set of the night, Matt went to the bar for the next round. Louise joined him, slipping an arm around his waist.

'If I were Lorraine, I'd feel very lucky to have you,' she shouted to him.

'What?' Matt indicated that he couldn't hear her.

Louise sighed. It had taken all her courage to say it once. She didn't feel brave enough to repeat it.

'I said, let's get wasted,' she yelled.

While Louise became more and more inebriated as the night wore on, Charley was having the time of her life. She and Sophie had given the boys some money earlier that day and they'd arrived tonight with a bottle of vodka and a few cans of lager. Connor passed for eighteen easily, especially with his older brother's ID.

They were watching *Bridesmaids,* which was something that Charley had seen several times already, but tonight she had far more important things to do than watch the TV screen. It was half past nine and she and Connor sat side by side on the settee, his arm draped casually around her shoulders. Across the room, Sophie was squashed in next to Owen on the armchair.

Charley couldn't believe that she was sitting with Connor Blackstock. Despite fancying Aaron before the blowjob saga, she'd fancied Connor for months now. Most of the girls in her year at school did, he was such a catch. And he was even nicer close up. He had a slight bit of stubble on his chin, a silver chain around his neck and the smell of something gorgeous wafting from him. His eyes were dark and moody, his lips unbelievably kissable, drawing her to them, and even though it made her think of Alex, wonder what he looked like, she thought maybe it would be okay if she did have a bit of fun with him. The pact she'd made with Sophie said it had to be someone special, right? Connor *was* special, even though she hadn't kissed him yet.

Pushing away all thoughts of common sense, Charley glanced over when she heard a slurping noise. She squirmed. Owen was snogging the face off Sophie. *She* didn't seem to be having any problem with the intricacies of the pact. But how embarrassing, and while she sat in the same room, next to Connor! She knew he'd heard them too, as his head had turned at exactly the same time. He glanced at her and they both grinned. Then he moved towards her slowly, his hand at the back of her neck. Well, at least Sophie's slurping had been of some use.

Charley gasped when his lips met hers, but not due to passion. Connor's kiss was all tongue and she could hardly breathe as he tried to ram it down her throat. She moved away slightly but he took this as a cue and pushed her back into the sofa. With his weight pinning her down, Charley thought she might as well try and get into his kiss. He'd slowed down the exploring with his tongue. That's because his hands had taken over.

'Erm.'

Charley glanced up to see Owen and Sophie standing up.

'We're just going to get a drink from the kitchen,' Sophie managed to say before Owen dragged her away by the hand.

Once they'd gone out of the room, Connor kissed her again and she relaxed a little. It was one thing to want to share details with Sophie but she didn't want to do anything at all in *front* of her. The feelings jiggling around inside her felt so good, like fizzy sweets exploding inside her tummy. She kissed Connor back, using her tongue to flirt with his now, while she ran her fingers through his hair. Without warning, they lost balance and rolled onto the floor with a thud.

'Ow,' they both said in unison before laughing. Then the kissing began again. For a few minutes, it was fine but with more room to manoeuvre, Charley felt Connor's hand beneath her rib cage. It lightly brushed her breast before falling on it and squeezing roughly. Trust her to put on a dress, she cursed inwardly, pushing his hand away. Now he wouldn't be able to get inside it without going all the way up. It didn't deter Connor. She felt his hand move down over her dress, trying to find the hem. He slid his hand up her leg, further, further, not stopping with his lips on hers for a second. She froze for a moment when he reached the side of her knickers. But his hand continued upwards, up and over her ribs to rest on her breast. She gasped as he touched it, gently at first, then a little too roughly. She wanted to tell him it wasn't an orange but he seemed oblivious to her.

And then she felt it, his *thing* hard against her leg. She pulled away for a moment. After all the things she'd discussed with Sophie about how far they were both willing to go, when it came to the crunch she just wasn't sure.

'What's up?' asked Connor abruptly.

'Nothing.' Charley shook her head quickly. 'I just thought I heard something.'

'It's probably those two in the kitchen.'

Connor kissed her again. His hand was still inside her dress, but she moved it down as he squashed her breast again. But then his hand moved lower and she realised he'd taken it as a sign that he could touch her. His fingers found the front of her knickers and slid underneath the material. She froze again, this time out of curiosity, as he tucked his hand in and moulded it around her. After all the vodka she'd drunk, she felt slightly light-headed. Warm feelings were flooding her body, things she'd never experienced before. It felt really good as he moved his hand back and forth over her…

She sat upright and pushed his hand away. 'What the hell are you doing?'

'Well, you've never had that done to you, from what I hear,' Connor replied shortly.

'What – what do you mean?' Charley could hardly speak.

'After what Aaron said, I know this is our first date but I thought if I got you off, you'd do the same to me.'

Charley pushed Connor away, stood up and straightened her dress. She could see herself through the mirror above the fireplace. Her face was flushed, her neck too. Her eyes shone underneath far too much makeup. But inside, those first feelings of passion had disappeared entirely.

'You came for a bet, didn't you?' she said quietly.

'No, I didn't.' Connor lay back on the carpet with a sigh. 'I do like you, Charley. But I did want to see if the rumour was true.'

'And I suppose you're going to make nasty things up about me too and spread them all around the school, aren't you?'

When Connor shrugged, Charley wished she had the nerve to kick him where it would hurt him the most.

'There's nothing to tell anyway.' Charley was close to tears now. 'I want you to go.'

'But we've only just started.' Connor grabbed her hand and tried to pull her down again. She snatched it away sharply. 'No. Sophie! Sophie, where are you?'

A moment later, Sophie came rushing in to the room. She was tucking in her T-shirt, lipstick smeared all over her face. Owen followed close on her heel, fastening the buckle to his belt.

'What's up?' asked Sophie.

Charley didn't know what to say now that Sophie had come in to help her. But Connor was done. He got up from the floor.

'Don't worry, I'm going,' he said. 'No point wasting time on a dick tease like you, anyway.'

Charley waited for them to leave before bursting into tears.

'What happened?' asked Sophie. 'Did he push you too far?'

Charley opened her mouth but no words came out. She was unable to explain. Why had she stopped him? Why had she been so frightened? She couldn't understand it. She'd wanted Connor to touch her, feel her up. Why couldn't she let herself go?

She looked sheepishly at Sophie. 'Did I ruin things for you, too?'

Sophie sat beside her and gave her a hug. 'Course not. There'll be plenty of other opportunities. He had a big willy though.'

Charley laughed. She couldn't help it.

Sophie laughed too. 'To be honest, I was a bit scared that if he tried to put it in, he'd split me in two. So I'm glad you shouted when you did.'

Charley laughed at this even more. She grabbed the bottle of vodka, pleased to see it was half full.

'Let's get wasted,' she said, mirroring her mother's words without knowing.

Sophie grinned and turned the volume up on the television. 'Ooh, he's got a sexy arse.' She pointed at the young lad on the music video.

It was enough to make them roll around with laughter again.

CHAPTER TEN

Sam opened her eyes to Sunday morning with a heavy heart but a very clear head. She'd been trying to ring Reece all day yesterday but with no answer from him, had gone to bed quite early the night before. It had taken her ages to get to sleep and then she had woken up numerous times before cat-napping and waking for good at six a.m. It had given her ample time to think things through and now she realised that Reece turning up unannounced on Friday evening might have been the best thing that could happen to them.

Sam loved Reece but wasn't sure she was in love with him any more. Even though a part of her was relieved that she wasn't going to break his heart by ending the marriage, it didn't make her feel any better knowing that Reece probably felt the same too. They'd been together since forever. Sam couldn't help thinking that if they'd managed to have a child, maybe things would have been more solid. Ideally, they would have been a family now but after trying to conceive for five years, they'd decided to let nature take its course. Unfortunately, nature never had and as well as having different interests, the lack of children had made them grow apart rather than bring them closer together. And that's why, for her, it was better for Reece to work away than to be here all the time, constantly reminding her of what they should have by now.

Recently, she'd started looking at children in that way – in the *ticking biological clock* kind of way. She'd smile at babies in supermarkets and feel herself being pulled towards the rows of tiny clothes when she went shopping in Hedworth. Thirty-four was still youngish to have a child nowadays, so she knew she still had time, but Sam desperately wanted to become a mum, and soon. And although Louise's life had been hard as a single parent, it had hurt Sam to watch her bring up Charley, envying her having a daughter of her own.

Secretly she'd wanted to broach the subject of adoption, see what Reece's reaction would be. But as they grew further and further apart, it just hadn't seemed appropriate. Yet another weekend had gone, and then another, and another. And now she doubted if he'd ever come back, apart from one last time to collect his belongings, maybe tie up loose ends. Reece came home to hand her his keys on Friday. If Dan hadn't been there to put the nail in the coffin, she could have fought for him and he might have been willing to try again. But now it was too late.

She sat up in bed and hugged her knees, deciding that she wasn't going to give up on Reece. They had been together for sixteen years; he was worth fighting for. She'd ring him again later to see if he'd answer this time. She had to try and make him see that she hadn't cheated on him. That she'd stopped things from going too far with Dan, because it was Reece that she loved. Their marriage couldn't be over just like that. Could it?

'What a mess,' she said aloud for the umpteenth time that weekend.

* * *

Louise woke up at ten thirty. Her head felt like someone was repeatedly hitting it with a brick, her mouth dry and smelling nasty. She looked around the room, her clothes and shoes thrown anywhere as she'd removed them quickly to climb into bed, to stop the room from spinning.

Like a good girl, she'd stayed at the pub with Matt and his friends until eleven as planned and then he'd insisted on walking home with her. She recalled messing around with him – at one stage she'd pushed him into someone's hedgerow, laughing loudly as he'd bounced back at her. She remembered singing with him, and checking on Charley once she was home, finding Sophie top to toe in the bed next to her.

After showering, she went downstairs. Charley and Sophie were sitting at the kitchen table, both still in their pyjamas. Charley looked a little green, her head resting in her hands.

'You look like I feel,' Louise said to Charley, after flicking on the kettle. 'What's wrong?'

'I've got a terrible headache.' Charley winced as she'd moved her head slightly.

'Oh, dear. You're not coming down with something?' Louise reached over and placed a hand on Charley's forehead. 'You're not hot.' She sniffed, then drew her head back as she smelt a familiar smell coming from the two girls. 'Have you been drinking?'

'We had a little bit last night,' said Charley.

Louise sniffed again. 'What did you have? And where did you get the money from?'

'I bought it, Louise,' said Sophie, hoping to take the blame for Charley. 'My mum gave me some money and I – I bought a bottle of vodka.'

'Vodka?' Louise's face was like thunder as she stared at Charley.

'I'm nearly sixteen!' Charley retorted.

'You're still a child! And you'll do as you're told in my house.'

'It's not your house. It belongs to the bank until you've paid off your mortgage.'

'Don't be cheeky – and stop trying to change the subject. Have you any idea how much trouble I would be in if you were caught with alcohol underage?'

'Whatever.' Charley rested her head on the table for a moment.

'Was there anyone else here with you, last night?'

'No!' Charley sat upright so quickly that she felt the room start to spin.

Louise pointed a finger close to her daughter's face. 'If I hear from any of the neighbours that you had boys around, Charley Pellington, I'm going to –'

'We didn't have anyone around!' Charley fibbed then looked to her friend for support. 'Did we, Sophie?'

'No, Louise, we didn't.' Sophie fibbed too. But it had the advantage of calming Louise down.

'Booze and boys at your age just don't mix,' Louise addressed them both. 'I should know.'

'Yes, *you* should know.' Charley's tone was snide.

Louise went to speak but chose to pause for a minute. 'You might think I'm being mean watching out for you like this,' she said eventually, 'but I'm not. I don't want you making the same mistakes that I did.'

'Like having me,' said Charley.

'No!' Louise sighed in exasperation. 'You know I didn't mean it like that.'

'Yes, you did!' she snapped. 'Just because you got pregnant when you were young doesn't mean that I'm going to. It's not the law.'

As Louise stood with her mouth open, Sophie, sensing the tension in the air, jumped up. 'I think I'd better be off,' she said. 'I'll see you later, Charl.'

Charley nodded and grimaced again. Her head. She hated vodka more than she hated Connor Blackstock right now. This morning, she'd woken up to three text messages asking if it was true he got her off last night.

Louise finished making her coffee, slid the one she'd made for Charley across the table and sat down in the chair that Sophie had just vacated.

'That was a bit below the belt, don't you think?' she said. When Charley said nothing, she continued. 'I only say these things because I care.'

'Yeah, right.'

'I want you to see a bit of life before you settle down. I want you to do well at school and explore the world, see where the day takes you. I don't want you to be stuck in Hedworth like me.'

Charley started to speak but Louise went on. 'You may think you have it hard but believe me, life gets harder. Mistakes made now will haunt you forever.'

'I had a drink, Mum, not a baby like you.'

Louise slapped the palm of her hand on the table. 'I had a drink and look where it got me.'

Charley's eyes filled with tears. 'It got you *me*, remember. All the times you talk about lost chances, you make me feel like it's my fault.'

'No, Charl. I didn't mean—'

Charley prodded herself in the chest. '*I* was the mistake you made. How do you think that makes me feel when you go on all the time about you never having any chances in life? That you never made it any further than living in a tiny terraced house? It makes me feel guilty, especially as you've never told me who my father is, denying me the chance to get to know him. I have a right to know who he is but you—'

Louise leaned across to touch her hand but Charley pulled it away abruptly. She stood up, scraping the chair across the floor. 'I hate you. You're so selfish I'm surprised anyone would want to spend time with you. No wonder you're lonely.'

'I'm not lonely!'

'Yes, you are. I hear about you in the nightclub. Damien Masters goes to my school – he tells me what you get up to with his dad because you can't get a man of your own. It's embarrassing, Mum, and hurtful when they call you a slapper and say that I take after you. It's not fair.'

Louise paled. Charley knew about Rob Masters and was turning the tables, telling her off now. How did that happen?

'Now listen here, young lady,' she said, trying to exert her authority. 'What I do in my private life is up to me.'

'And what I do in mine is up to me! You don't have any right to tell me off. I'm actually better behaved than you, and you should give me credit for that.'

Louise looked up as Charley stormed out of the room. She jumped as the kitchen door banged shut, closed her ears to the thunder of feet going up the stairs.

'That conversation went well, Louise,' she spoke to an empty room before raising her mug into the air in a silent salute. Yet what Charley had said brought tears to her eyes. Her daughter was getting teased for her sluttish ways, for everything she did at the weekend, when all Louise set out to do was forget about her miserable life and have a bit of fun.

But, every day, Charley was taking in everything that she did. Louise *wasn't* setting a good example. Calling her a mistake was wrong, for starters. She wasn't a mistake, nor a burden, but sometimes she wished Charley had come later in life, when she had been settled with the right man, and had been more mature about motherhood.

Louise wouldn't swap her daughter for the world. Maybe she needed to show her that.

Charley ran upstairs and threw herself onto her bed. Sometimes she hated her mum so much that she couldn't find the right words to express herself. What was it with her? She got a little bit tipsy on vodka and Mum thought she could lecture her, when she came home drunk EVERY weekend. Charley wished Louise was like normal mothers, who take their daughters out shopping or for coffee – or even to the cinema. When was the last time they went anywhere together? She sat and thought about it but couldn't remember.

And now she had to put up with all this rubbish about Connor too. Charley hoped she wasn't going to get it in the neck at school tomorrow. She couldn't believe he'd start another rumour. She'd had enough with the one last week.

She sat up, and stared at herself in the mirror on her dressing table. What was wrong with her? Why wouldn't she let a boy touch her? Her mother certainly didn't have that problem. Why was Charley such a prude? Was it because she thought more of herself than her mum did? She thought she could do it but when it came down to it, she was scared. What *would* happen if she got pregnant like her mum did?

She was right about one thing, though. Charley didn't want to have a baby tying her down. As soon as she was old enough, she was leaving Hedworth and going to London.

She'd get a job on a magazine, become a writer. She'd make something of herself, even if her mum hadn't.

A message pinged in on her phone. It was from Alex.

> AP: How goes it, C?
>
> CP: Crap as usual. I hate my mother.
>
> AL: I hate my dad too. Got a bollocking for not doing my chores again. What are you doing today?
>
> CP: Not sure. Might hang around the shops with Sophie. You?
>
> AL: Not much to do here either. Wish I could come and see you. We could hang out together.
>
> CP: Me too. I wish you weren't so far away.

Charley sighed. She did too. She wished she could see Alex, chat to him face to face. Maybe he would understand how she was feeling. Lonely, abandoned, hurt. Why was life so cruel?

After what happened with Dan, Sam hadn't expected to hear from Reece until some time had elapsed and he could think straight. She'd left another message on his phone but didn't hold out much hope of a reply. So it shocked her when, at two thirty, she received a text message to say that he was on his way over to see her.

She opened the door to him, feeling nervous, not knowing what to expect. From the bags under his eyes, he looked like he'd had no sleep either. He entered, and paced the hallway until she'd closed the door. They stood in silence, neither of them knowing what to say.

'I didn't think you'd want to see me so soon,' Sam started.

Reece shrugged. 'I've stayed at my parents' place since Friday.'

'Oh!' Sam had automatically thought he had gone back to Sheffield after their row.

'Well, there was no way I wanted to stay here after … why did you do it, Sam?'

Sam cringed inwardly. 'What exactly do you mean by 'it'?' she asked.

'Do I have to spell it out to you?'

'Not really, but you need to know that I didn't do what you think I did.'

Reece looked confused.

'I didn't sleep with Dan.' At the mention of his name, Sam saw her husband flinch. Tears welled in her eyes.

'Then what did you do with him?' he asked. 'Those were some flowers.'

Sam felt her bottom lip start to tremble as she saw the pain in his eyes. Thankfully, she'd had the sense not to take the bouquet from Dan.

'Shall we go and sit down?' she suggested.

They went into the kitchen, she made coffee, and they sat in the conservatory. The winter sun streamed in, it looked such a lovely day. With a pang of regret, Sam thought that they should have been out somewhere enjoying it. She closed the blinds, sat down and began to speak.

'So, you only kissed?' Reece asked afterwards.

'Yes.' Sam left out the part where Dan had his hand in her pyjama top ... he didn't need to know every detail. 'Yes,' she said again.

Reece looked her straight in the eye. 'You hurt me so much.'

'I never meant to.' Sam cursed as tears poured down her face. She hated crying when she was in the wrong. It made her feel weak. But she truly was sorry for what she'd done to him.

'What would have happened if I hadn't come back?'

'If I was going to do anything, it would have happened by now,' she said truthfully, although purposely omitting the details. 'I'd been having doubts about us and he – he was there to give me what I needed, I suppose. I know it was wrong, but I just wanted some affection. I missed having you around, and I wasn't sure that you even wanted to be around any more. When you did come home at weekends, it wasn't right, was it? We'd become like strangers and it hurt. And, even though I want to make it better between us, I don't know how to.'

'So you thought sleeping with another man would do the trick?'

'I didn't sleep with him!'

They were silent for a moment, each lost in their own thoughts. Sam studied Reece while he stared through the window, working out what to do next. Would he accept the job in Hedworth and come home or would he leave for

Sheffield and not come back? She could almost see a pendulum in his mind swinging backwards and forwards. Yes. No. Yes. No.

'Come home,' she pleaded. 'Let's see if we can work things out.'

'I don't know. It hurt me so much to think—'

'I won't hurt you. I'll never hurt you, but don't you see? We've both let things slip. You've been such a huge part of my life. You were there for me when my dad died, but I've been lonely for so long and our marriage felt so stale. I was upset that maybe it was me who couldn't give you children, that maybe we would have been closer if I had. My attraction to Dan was just because I want to feel desired after so long of being part of the furniture.' She paused. 'If you come back to Hedworth, maybe we could get back what we had. I— I really do love you.'

'I don't know.' Reece swallowed. 'I'm not sure that I trust you now.'

Sam frowned. 'That's a bit unfair. I've had to trust you when you've been working away for all these years. Don't tell me there haven't been any women who attracted your attention over in Sheffield?'

'They haven't exactly been falling at my feet.' He gave a weak smile.

'You know what I mean.'

'I know that seeing *him* on our doorstep, thinking that you and him …? Well, it made me so angry. You're my wife, Sam.'

'Then come home.' Sam reached across to touch his face, wiping away the lone tear that trickled down his cheek. 'Please, let's try again.'

CHAPTER ELEVEN

The next day, Hedworth market hadn't just got the usual Monday-morning-blues feel to it. It had all-round-abysmal stamped over it. Louise was hardly speaking, still upset by Charley's accusations and talk of letting her down. Nicci was in a mood after 'suffering Jess whinging all weekend' and Sam? Sam was a complete mess and didn't really notice the cold shoulder she was getting from Louise. As if that wasn't bad enough, over the aisle, Jess was getting down to some serious flirting with Ryan. Enough to put Matt in a bad mood and for Louise to notice too.

'What's with Jess hanging around the boys' stall?' she asked Nicci. 'She's been chatting to Ryan more than she's been working on her own stall. I thought she was supposed to be helping her dad so your future mother-in-law could take some time off.'

'She should be.'

'Well, she's spending more time across the way with our Ryan. If she doesn't watch what she's doing, I'm going to have words with her soon.'

'She could just be being friendly,' Nicci snapped. 'Not everyone's man mad like you.'

Louise turned to her sharply. 'Hark at you, sticking up for her. And what do you mean, man mad like me.'

'You know what I mean,' Nicci blushed.

'No, I don't,' Louise disagreed. 'Care to enlighten me?'

'Care to serve someone?' Sam stood in the doorway of the back room, pointing out to a small queue forming. 'Can you keep your focus on this stall for a change?'

'Flipping heck, not you as well. What is it with everyone, lately?' said Louise. 'Yes, Mrs Danson. What can I get you?'

As she served the waiting customers, Louise covertly watched Jess. She was really lapping up the attention from Ryan, leaning across the counter so that she could be nearer to him. She saw Matt's face once or twice. He was scowling and it didn't suit him. Matt was one of the most happy-go-lucky people she knew.

Once she got a lull in customers, Louise would go over, see if he knew why Ryan and Jess had become thick all of a sudden. She knew her brother had wandering eyes and hands after the last time, two years ago, when he'd had an affair. She'd thought he'd really messed up but her sister-in-law, Sarah, took him back after a temporary split.

'How are you feeling now?' she asked Sam who had come out of the back room, trying to get into her good books again.

Sam frowned. 'Oh, I'm fine, thanks. I'm sorry about Saturday night. How about I make it up to you this weekend?'

Louise smiled sarcastically. 'Great. Something to look forward to. Being let down again at the last moment.' She saw Sam's jaw drop. 'Wait, I'm kidding!'

Sam didn't look too sure as she disappeared into the back room again. Louise cursed quietly. Why couldn't she learn to keep her big mouth shut? She looked across at the stall opposite to see that both Ryan and Jess had disappeared. She went to the edge of the stall and looked either way down the aisle but she still couldn't see them.

'Where's Ryan?' she shouted across to Matt.

'Stock room,' said Matt.

'What are him and Jess up to?'

Matt shrugged. 'Could you just watch the stall for a moment?'

Louise nodded but before she could pry any further, she spotted Dan Wilshaw walking towards them.

'Hey, the Lone Ranger returns,' she said. 'I hope you've come to put a smile on Sam's face. She's a right moody sod this morning.'

'Butt out, Louise.' Sam pushed past her and into the aisle. Grabbing Dan's arm, she marched off with him. 'Be back in ten minutes.'

'Oh, great, I get to mind two stalls now?' She turned back to Nicci with a huff.

When Reece had left yesterday, telling her that he needed time to think about things before coming to a decision, Sam had texted Dan, asking if they could meet. She felt it was only fair to explain things to him face to face rather than over the phone. She hadn't been surprised when he didn't reply but she hadn't expected to see him here at the market this morning.

They went outside to the back of the building, out into the staff car park. After the bright winter sun of yesterday, the sky was grey and it was drizzling slightly. Two smokers huddled together underneath the shelter.

'I'm sorry,' Sam said after it was obvious Dan wasn't going to speak first. 'I didn't know he was going to turn up like that.'

'I wouldn't have come if I'd known.'

'In fairness, I didn't know you were coming either.'

Dan gave a half smile. 'Trust me to be spontaneous. I thought I'd surprise you.'

Sam smiled. 'I think you surprised yourself.'

Dan reached for her hand. 'It was so awkward. I had no idea what to do.'

'I don't suppose any of us did.' She left it in hers for a moment. 'It felt like I was in a sitcom. I was half expecting a studio audience to gasp.'

In silence, they pretended to watch a lorry that was reversing in front of them.

'Do you still love him?' Dan asked afterwards.

'Yes.' Sam wasn't going to lie any more.

Dan dropped her hand.

'I'll always love him,' she said. 'I've known him so long, since we were teenagers. It's hard not to remember a time when he wasn't around. But that's where the problem lies. We became too familiar.'

'How can you become too familiar? Too complacent, you mean.'

'Not exactly. We weren't together enough.'

The reverse warning beeps stopped on the truck and the brakes hissed. The driver got out with a slam of his door.

'What do you want to do?' Dan asked.

Sam looked away for a moment. She didn't have a clue how things would work out between her and Reece but she couldn't string Dan along. It wasn't fair to him.

'I have to let you go,' she told him. 'I can't play around with your feelings.'

'But can't you see what we'd started might be good, it might even be better? I can give you just as much as Reece, more in fact. I could be here for you every night and not just at the weekends.'

She shook her head.

'So you used me.'

'No!' Sam looked up, horrified that he would think that. 'I was unsure of what I wanted, and I thought it was you.'

'You did use me.'

'For all I know, I could be making the biggest mistake of my life, but please, I have to give my marriage the chance it deserves. I want to stay loyal to Reece. I tried not to get attached to you, and yet I know I was developing strong feelings for you. But I owe it to my husband to try and make it work.'

Dan folded his arms and looked into the distance.

'I'm sorry if I hurt you,' she added. 'But I never intended you to feel used.'

Silence fell between them.

'Are you sure?' Dan asked eventually.

Sam nodded slightly. She wasn't sure at all, really.

'I can't persuade you otherwise?'

With tears glistening in her eyes, Dan pulled her into his arms and hugged her tightly. Sam hugged him back, breathing in the scent of him for one last time. As they pulled apart, she felt her shoulders relax for the first time since Friday evening.

'See you around, then.' Dan kissed her lightly on her cheek before walking away.

Sam watched him, feeling deflated but okay with herself. Sighing, she went back to the stall.

While Sam was outside deciding her future, Jess was hoping to secure hers. She and Ryan were in the stock room. It was the only place that she could think of to get him on his own without Matt scowling at them or one of Ryan's sisters butting their noses in. Or being asked to come back to the stall because she'd been missing for the past half an hour.

She looked at the list her dad had given her. Cola cubes, Kopp Kops and sherbert lemons. She'd remembered them fondly before she'd come back to Hedworth. Now after eating them whenever she'd weighed a bag out for a customer, she was sick of the sight – and the smell – of them all.

She reached up, trying to see the top of the shelving unit, knowing that a flash of her stomach would be on show. She glanced back at Ryan. Yes, he was looking. Good boy.

'Can I pass you these down, please?' she asked.

Ryan read the label on the plastic bottle. 'Sherbert lemons? I bet you'd like something more substantial on your tongue.'

Jess giggled. 'Cheeky!'

'I bet I have something that tastes just as good, too.'

She placed the tip of her index finger into her mouth suggestively. 'I don't know what you're insinuating,' she remarked. 'They were merely on the list, along with Cola cubes and aniseed balls. I like aniseed balls. Something for me to roll around my tongue.'

'Do you have to be such a tease?' Ryan moved in closer but the door opened behind them. Seeing that it was Matt, Jess stooped down quickly so that she was hidden behind a pile of boxes.

'Ryan, I need you on the stall, mate. What the hell are you doing in here?'

'Just after some ... some clips.' Ryan pretended to search around, jumping slightly as he felt a hand creeping up the inside of his leg. 'I could have sworn we had some.'

'Where's Jess?'

'She slipped into town for something. Haven't seen her since.'

The reply throwing Matt a little, he snapped back. 'Well, hurry up then.'

The door closed behind him and Ryan breathed out a sigh of relief. He looked down at Jess, her hand up to his thigh by this time. 'What are you doing? I nearly had a heart –'

The door opened again and Matt was back. Ryan held his breath as the zip went down on his trousers.

'While you're there, mate, can you see if we have any cans of WD40?' Matt shouted.

'Will do.' Ryan's voice came out as a squeak as Jess slipped a hand inside his pants. He cleared his throat. 'Be with you in a minute.'

The door closed again. Ryan sighed with relief. He pulled Jess to her feet, quickly fastening his zip.

'You can't do that here!'

'Don't be ridiculous. No one will see us.' She moved towards him, stopping with her lips an inch from his. 'And we're going to get it on sooner or later, aren't we?'

'Maybe.' Ryan's voice was thick with lust.

'So it won't hurt if I give you a little something to remember me by?'

She kissed him, searching out his zip again. This time there was no hand to stop her.

CHAPTER TWELVE

For the second morning in a row, Charley got back into bed as soon as her mum left for work. The second morning in a row that she wouldn't be going to school again because of the rumours.

It had started yesterday afternoon when word began to spread about what she and Connor had got up to and by last night, she'd had to switch off her phone again. She'd had emails too and comments left on Facebook about what she'd supposedly been doing. If anyone had doubts about what she had got up to with Aaron, she knew they'd disappear after Connor had added fuel to the fire.

What was it with everyone? Why did her so-called friends want to ruin her life? As usual, Sophie had got away with things and she'd stopped Owen from going all the way with her. Although that was probably because Charley had shout-ed out for her friend when Connor had – oh, no, she was still embarrassed just thinking about it.

Charley knew girls of fourteen, sometimes thirteen, who had sex, but she couldn't see what all the fuss was about. However, she realised that her time with Connor had un-leashed some feelings inside her that she'd never felt before. She couldn't even share her private thoughts with Sophie, which was unusual.

She sent her friend a text message to say that she wasn't going in to school. She couldn't face all the teasing again. Everyone would be staring and laughing at her, wondering if she really did put out like the boys had said. She knew girls in her class would make snide remarks. She wasn't the guilty party but they wouldn't care.

It wasn't fair. Why should she be picked on because she wanted to stay special to someone? She just wasn't ready to go that far yet. Stupid thing was, if she had given them what they wanted then she probably wouldn't even be getting talked about. Charley reckoned it was only because her and Sophie made up that stupid pact, that they were trying to stay virgins instead of sleeping around that had given her a reputation. As a dicktease! Life was so unfair. She seemed damned if she did and damned if she didn't.

Charley's message was returned, letting her know that Sophie was on her way over. It was only quarter past eight, so she logged on to Facebook next. Ignoring the comments that people had left about her again, she noticed a smiley face in reply to her comment telling one of them to go stuff themselves. She'd been mortified when she'd thought of Alex reading all the abuse last week, after what had happened with Aaron, but he'd been really helpful and they'd chatted it through within a few emails. He'd told her to ignore them all, not once questioning if any of it was true. Now, she couldn't believe it was happening again and prayed that Alex didn't start to believe the lies. She clicked on to see if he was online but he wasn't there. He must have gone to school.

When Sophie arrived, Charley made them both tea and toast before sitting on the settee next to her. They sat in companionable silence while they ate, watching some house renovating programme.

'He's such a cool guy.' Sophie sighed longingly as she ogled the young presenter. 'I think I'd like to date an older man.'

'Really?' Charley wrinkled up her nose. 'I'm not sure I would. He's old enough to be one of our teachers.'

'Oh, I meant someone as old as say, twenty. With a car, preferably.'

'Someone that old would be far more mature than anyone from school anyway.'

'I can't believe you're getting grief again,' Sophie sympathised.

'Me neither,' she said sadly.

'Aren't you curious though? To know what it's like?'

Charley shrugged. 'I'd rather not get pregnant.'

'Oh, there's ways around that. I'm going to look into going on the pill. Do you want to come with me?'

'No!'

'Why? If that's the only thing that's putting you off, maybe—'

'It's not. I just thought we weren't going to, not yet.'

Sophie took off her shoes. 'Maybe you should put out, just a little.'

Charley stared at her with wide eyes when she saw her best friend blush.

'Because you have?' Charley gasped. 'You have, haven't you?'

Sophie nodded and giggled. She pulled her legs underneath her and grabbed a cushion, hugging it to her chest.

'With Owen?'

Sophie nodded again. 'I met him again last night. His parents went out so we were all alone in his house. W—'

'Did you go all the way?' Charley interrupted, fearing for herself if she had. Where would it leave her if Sophie had done the deed?

'Not all the way,' Sophie admitted. 'But I was thinking about it the next time we meet.'

'Oh.' Charley was so surprised she couldn't think of anything else to say.

'You're not mad, are you?'

'No.' Charlie shook her head. 'Just a little shocked.'

'It's a natural act, you know, not a crime.'

'It is until you're sixteen.'

'I'm sixteen in a couple of months. Besides, everyone has to do it some time. And I've fancied Owen for ages. It just feels right. And I want to … I want to see what it's like.'

Charley did too. Why couldn't she let herself go? She'd liked what Connor had been doing but she'd got scared. And every time she'd let him get near to her, she had her mum's words running around inside her head. Charley didn't want to make the same mistakes she had; be trapped at such a young age with a baby to bring up.

'Come on, then.' She flicked her feet up onto the settee too. 'Tell me all about it.'

Tuesday evening, Nicci was in bed with Jay. Nothing unusual in that, except it was six thirty in the evening and they'd only just eaten. After dinner, Jess had gone out to do a little late night shopping so they'd spotted an opportunity to be alone. Honestly, it felt like going back to being a teenager again, waiting for her parents to go to bed before she could have a quick grope with her latest boyfriend. It just didn't feel right getting down and dirty when you knew your sister-in-law was in the next room and could probably hear everything.

'I wish she'd hurry up and move out,' said Nicci as she ran a hand lazily up and down Jay's chest. 'As much as I can be quiet, I'd rather be noisy.'

'Yeah, me too. I love it when I make you moan.' Jay gave her a quick squeeze. 'It won't be for much longer now.'

Nicci sighed. 'Are you sure about that? She looks as though she's settling in.'

'She hasn't been here that long. Give her a break.'

'But I like it better when there's just you and me.'

'Me too, babe. Me too.'

'Do you?'

'Hmm?'

Nicci could tell that he was falling asleep. She nudged him. '*Do* you think it's better when it's just you and me?'

'Yeah.' Jay yawned. 'It's you and me to the end.'

She turned towards him and propped herself up on her elbow. 'Then let's get married.'

Jay's eyes shot open. 'Where – where did that come from?'

'It came from the heart, silly,' she said, trying not to feel too embarrassed for blurting it out. 'I know we've discussed marriage before and you've always wanted to wait because of your past experience with your ex-wife, but, well, I think it's the right time now, so I thought I'd ask you.'

'Oh.' Jay laughed a little.

Nicci lay back down, as the atmosphere in the room became loaded.

'Don't you want to marry me?' she asked quietly. She didn't want to hear Jay say no but she had to be sure. Now that she'd broached the subject, she might as well find out the reasons why.

'Of course I want to marry you,' he said. 'I just want to get some money behind us first.'

'But it doesn't have to be expensive. I don't want a big church do or a castle – or even a huge hall. I just want –'

'Do ordinary people really get married in castles?' Jay broke in. 'I mean, isn't it just celebrities?'

Nicci slapped his chest playfully. 'I said I don't want a castle, you dope.'

'That's okay then. For a moment, I thought you were going to get me dressed up in some medieval gear and demand a banquet.'

Even though he was making a joke of things, Nicci felt better as he pulled her into his arms again.

'It might be good fun to eat from the plate with my hands, though.'

'Huh,' Nicci snorted. 'That's nothing new.'

Jay rolled on top of her and pinned her down by her hands, she thought with the intention of tickling her, but instead he just stared at her for a moment. Then he smiled.

'I love you, Nicci Pellington.'

'Then marry me,' she repeated.

'I will, just not yet.'

She pouted. 'Yeah, right.'

'Shut up.' He kissed her gently on the lips to stop her from complaining any more.

But it didn't stop her from worrying. She'd said that she didn't need anything expensive so why was he so reluctant? He loved her, she was sure of that much.

Maybe in time he would come around. After all, she had sprung it on him. Besides, she'd made a vow with herself, she never wanted to end up as lonely as her big sister.

Jess was trawling the shops at a late night retail centre a few miles from Hedworth, trying to find something to cheer herself up. She picked up a silk, plum-coloured bra and brief set and located its price tag. It was more than she'd normally spend but she felt like treating herself. And she knew she'd be showing it off soon to Ryan, now that she'd given him a taster of what was to come.

She paid for the item, already dreading going back to her brother's house as she put away her change. She wasn't sure she could stand another night with Jay and Nicci cuddled up together on the settee while she sat on the armchair like a gooseberry.

As she made her way into the next shop, her phone beeped. A text message. It was from Ryan.

'Great to spend a little time alone today. You blew me away ;)'

Jess giggled. He was such a pushover. Then she thought of an idea. Maybe there was another way to prolong going home tonight. She quickly texted Ryan back.

Two minutes later, she had her reply. Her smile widened when she read it. Ryan could only spare half an hour. Yeah, right. She couldn't help but laugh as she made her way to the car park where they'd arranged to meet. All it had taken was one quick blowjob for him to sneak away from his wife and kids.

Men, they were so gullible at times.

The past few days, Nicci's mind had been in turmoil. Since blurting out her innermost thoughts to Jay, she'd thought of nothing else but the wedding. She hadn't told anyone that she'd proposed to him but she couldn't help thinking that if they didn't just get married, they'd never do it. There would always be one more thing to get in their way. Would they ever have enough money? Would one of them lose their job? Would one of them become ill? Would she always dream about a wedding that she'd never have?

But then she'd got to thinking that maybe Jay was just scared of the whole idea of arranging the big day. Nicci had seen some of her friends being swept away by the whole idea of the romance of the wedding and spending thousands of pounds on their dresses alone. Although Nicci was a girly girl, she didn't want any of that splendour. She just wanted to marry the man she loved in front of her family and a few friends. If Jay was scared of the cost of it, she could easily get it done on the cheap.

So when she'd started to search online – just to have a little check of the prices of venues and cakes and flowers, she told herself – and she'd seen the amount of things on offer to make that special day perfect, well, Nicci had got a bit carried away. In fact, she'd clicked on a few buttons, purchased a few items and found she couldn't stop. And when she saw a hotel with a cancellation for Easter weekend, well, in no time at all, she'd convinced herself that it was what Jay wanted. After all, she was only making life easier for him, wasn't she?

It was over the family Sunday lunch at the weekend that Nicci confided in Louise. Sunday lunches at the Pellingtons were a real family affair. Once a month, they'd all gather at their parents – Ryan, Sarah and the twins, Abigail and Amelia; she and Jay; Louise and Charley, and Matt sometimes tagged along too. Sometimes Sam and Reece came. This weekend, Jess had blagged an invite. Nicci wasn't too pleased about it. But, as Jay had pointed out, if Matt could come along, then Jess could.

Everyone was there when they arrived so it took her a while to get Louise alone. In the end, she followed her upstairs as she went to use the bathroom. She sat down on the top step and waited for her to come out.

When the door opened, Louise jumped when she spotted her. She held her hand to her chest. 'You gave me a fright sitting there. What's up?'

'I need some advice.'

'From me?' Louise laughed. When Nicci didn't follow suit, she sat down next to her. 'Whatever's the matter?'

Nicci told her about the proposal. Louise let out a squeal and clasped her hand to her mouth. Horrified, Nicci turned the colour of beetroot.

'Really?' Louise whispered this time.

'Yes, but—'

Nicci didn't get any further as Louise gave her a hug, squeezing so tightly she could barely breathe.

'Ohmigod,' said Louise. 'My little sister's getting spliced at last. Have you set a date?'

'Yes, Easter weekend.'

'Next Easter?'

'This Easter.'

'That's less than three months away! Don't weddings have to be planned at least a year in advance?'

'As long as the venue is available, anything else can be worked around. There was a cancellation and I just went for it.'

'Really?'

'Really.' Her tone was defensive.

'So how did he pop the question?' Louise could barely contain her excitement. 'I mean, you've been wanting him to ask you forever.'

'I asked him.' Nicci started to look uncomfortable.

'No!' Louise clasped her hand to her mouth. 'Wow,' she finally said. 'This is fantastic.'

'You can't tell anyone,' Nicci told her.

Louise frowned. 'What do you mean?'

'Well … we didn't exactly agree on that date.'

'You mean Jay wanted another date? Did he want to wait a bit? Because if he did, don't worry about it and get it booked. Men don't like weddings and—' She stopped when she saw Nicci's face. 'What?'

'I haven't told him.' Nicci gnawed at her bottom lip.

Louise gasped. 'You mean he doesn't know?'

Nicci shook her head. 'I want to arrange it all, for a surprise.'

Louise whistled softly. 'Wow, that's a brave thing to do. Have you really thought this through?'

Nicci nodded. 'What do you think?'

'I'm not sure.' Louise paused. 'Don't you want Jay to get involved in anything?'

'Men don't want to know the intricacies and arrangements. I just thought it would be a nice thing to do for him. Show my gratitude.'

'Show your— you're marrying the man, not thanking him for putting up with you.'

'I think it's a bit of both.' Nicci grinned. Then she whispered. 'I'm getting married, Louise. In less than three months' time, I'm going to be Jay's wife!'

Louise hugged her sister. 'It is exciting news, even though it's all so secretive.'

'Will you be my chief bridesmaid?' Nicci asked.

'I'd love to!'

As Nicci smiled at her, she prayed Louise would keep her secret. If Jay found out what she was doing, he'd go mad that she'd spent so much money already. Still, it was their wedding day. And as much as she said she wanted to do it on the cheap, well, she should have the best, right?

'Tell me what you've planned so far,' Louise said, interrupting her thoughts.

'I've booked a hotel for the reception,' Nicci began.

'Already?' Louise sounded shocked.

Nicci nodded, eyes wide like a child's. 'I went to see a place ... and it was so beautiful. You remember when we used to talk about weddings as kids? I wanted a big hall or a marquee? Now that the law has changed and we don't have to get married in a church, this place is just what I ever dreamed of. And I've seen a gorgeous dress. It's off white, with a fitted bodice and . . .'

As Nicci told Louise about her big plans, Jess stood at the bottom of the stairs, tucked in the door frame of the hallway. Her fingers clenched into a fist, she had to stop herself from dissolving into laughter. How pathetic that Nicci had to plan a wedding in secret just to get someone to marry her. And to deceive her brother? Well, it just wasn't on.

She'd have to tell Jay. There was no way she could let him be tricked into getting married by Nicci. He needed his head examining even being with her anyway, Jess thought. Nicci was so wet.

As she heard the two women coming down the stairs, Jess slipped back into the kitchen unnoticed. Ryan was chatting to Jay so she went over to them. But Ryan hardly looked at her.

'Oi.' She prodded him sharply after a few minutes of being ignored. 'Aren't you speaking to me?'

'Course,' said Ryan, trying not to panic as he saw Jay look at Jess oddly.

But Ryan still wouldn't look at her and Jess knew why. His wife, Sarah, was sitting no less than three feet away from them. Jess studied her out of the corner of her eye. Sarah sat with her mother in law, Sandra, while her daughters played a game on the floor in front of them. Sarah Pellington wasn't a yummy mummy but neither was she a slummy mummy. She wore clothes that matched her age, which Jess reckoned was near or the same as Ryan's. Her daughters shared her blonde hair, blue eyes and dimples either side of their mouths.

And she hadn't let herself go, which had been Jess's first thought when Ryan started to pay her attention. She was glad now that she had manipulated her brother into getting her invited for lunch. It served Ryan right for feeling uncomfortable with her here.

She watched as Nicci joined them, giving Jay a quick peck on the cheek. As they cuddled up and started to chat, she leaned into Ryan slightly.

'No one will guess what we're up to if you just act natural.'

'Natural?' Ryan baulked. 'How can I act natural when you're here and my wife is over there? I feel like a right bastard.'

'Don't worry, babe,' she whispered. 'We're not the only ones with a secret. And ours is nothing compared to what I've just heard.'

CHAPTER THIRTEEN

With no interest being shown by Ryan, Jess decided to head off back to her brother's house after lunch without Jay and Nicci, on the pretence that some exercise would do her good after the amount of food she'd just consumed. If truth be known, she'd found the atmosphere stifling after a while. All those people paired off and playing happy families wasn't quite her thing.

As she walked, she thought about the conversation she'd overheard between Nicci and Louise. It was sneaky and the more she thought about it, the more she knew she should do something to stop it. By the time she got back to the house Jess had convinced herself that it just wasn't fair to Jay if she let it go ahead.

She took off her coat and ran upstairs into their bedroom, searching for clues. The room was all red and black, cushions piled up on the bed. Photographs that looked like they'd been taken by a professional photographer were spread across one wall. Tasteful but sexy photos, she realised. Peering closer, she laughed at Nicci's attempt to appear sultry, before grimacing as she saw her brother's bare chest on show in one of them.

On a makeshift desk over in the far corner, Nicci's laptop was open. Jess wiggled the mouse to find it was still on, but it was password protected. After trying a few names, she gave up. She glanced around the room, wondering where Nicci would hide something secret. She tried under the mattress. She looked in the wardrobes, even inside shoe boxes and handbags. But she couldn't find one single list or wedding magazine or anything that would incriminate her.

Disheartened, she went downstairs to the kitchen and made coffee, her eyes scanning the room. It was then she spotted a notebook with a bright pink spine, tucked in between the cookery books on the shelving. Jess got it down and opened it. *Bingo*. Written on the first page was 'Nicci and Jay's Wedding Planner.' Nice one, Nicci, she thought, smiling to herself. Jay would never find anything there.

She sat down at the table and rifled through it. Nicci had certainly been hard at work. There were cuttings of dresses and flower arrangements shoved in the front pages. Printed details from the internet of wedding fancies and shoes. She found details of the hotel that she'd heard Nicci talking to Louise about.

A note by the side of it read: 'Sent deposit £400.'

Next were caterers: 'Sent cheque £534.'

And cars: 'Sent deposit £250.'

Underneath those entries were written a number of things that needed to be sorted out, along with some rough estimates of prices. Jess quickly totted them up in her head. They came to nearly £10,000. Wow. She'd heard Nicci say it was going to be cheap and low key too. Not at these prices, it wasn't.

She paused for a moment. Since she'd been back in Hedworth, Nicci had been a right bitch to her. And after what Jess had gone through with Laurie, having to move back from her glamorous life in London to a shabby sweet stall in Hedworth, she didn't want to see someone else being happy. Perhaps her brother would tell Nicci to cancel it all. And maybe he'd see her for what she really was too; a scheming, devious cow who was after his cash. She must be creaming money off their joint account at this rate.

Forty minutes later, the front door opened. Jess jumped up and stood on the chair she'd pulled across from the kitchen table in readiness, then reached up to the shelving where she'd put the notebook back. As Jay and Nicci burst into the kitchen, laughing, she made it look as if she'd slipped and knocked it off the shelf.

'Oh, sorry,' she said, raising her eyes to the ceiling. 'Clumsy me. I was after a cake recipe. Thought I might do a little baking. You wouldn't mind, would you?'

Nicci paled as the contents of the notebook scattered over the kitchen tiles like confetti.

'Those are *mine*! She quickly dropped to her knees, trying to gather up as many as she could. Jay bent down to help her. He picked up a brochure, an invitation sample and a pile of handwritten notes, handing them to her before picking up some more. He was about to give her that pile too but pulled back his hand and studied the top piece of paper.

'What's this?' he addressed Nicci as he held up a photo of a model wearing a wedding dress.

'It's a— it was going to be a surprise.'

'A wedding dress?' Jay flicked through a couple more. Nicci glared up at Jess, who was smirking.

'Oops,' she said all innocently. 'Is that a secret notebook? What's in it?'

Suddenly, Nicci realised that she'd been set up.

'You bitch!' she shouted before bursting into tears. 'You've ruined everything.'

'What are you talking about?' Jess held up her hands in mock surrender. 'I was only after a cake recipe. What's that you've got, Jay?'

Jay was speechless. Flicking through the notebook, he became more enraged by the second.

'Will you give us some space, Jess?' he managed to say eventually.

'Of course,' Jess said sweetly as she got down from the chair and left the kitchen, inwardly congratulating herself. She hadn't even got to the top of the stairs when she heard raised voices. She grinned, thinking,

Bang goes the secret wedding.

Downstairs in the kitchen, Jay yelled at Nicci. 'You had no right to do this!'

'It was a surprise!' Nicci sobbed. 'I was going to tell you as soon as it was all organised. I know how you'd hate all the planning so I thought if I did it for us then all you'd have to do is turn up and—'

She stopped talking. All colour had drained from Jay's face, and his shoulders drooped. He looked like he was going to pass out. Panic set in. Had she read the signs wrong the other night? Was he only saying that he wanted to marry her to get her to stop talking about it? Men were good at that. They'd deny you'd said anything of the sort.

'I thought you wanted to marry me,' she whispered.

'I do! But—'

'There shouldn't be a but!'

'We don't have the money right now.'

'We can save it by Easter. I haven't spent that much.'

'Really?' He chucked the book at her. 'Have you added all that up? It must come to a small fortune.'

'I had to pay more for short notice.'

'Have you ordered everything?'

'Not yet, but—'

'Then don't.'

'But I—'

'And see if you can get those deposits back.'

Suddenly, Nicci shook her head defiantly. 'No,' she told him, knowing that if she cancelled everything there'd never be a wedding this year. She'd have to call his bluff. 'It's all done.'

'Then you'll just have to undo it all.' Jay threw the book onto the table and walked out of the room.

'Wait!' Nicci shouted after him but he kept on going, out into the hallway and through the front door.

Knowing there wasn't any point following him, she let him go. Running upstairs to have it out with Jess, she stormed in her room to find it empty. So too was the rest of the house. She must have slipped out while they were arguing. Wait until she saw her. She wanted her out of their home now.

In the kitchen again, she flopped into a chair, covered her face with her hands and sobbed. What had she done? Even though she had ignored the nagging voice inside that said she was getting carried away, she'd thought she was doing the right things.

Now it seemed as if she'd ruined everything.

Although Sam's weekend hadn't ended in tears, it had been a quiet one. And a lonely one too, even though she'd received a few text messages from Dan. He wanted to meet up with her again, despite her replying to previous messages to say that wouldn't be right.

Reece had rung on Friday night and told her he wouldn't be coming home that weekend, or the next, as he wanted to finish off the job he was contracted to do. Sam knew it was probably more to do with him needing more time to think, and that was fine with her. If he did come back, it had to be the right decision for both of them.

By the time Saturday evening rolled round, she still hadn't shared the details with anyone. Luckily, Louise wasn't begging her to go out that night. Earlier in the day, she'd grabbed a cheese topped bloomer and a large cream cake from Mr Adams' stall. She took it home and gorged herself silly on toast topped with more cheese. Simple, stodgy comfort food was what she needed.

On Sunday, the usual routine kicked in – washing, cleaning and ironing. By mid-morning, her chores were done, her house was shining and her mind still refused to switch off. Would they be doing the right thing if they started again – was it what they wanted? Was it really going to work? She knew they'd never know until they tried, and she had missed Reece being at home. But people could still be lonely in a relationship.

After mooching around for the rest of the day, by Sunday evening, as she settled down to watch *Downton Abbey*, Sam had convinced herself that after three weeks apart, she'd be really looking forward to seeing Reece. She wanted to be part of a couple again. She wanted to experience the butterflies that Dan gave her, with Reece again. And that couldn't be a bad thing, could it?

After a restless sleep, Nicci dragged herself into work on Monday morning. Jess had come in late the night before and gone straight to her room to avoid confrontation on her return. Nicci had wanted to charge upstairs and have it out with her but she needed to speak to Jay first.

He hadn't come home until just before midnight, and then he'd gone to bed without a word too. She'd had the silent treatment that morning as well. She wasn't sure what to do next – talk to him that night when she got home or leave it until he was calmer, after he'd had time to think things through. Either option was going to be a nightmare.

'Morning,' Louise greeted, as she got to the stall. 'How's the bride to be?' she whispered as she took off her coat.

Nicci was barely able to hold back her tears. She had to tell Louise what had happened. She was the only one who she had confided in about planning the wedding. And she might be better doing that than waiting for Jess to come over later and blurt out the secret to everyone, humiliating her even more.

'I don't know what to do,' she told Louise when she'd quickly run through it all. 'Why doesn't he want to marry me?'

'I'm sure he does but I'm not sure he'd want to be tricked into it.' Louise was always one to speak the truth.

'What do you mean?' Nicci frowned.

Louise hauled a sack of carrots up and began loading them into the display rack. 'I mean, he's not really been that keen before.'

'You think I pressurised him into it?' Nicci accused.

'No, I didn't mean that.'

'Yes, you did.'

Louise rummaged for the dregs in the bottom of the bag and scrunched it up once it was empty.

'What are you two bickering about?' Sam shouted through from the back room.

'Nothing.' Nicci glared at Louise, hoping that she wouldn't say anything to Sam.

'We were discussing *Wedding Belles,* said Louise when Sam appeared in the doorway. 'Aren't we always? Nic's mad about that show!'

Nicci left Louise and Sam chatting as she went off to the toilet. The weekend's television was always the topic of conversation on a Monday morning. Usually it made her laugh, but not today. Not when all she could think about was this wedding and not anyone else's.

What the hell was she going to do? If she cancelled the bookings she'd already paid deposits for, she'd lose all that money. It seemed a ludicrous idea. And she really wanted to get married.

She wrote a text message to Jay. Then she deleted it. Then she wrote another, this time adding kisses. Each time the words looked wrong, the tone too harsh. But she desperately needed to talk to him. In the end she settled on something and pressed send.

'Jay, please can we talk tonight? Nx'

Nicci washed her hands at the basin, the woman staring back at her looking frazzled and vulnerable. She pulled up her shoulders and took a deep breath. There was no point dragging this out. She would have it out with him tonight, as soon as she got home. Find out the real reason Jay didn't want to marry her. And if Jess was in, she could either go to her room or get out of the house until they'd sorted things. She had no time for her now anyway. This was her fault.

For the rest of the day, Nicci clock-watched. She added up stock with Sam, cleaned down shelving with Louise, finished serving the last few customers and was out of the door the minute it turned five thirty.

When she got home, Jess was nowhere to be seen, but Jay was sitting at the kitchen table. His face looked as pale as it had been yesterday, when he'd seen her pink notebook. In front of him were a pile of envelopes.

'You need to see these,' he said. He pushed them towards her, not meeting her eye.

Nicci slipped off her coat. 'What are they?' she sat down across from him.

But Jay didn't offer any explanation, just looked down at the table soundlessly.

She took the first letter out of the envelope and read it. Then she took out the next, and the next. Her hand covered her mouth as she saw the sums detailed on the statements. £2,000 owed on one. £792 on another. £3,000. £800. Then the final one: £8,263.47. Mustn't forget the forty-seven pence.

Nicci glanced up at him for an explanation. 'You owe all this money?'

Jay nodded, still unable to look at her.

'But, how?'

'It was before we met.' He finally raised his eyes. 'When Sharon left me, you know she took everything.' Nicci knew that his ex-wife had met another man and left Jay suddenly, a couple of years before she had started to date him. 'She also left me with a mountain of debt that was in both our names. She wouldn't pay anything towards them and as the companies knew my address and not hers, they latched on to me for payment. And every few months they wanted more and more. When the house was finally repossessed, the building society wanted so much back per month that I couldn't afford to pay off these debts too.'

Nicci picked up the first bill – Kitchens Unlimited. 'You still owe money for a kitchen?'

'Ironic, isn't it?' Jay sighed. 'I still have to pay for what I no longer have. Since I've met you, I've been able to keep up with the payments if I did a bit of overtime. But I can't afford to pay for a wedding too.' He reached across for her hand. 'That's why I was angry yesterday. I want you to have the best of everything but I want to pay for it all.'

'That's a little bit sexist, don't you think?' Nicci remarked. 'I go to work too.'

A faint smile appeared on his face. 'You know what I mean. How can I get married again when I haven't finished paying for mistakes from my first one?'

'I still can't see why you didn't tell me about it all.' She pointed to the pile of letters.

'I was too embarrassed. I hate how I was left to fend for myself. It wasn't my doing, it was hers. She always wanted the best of everything and I – well, I was always a soft touch. I tried my best to get out of the mess but I just got in deeper and deeper. I'm so sorry.'

Nicci smiled then. She couldn't help it. Here she was thinking that Jay didn't want to marry her and all the time it was because he had money problems. She leaned across the table and kissed him.

'You big dope,' she told him. 'I've been worried that you were trying to get out of things.'

'No. I really do want to marry you.'

'It doesn't matter.' She kissed him again. 'None of it matters as long as we're together. Who needs a marriage certificate when they have what we have? I'm not giving that up for anything.'

Jay smiled then, and she knew this time it was with relief.

'Jay, will you unmarry me?' she asked.

He laughed, only stopping when he leaned forward to kiss her.

Jess couldn't believe she could hear laughter coming from the kitchen when she got in. Really, were they so loved up that they couldn't stay angry with one another for more than a night? If so, she'd seriously underestimated Nicci.

She walked into the kitchen to find her brother and what still seemed to be her future sister-in-law holding hands across the table, heads close together.

'Oh, you're not at it again,' she said.

'We are indeed,' said Nicci. 'Nothing – or no *one*,' she looked pointedly at Jess, 'will stop true love.'

Jay sniggered. 'I think that's a bit too lovey-dovey for me.' He smiled at Jess who was scowling. 'But I am happy we got things sorted.'

'Well, that's wonderful news.' *Not.* Jess forced out a smile before leaving the room. She made her way upstairs and pushed open the door to her room – the box room, that tiny room that everyone saved for their first addition to their family. It was only big enough to fit in a single bed and wardrobe but how she wished she had a man and a house and a box room right now.

Tears welled in her eyes as she heard the laughter from downstairs. Why couldn't she be that happy? Why couldn't she be in love with someone who loved her back in just the same quantities? What sort of future was she going to have now?

CHAPTER FOURTEEN

After Louise had constantly badgered Sam all week about another attempt at a girlie night out, Saturday evening at nine thirty found them both in Atmosphere, a popular wine bar in the centre of Hedworth. The place was packed and it was standing room only.

Even though Sam didn't really want to be out on the town, she liked it in Atmosphere. It had the feel of a retro American bar, with embossed steel plates advertising such things as tea and peanut butter, adorning the walls along with posters of Marilyn Monroe, James Dean and a young Elvis Presley. World War Two pilots' uniforms and memorabilia could be seen displayed behind glass cabinets. There was even a Harley Davidson motorbike situated in an alcove above the stairs.

Here, Sam could enjoy herself, have a conversation because the music wasn't hurting her ears, and she could actually see people who were older than her. In most of the places Louise usually dragged her to, she wouldn't have been surprised to see Charley and Sophie lurking in the background. How did she get to be so old and, well, *past it,* when it came to going out on a Saturday night?

'So, come on. Spill the beans,' said Louise, after they'd got a drink each. 'Are things okay between you and Reece now?'

Sam froze as she knew she hadn't told anyone what had happened between them.

'What do you mean?' she asked.

'The last time we went out, you spent most of it moaning that you wished Reece would come home for good, so that you could feel like you were still a couple. Then there was this thing with Dan and since then, you've hardly mentioned either of them, come to think of it.'

'Reece and I are fine,' Sam nodded fervently, moving forward slightly as someone wanted to get past them. 'And I ended it with Dan.'

'What?'

'Oh, come on, Louise,' Sam protested. 'It was wrong what I did with him and—'

'What do you mean, what you *did* with him?' Louise gasped, her eyes widened. 'Did you do more than snog Dan Wilshaw, you dirty cat?'

'No!'

'Then what?'

'Just nothing, okay?' Sam almost shouted.

'Okay, okay. Keep your hair on.'

They sat in silence for a while. ALouise knocked back her drink and went to the bar for another round, Sam cursed herself inwardly for slipping up. Despite his constant efforts to get in touch with her again, she hadn't told anyone what had happened between her and Dan. But if Louise got wind of it, even though she had her fair share of secrets, Sam knew she'd be livid that she hadn't told her and then she would be worrying that Louise might slip up. She'd spoken to Reece again last night. He was coming from Sheffield to see her tomorrow for a couple of hours and she was looking forward to it.

Not wanting to mope on her night out, she watched as Louise chatted to some man at the bar. She smiled as she saw them laughing together. Louise was good to be around, most of the time. It wasn't that Sam didn't want to share things with her best friend. Usually she would, and gladly. But if she told Louise what she and Dan had done, and then that Reece had left, she'd put two and two together and make four which, unfortunately, would be the right answer. And Sam didn't want anyone to know how disgusted she felt with herself, especially if Reece decided to come back. So the fewer people who knew about it the better, as far as she was concerned.

Louise returned with their drinks and she and Sam clinked glasses. The wine flowed and before they knew, it was nearly midnight.

'I'm bushed,' Sam told her later when they were re-applying lippy in the loo. 'Shall we grab a kebab and head off home?'

'Nooooooo!' Louise flung an arm around her neck. 'It's too early. You and me are going clubbing.' She held up a hand when Sam started to protest. 'I haven't been dancing with you in a long while. I fancy a good boogie. What do you say?'

Sam paused. She couldn't recall the last time she'd had a dance. And if it meant getting Louise off her back for a while before she had to do it again, she might as well give it a shot.

She nodded. Louise squealed like a pig, much to the fright of some of the teenagers re-applying Mac lip gloss.

Twenty minutes later, they headed to Rembrandt's, the best in nightclubs that Hedworth had to offer. Once they were inside, Sam decided to forget about everything and have a dance with her best friend. And maybe, if they stayed on the dance floor, Louise wouldn't have time to meet a man and leave her alone …

Matt woke up with a jolt to see it was nearly half past one. His arm was dead where he'd been leaning against it. He stretched, yawning noisily. The television was playing something he couldn't recall watching. All he could remember was Charley going to bed shortly before midnight.

He really enjoyed watching over Charley. In her own sweet way, she reminded him of Louise when she was younger; sassy, cocky and full of life. Yet tonight he'd noticed she'd been a bit subdued.

He'd cracked a few jokes with her, which had raised the odd smile but that was all he'd got. Something was bugging her but he'd have to find out in her time. Matt knew better than to goad her into anything. She'd talk to him if she needed to.

He went through to the kitchen and made himself tea and a piece of toast before settling down in front of the television again. He could go to bed – there was one made up for him in the spare room. Louise would let herself in, albeit somewhat noisily, he knew from experience. But he always stayed up until she got back, waiting for her to check in. He couldn't sleep until she was home so what was the point of going to bed and lying awake tossing and turning anyway? Besides, he knew Louise was always happy to see him, despite whatever he heard she'd been up to with Rob Masters.

Matt watched an old movie for a while before his eyes shut again.

Sam glanced at her watch. Through squinting eyes, she peered at it again. Was it really nearing two a.m.?

Coming out of the ladies' for the umpteenth time since they'd arrived at Rembrandts, she searched around for Louise, only to find her on the dance floor, arms wrapped around Rob Masters as she snogged the face off him. Oh dear. If Louise didn't want to feel bad about herself on a Sunday morning again, she'd better rescue her. She tapped her friend on the shoulder.

Turning towards her, lipstick smeared all around her mouth, Louise beamed and pulled her into a bear hug. Sam found her head being crushed into Louise's chest.

'I'm ready to go home,' she shouted in Louise's ear afterwards.

'I can't hear you!' Louise shouted back.

Sam took her hand and pulled her towards the edge of the dance floor. When she turned to speak to her, she couldn't believe Rob had come over too, until she noticed Louise's firm grip on his arm.

'We're going home,' she told Rob, prising Louise's hand away.

'But I don't want to go yet.' Louise dragged Rob's arm up and pulled it around her shoulders. 'I'm okay with you, aren't I, Rob?'

Rob nodded. 'Yeah, course, babe.'

'Oh no.' Sam wasn't having it. 'I'm not leaving you behind so that you're embarrassed about what you get up to again.'

Louise's eyes nearly came out of their sockets. 'I'm not embarrassed,' she told Rob, stretching up to kiss him.

'Rob, have you any idea how you make her feel every weekend when all you think she's good enough for is a quickie?' said Sam. 'Louise hates herself every Sunday morning because she's been weak enough to fall for it again. She doesn't want to sleep with you. She's just lonely and you'll do at the end of the—'

'Oi!' Louise jumped in. 'I ...'

Sam held up a hand to silence Louise and continued to speak to Rob.

'If you actually like her, why don't you start dating? Act like a normal couple, not just two sad and lonely people at the end of a night out.'

'Okay, okay, you've made your point.' Rob held up his hands in surrender. 'I know when I'm being ambushed. I'll see you around, Louise.'

'Wait!' Louise shouted after him as he walked away. With a glower, she turned back to Sam. 'What did you say that for, you cow?'

But Sam wasn't listening anymore. She didn't drag Louise away kicking and screaming, but Louise did plenty of protesting as they left the nightclub.

'I can't believe you did that,' Louise continued to complain as they got into a taxi parked outside the entrance. 'I was ready to have a good time.'

'I was saving you from yourself.'

Sam slammed the car door shut behind them, giving the driver Louise's address. Although her house was the nearest to the city centre, she needed to make sure that Louise was home before she could relax. In her drunken state, she wouldn't put it past Louise to ask the driver to take her back to Rembrandts to finish what she'd started once Sam had got out.

'Yeah, right,' Louise slurred. 'More like you're jealous because you're not getting any.'

'Don't be disgusting.' Sam turned her face and stared out of the window.

But Louise wanted to argue. 'Well, I doubt you and Reece have sex any more.'

'Louise!' Sam remonstrated, appalled to see the taxi driver smirk through the rear view mirror.

'Well, come on.' Louise sat forward and ended up with her face in Sam's shoulder as the driver took a corner. 'You only see him for one night a week. What do you do for the rest?'

'I'm not arguing with you when you're drunk,' Sam told her. In this state, it was better for Louise to think she'd had the last word.

'And you must be frigid,' Louise added.

Despite herself, Sam wouldn't let those be the last ones.

'That's enough. You don't know anything about it.'

'Whassup? Truth hurt?'

They sat in a stroppy silence for the rest of the journey. Sam was grateful to see Louise's road when it came up ahead. At least now she'd get some peace.

The taxi came to a halt and Louise handed the driver money to cover the fare so far. But then she struggled to get out of the door. Cursing, Sam tried to help her.

'Would you sound your horn a little, please?' she asked the driver as they practically fell out onto the pavement. 'I've a feeling it'll be quicker than this one trying to find her keys.'

The light went on in the hallway as they walked up the path and shortly afterwards, Matt came to the door and stepped out towards them. Sam held onto Louise in case she fell.

'Hello, gorgeous,' Louise smiled at Matt, as Sam transferred her into his arms. 'Ya missed me tonight?'

'Like a hole in the head,' Matt muttered. 'I can't believe you're in this state again. Come on. Let's get you into bed.'

'Ooh, I'll let you take advantage of me, ifyerlike.'

As Sam left in the taxi, Matt helped Louise upstairs.

'I love you, Matt Ratcliffe,' Louise slurred as she dropped onto her bed.

'I love you too, you drunken tart.'

Matt slipped off her shoes. Louise was so drunk she was like the sacks of potatoes that she emptied day after day. Hearing her snort, her eyes already closed, he tucked her under the duvet and sat down on the bed beside her.

Lying on her stomach, Louise snored gently. He watched her for a while, wondering what she'd been up to. Tenderly, he brushed her hair away from her face so he could see her. Her make-up was smudged everywhere but she was still beautiful to him. If only she could look at him as more than a friend, he'd look after her. He'd provide for her and Charley. He'd make Louise feel loved so that she didn't have to sleep with other men to feel wanted.

Ever since he'd started to hang around with Ryan and Jay when they were teenagers some twenty years ago, Matt had always had feelings for Louise. He'd watched from the sidelines as she'd turned from a girl into a lady – a kick ass lady with a kick ass attitude. It had been worse when she'd found herself pregnant with Charley.

The pregnancy had shocked him at first but it didn't dampen his feelings towards her; he still wanted to be with her. But even though Matt and Louise had been out on a few dates when they were younger, Louise hadn't really wanted things to become more permanent. Her mind seemed to be elsewhere, on someone else rather than him. In the end, he accepted that the only way he would get to be part of her life was to stay friends with her, to become the person that she could always turn to, rely on.

Annoyingly, she'd often taken advantage of him. Now Charley was fifteen and it wasn't so bad, but when she couldn't be left alone for any length of time, Matt had become an unpaid babysitter. Although Ryan and Jay constantly told him that he was a mug, he didn't mind so much. Looking after Charley was something he loved to do. He couldn't wait to find a woman of his own and settle down to start a family.

But as time went by, somehow, he could never find the right one. His relationships would finish after a year or so – mainly because he spent so much time with Louise and Charley.

When she'd found Brian Thompson and ended up getting married, he'd wondered if it was too quick. They'd only been together a few months but they seemed to love each other nonetheless. And for a while, things changed between him and Louise. It meant he couldn't pop around just for a chat or a takeaway. Matt missed both Louise and Charley.

So when the marriage was over, he was there for her again – even if it was with a comforting arm around her shoulder, rather than in her bed. In the back of his mind, he'd always hoped that Louise would be his eventually, especially as Charley saw him as a father figure. But even then, Louise didn't notice him. Matt knew she thought of him as just a good friend. He'd been around for so long it was as if he was part of the paintwork, part of the family. Someone there for her and Charley; someone who could be relied on but not loved.

Still, at least he got to look out for her, even if it was in just a tiny way. And no matter what, he knew he'd always be there for her. Maybe one day she'd change her mind, see that he loved her. Maybe one day she would love him too.

Louise was snoring loudly now. He went to fetch a glass of water and a packet of paracetamol and placed them by the side of the bed. Then with a heavy heart, he left the room.

Arriving home after dropping Louise off, Sam let herself into her hallway and stood for a moment in the silence. Still a little tipsy, the emptiness distressed her and she burst into tears. She really didn't want to go clubbing every weekend to find someone to care for her. No wonder Louise went off with Rob Masters as often as she could. If she had to come home to a house as empty as this one felt right now, she'd soon be getting her kicks up some dark alley.

In the space of one evening, she'd realised just how lonely Louise must have felt after being on her own for so many years. Even though Reece hadn't been around as much as she would have liked him to be, Sam had always known she had him as her other half. The awareness was always there that he was only a drive down the motorway if she needed him.

Feeling the urge to talk to him, she kicked off her shoes and located her phone. Through watery eyes, she flicked through the contacts to find the one she wanted. Her fingers hovered over the button. It was nearly three a.m. now. Should she ring him? Of course she shouldn't. She would see him tomorrow.

Feeling alone and wondering how she had made such a mess of her life, Sam dropped onto the settee and sobbed into the cushion.

CHAPTER FIFTEEN

The next morning, Jess didn't feel like getting up. What had she got to look forward to? A Sunday with the loved-ups cooing over the breakfast table, letting her know for certain she had overstayed her welcome? Both her brother and Nicci had been cold with her since she'd tried to sabotage the wedding, but at least they had said she could stay a little longer. It wasn't an ideal situation, but what else could she do? She had nowhere else to go.

The day was going to drag. She couldn't even go shopping as she didn't want to spend any more than was necessary. She'd be needing to buy things for the baby soon.

Thinking of her predicament made her think of Laurie, wonder what he would be up to right now. No doubt, he'd be spending the day with his wife and children while she was alone again. She wondered if he'd thought about her at all since she'd been gone. Remembered the happy times they'd shared, the love-making as well as the sex.

If she was a cow, Jess would have made sure his wife knew about his extramarital bliss, plus the baby, and she would have gone after him for maintenance when the child was born. But even though Jess was needy, she didn't want to do that to him. She'd just have to make someone else fall for her now, someone like Ryan. He was as needy as her.

Desperate for the bathroom, she swung her legs up and out of the bed. As she stood up, she felt nausea rising and only just managed to get to the the toilet in time to throw up. Morning sickness, ugh. She couldn't wait for that to be over and done with.

She sat on the side of the bath waiting for her colour to return. The tears pouring down her cheeks took a long time to stop.

Louise opened her eyes slowly, knowing full well that she already had the headache from hell, even if she hadn't woken up properly. She'd been dozing for a while now, every now and then the voices of Charley and Matt floating up from downstairs. She'd been wanting to join them for ages but equally didn't want to get out of bed for fear of feeling worse than she did.

In the end, she didn't have to. There was a knock on her door.

'I've a mug of coffee if you're awake and decent,' Matt spoke through the door.

'Come in,' Louise croaked. She coughed to clear her voice as Matt came in.

He wafted a hand in front of his face. 'Morning, drunkard,' Matt greeted her. 'It smells like a brewery in here.'

'It's not that bad.' Louise attempted to rise on one elbow but her head began to pound so she lay back again.

'Did you take the painkillers I left out for you?' Matt plonked the mug on the cabinet next to the bed.

'Yes, thanks.'

'You were in a right state when you came in last night.' He sat down on the bottom of the bed. 'I worry about you when you get like that.'

'I'm fine.' Her voice came out as a croak again and she took a sip of water. She couldn't look Matt in the eye. 'I didn't say anything I shouldn't, did I?'

Matt sniggered. 'Just the usual stuff – how much you love me and I'm such a good friend.'

'It's all true.' She still couldn't look at him, already feeling her cheeks burning.

'You're flushed,' Matt noticed. 'Are you feeling ill or just hungover?'

'Is there a difference?'

'I suppose not.' Matt clapped a hand on his thigh before standing up. 'If you're staying in bed, I'll head off home. But if you're thinking of getting up, I'll do us a fry up?'

Louise felt her body spasm at the thought of anything greasy. 'Not unless you want the contents of my stomach on the plate too,' she replied.

'Ugh, you are gross at times.' Matt stopped and turned back just before he got to the door. 'I'll do me and Charley a breakfast anyway. If you want to join us come down.'

'Like this?' She pointed at her pale face.

'Yes, you'll be fine in your jim-jams.' He stared at her but she looked away.

'Okay, I'll see you tomorrow then,' he smiled. 'I'll text you later to see how you are.'

As soon as he was gone, Louise regretted not going downstairs with him. She knew she was in for a long recovery back to the land of the non-drunk. Still, she couldn't resist trying one more time to get out of bed. When the room began to spin, she sat down again promptly. She'd have to miss her time with Matt this morning.

Despite her head pounding that morning, Sam had got up early to prepare for Reece's arrival. Every time she glanced at the clock, she had butterflies in her tummy. She cleaned the house from top to bottom, as she did every Sunday morning, but this time it seemed different. This time she cleaned the windows – and the oven! It was as if everything had to be perfect. Pull yourself together, it's only Reece, she chastised herself as she made sure there wasn't any litter on the driveway that had blown in with the wind last night. Then she paused.

It's only Reece.

Those words spoke volumes said in that context. Because it wasn't only Reece this time. It was Reece, her husband who wasn't sure if he wanted to be married to her any more. And maybe the fact that she'd thought it's *only* Reece had been the problem all along – that she took him for granted.

The visit loomed as she prettified herself. Despite the tears of the previous night, and the pallor of her skin due to excessive alcohol and a late night, she managed to look half decent for his arrival. He arrived promptly at two o'clock, his eyes focussing on anything but her. Already it was as if they didn't know how to act around each other.

She hadn't asked if he wanted anything to eat but had assumed and made a Sunday roast, really making an effort to cook it just as he liked. It hadn't been a good idea because at first they'd sat in silence while they'd eaten. Then the small talk began.

'How's the stall?' Reece asked.

'Doing fine,' Sam nodded, pleased to have something to talk about. 'That range of organic chopped mixed fruits that we sourced are doing well.'

'That's great. I did wonder if they might not take off. And how are the staff? Is Lou being her obnoxious self still?'

'As ever.' She grinned now. 'She's fine - still messing around with Rob Masters, although I managed to keep her from his clutches by going out with her last night. Not sure I want to do it again, though. Clubbing's not really my scene.' Her grin faded. 'And do you remember Jay's little sister, Jess? She's back in Hedworth.'

'Oh?' He looked up at her.

'She's working on the sweet stall. I was surprised, to be honest. I mean, who would swap London for Hedworth indoor market selling strawberry bonbons and liquorice all-sorts? I couldn't begin to—'

'Sam,' Reece interupted, holding up a hand. He gulped before saying the words she'd waited to hear. 'How would you feel if I moved back in?' Nervously, he glanced at her while he ate a spoonful of apple crumble and custard. 'Are you able to give us another try?'

'I thought you'd changed your mind,' she confessed.

'I'm not going back on anything,' he said. 'What about you?'

Sam grinned as she shook her head. 'We've always been good together. We just lost our way when—'

'When we couldn't have kids,' Reece broke in. 'We should have been more grown up about it, I suppose.'

'I'm not sure I realised anything was happening to us until it was too late,' Sam admitted.

'I think maybe it was easier for me to run away too rather than face it at the time. But if I do come back home again, what happens if we still can't have children? How would you feel then?'

Sam gnawed on her bottom lip before speaking. 'Is that what you thought? That I didn't want to be around you any more because I couldn't get pregnant?'

Reece shrugged. 'I'm not sure. It might have been me that didn't want to be reminded, I suppose. But even so, will it cause us problems?' He glanced at her, the anguish in his eyes clear.

'Neither of us know if we can have children with anyone else, though, do we?'

'Is that what you wanted to find out?'

'No!' Sam recoiled slightly at his suggestion. 'I – I just missed being a couple, I think.'

Reece went to speak but changed his mind. Sam cringed, wondering if he was thinking that she'd slept with Dan, so she could be pregnant with his child. But his next question removed any doubts.

'So, what do you think?' He smiled at her the way he used to do, cheeky yet unsure, before reaching across the table for her hand.

Sam nodded, relieved and hopeful. After all these years, how could they not try again?

The next morning at work, Sam had a spring in her step. Reece had stayed the night and despite their nervousness, they'd made love and again this morning before he'd set off really early back to Sheffield. She couldn't believe that he'd be home for good when he came back next weekend. She made a mental note to get a couple of pieces of sirloin from Derek's stall. And a fresh cream trifle too. And some decent wine on her trip to the supermarket.

She added a reminder to her phone to make an appointment to see the doctor too. Having spoken about children again, they were going to look into fertility testing once Reece was back for good.

Sam went outside to the skip with a handful of cardboard boxes. As she stamped on them to crush them down, she noticed Jay dropping Nicci off and waved to them. Once she'd finished, she looked up again to see that Jay was still sitting in his car, staring ahead. She walked over to him.

'Hey.' Sam dipped her head to come level with his window. 'How're things with you?'

'So, so,' he replied, not even managing a smile.

'Oh, dear, sounds ominous. You and Nicci haven't fallen out, have you?'

'We had a row but everything is sorted now,' he said. Then, he added, 'actually, Sam, have you got a few minutes to spare?'

'Sure.' Sam clambered in beside him. Suddenly, Jay was telling her everything. About the proposal, the secret wedding, finding the notebook, the argument with Nicci, the debt he had, the money Nicci had spent.

'Wow.' Sam was a little dazed by how much she had to take in. 'I bet that felt good to offload. So what happened next?'

'Since we made up we've sat down together and devised a new plan to pay off the money I owe, as well as put a little away each month towards a wedding in a couple of years.'

'And is Nicci happy with that?' Sam knew how much she wanted to get married. It was all she ever talked about.

'She says she is.' Jay drummed his fingers on the steering wheel. 'But it didn't make me feel good to see her so hurt. And all that money she's wasted because of me. Most of the deposits she sent are non-returnable. Either the order goes ahead or the money is lost. I wish there was a way round it all.'

They sat in silence for a moment, each mulling on their thoughts.

'I don't know what to do.' Jay sighed out loud.

'Hey.' Sam touched his forearm gently. 'It's not the end of the world. Nicci will understand. And having a roof over your head without any debt is always a top priority in my eyes. Plus, she did do it all without you knowing.'

'That's true, but she only wanted to do something nice to surprise me.'

'Even so …'

Jay struggled to keep his emotions inside. 'I really want to marry her. I've wanted to for ages now. I want to have kids and I – I love Nicci so much that I want her to have the best of everything. It killed me to keep it secret from her. Couples shouldn't have secrets. I'm actually glad it's out in the open now.'

Ignoring the guilt that she felt at the mention of secrets, Sam's eyes brimmed with tears, touched that Jay would share that with her. They always looked so happy together, him and Nicci, infuriatingly happy, in fact. There must be something she could do. An idea began to form in her mind.

'Does anyone else know about this?'

'No.' Jay shook his head. 'I know it's sneaky but I had to share it with someone. And I couldn't talk to Matt or Ryan. I just couldn't.'

'Well, why don't you turn the surprise around?'

Jay looked puzzled.

'How about we do something, oh I don't know, at the market hall? Dress it up to look all romantic, get everyone around the stalls involved, keep costs down and keep it secret from her until the day.'

'It's a bit far from what she wanted, don't you think?'

'Not necessarily. If we make it romantic and special, people will be talking about it for years to come. Nicci would love that.'

Jay was silent for a moment. Then he smiled.

'She did say that the most important thing is that we get married.' He paused. 'Are you sure that would work?'

'It'll be tricky, but yes, I think so.' Sam nodded. 'Do you think you can keep it a secret from her?'

'I can try my best. And if she does find out, perhaps she'll be happy that we're getting married regardless. Win-win in my eyes.'

Sam smiled. 'Quickly, there are two things I need you to do. The first is to have another look at that list she wrote and see if there's anything there to suggest a dress and shoes. Arranging little details without Nicci knowing is one thing, but a bride has to have the final say on her dress and accessories. If the dress she likes is too expensive, maybe we can get Cynthia on the fabric stall to make up something comparable? And Clara might have some similar shoes in Shoenique.'

'I'm on it.' Jay nodded.

'Then I need you to find out which parts of the wedding she's already paid money towards and I'll chat to them, see if we can salvage anything. At least if I tell them what we're doing initially, you can go and speak to them afterwards. Do you think you can manage that?'

'Yep.' Jay nodded again.

'Good.' Sam got out of the car. 'Then I suggest you get yourself off to work and don't mention that you saw me today. This is going to be some secret to keep.'

CHAPTER SIXTEEN

Sam walked back through the market, her eyes flicking onto every stall as she passed. Already, she was planning. Once Jay came back to her with what exactly she needed to do, then she'd get cracking on with the arrangements and start roping in people to help.

The first thing she needed to sort out was permission to hold a wedding in the market hall. With glee, she realised she'd need to make a list. Sam was one of life's big list-makers. Since being left on her own at such a young age, she had become uber-organised. It was the reason she'd been able to hold down the stall and the house.

A secret wedding, how romantic! She recalled her own. Reece proposed to her about a month after her dad's funeral, although they didn't get married straight away. Since Martin wouldn't be there, Sam didn't want a fuss. A small wedding in the local registry office had sufficed, so there was no need for anyone to walk her down an aisle. They'd gone out with a few close friends for a meal afterwards and then everyone had trooped back to their house for a knees-up where more people were invited.

As weddings went, for her and Reece it had been ideal. There was no falling out about colours and flowers, no bickering about who'd been invited and who hadn't and best of all, no terrible presents to laugh about, as everyone had given them holiday vouchers. They'd booked a week in the Canary Islands and set off the next month.

It wouldn't suit some but both she and Reece had enjoyed it that way, even though there had been tears when she'd wished her dad had been there to see how happy she was on the day.

Where was she? Ah, yes, the list. Melissa from the make-up counter could do Nicci's make-up and nails. She could ask Sally at Cupcake Delights to do the cake and Mr Adams to do the overall catering. It would seem fair for them each to do a bit. She knew they'd both want to. Everyone liked Nicci, she was always so upbeat and positive about everything. Most people knew Jay too.

Then there was Matt and Ryan. Well, there was only one job for those two.

The sweet stall – Jay had said he'd let his parents know of the plans, so there was no rush to tell Malcolm and Maureen but he'd have to ensure they gave Jess the minimum of information. Sam wouldn't put it past her to have sabotaged the wedding purposely. Still angry after Jay had told her what his sister had done, she'd wanted to confront Jess straight away. But she hadn't got time for that now as she had a wedding to plan. Maybe she should add it to her list of things to do!

'Oh, she's back at last,' Louise cried when Sam finally drew level with her own stall. 'I thought you'd driven to the incinerator to destroy the boxes, you've been that long. What kept you?'

Seeing Nicci close by, Sam shrugged her shoulders. 'Oh, I was chatting to Matt.' But as she passed Louise, she leaned in close. 'Actually, I was chatting to Jay, and he told me all about the scuppered wedding.'

Louise looked up quickly. 'I was sworn to secrecy.'

'Oh, never mind that. Let's go the café for a quick coffee. I have something to tell you.'

While Sam and Louise discussed the wedding, making a list of things that needed to be done for Nicci and Jay's big day, Matt had his head in the morning's newspaper, in between serving customers. Behind him, Ryan was making coffee.

'Hey,' Ryan passed him a mug afterwards, 'will you do me a favour, old buddy?'

'That depends on what it is and if it involves me being out of pocket,' said Matt.

'I just need you to cover for me while I, erm, attend to a little business.'

Matt looked up at Ryan. He could see his friend was watching the sweet stall – or rather, he was watching Jess. Suddenly, it all clicked into place.

'You've got to be kidding,' he replied.

'No.'

'And that's why you want me to cover for you?' When Ryan grinned, Matt shook his head. 'No way. I told you after the last piece of skirt that I wasn't comfortable lying to Sarah. I sure as hell won't do it again.'

'Aw, go on, mate,' Ryan pleaded. 'It's only this once. No one will know.'

'*I'll* know.'

'But it wouldn't be—'

'I said no!' Matt slapped his hand on the boxes piled up in front of him, causing a few people walking past to look around.

'I was only going to take her out for a drink after work one night, that's all.'

'Oh, right. So you wouldn't want to see her again? And you wouldn't want me to cover for you then too? And again and again?' Matt prodded him sharply in the chest. 'I know you of old, *buddy*. You've done this on me before and I won't be dragged into it again. The answer is no.'

'Fine. But it doesn't mean that I won't see her. I'll just have to think of another excuse.'

'Yeah, you do that, you selfish piece of shit.' Matt pushed past him and out into the aisle. He glared at Jess as he stormed past. 'Keep away from him,' he told her.

Fury rushed out of him. Why would Ryan want to mess around with Jess, and risk everything for a fumble with a cheap tart who was only after a bit of fun? Surely he could see what he had – a wife, children and a lovely home. Just what Matt had always wanted, yet Ryan was willing to chuck it all away.

* * *

At the bottom of the market, Charley and Sophie were sitting in the back corner of Jeff's café. It was half term and they were making the most of their break. Louise had treated them to breakfast and they were noisily tucking into bacon and eggs with fried bread, washed down with tea in striped blue and white mugs.

'Whatcha!' Charley shouted when she saw Matt. But he didn't stop, even though she knew he'd spotted them. 'Wonder what's eating him?' she said to Sophie as she poked the runny yolk of her egg with a piece of bread.

'Dunno,' said Sophie, following suit with her own. 'I wonder if your mum has said something nasty to him.'

'Probably,' said Charley. 'I just wish they could both see what everyone else sees. Matt's mad about her and Mum's mad about him but they pretend they don't love each other.'

'I know! Speaking of love, what's Alex got to say today?' Sophie mopped up the last bit of egg with the fried bread.

'He says he wishes he had the money to come to Hedworth and hook up.' Charley's face lit up with a smile. 'I wish he had too. I'd love to meet him in person.'

'Let me see his profile pic again.'

Eagerly, Charley got out her phone and located it for her, checking her messages first to see if Alex had got in contact since the last time she checked. 'Hang on, he's left me a reply.'

'Ooh.' Sophie leaned forward. 'Let me see.'

'No!' Charley pulled back the phone. 'I want to see it first. It might be private.'

'Since when has anything been private between me and you?' Sophie seemed a little put out.

Since Charley had found someone she could talk to who didn't go to her school, she thought. All the rumours that had been circulating about her had lessened, but the name calling hadn't and she was sick of it. Alex knew what people were saying because he could read her Facebook feed. But it didn't seem to be bothering him at all.

She read his message:

> 'I loved watching *Strictly Come Dancing* but don't tell anyone. Some of the dancers in it are quite fit. Not as fit as you are, though. You look lovely from your photo. That is you, isn't it? You haven't used someone else's photo, have you? LOL!'

Charley's grin widened.

'He likes the photo I emailed to him,' she said. This time, she let Sophie take the phone from her.

'He is rather cute, isn't he?' Sophie studied it before handing it back. 'Do you think he'll have any mates I can tag along with?'

'If only.' Charley sighed. 'He lives in Wales. It's miles from here.'

'There are plenty of trains that regularly go from Manchester. Or you could get a coach.'

'And they cost money I haven't got.'

'Why not work on the market stall? Sam's always after you to do a Saturday shift.'

'Hey, I might just do that!" Charley beamed. Ever since she could remember, she'd always been against the idea of working on a Saturday. Saturdays were for getting up late, going shopping and chilling with Sophie, not working with your mum, hurling potatoes and apples into pensioners' shopping trolleys. But if this thing with Alex developed, she could ask Sam again. Then she could go and see Alex.

Lost in a loved-up dreamy daze, Charley wondered what it would be like to kiss him. She sighed. It wasn't fair that he lived so far away.

'Shall we get going?' Sophie asked, the chair scraping noisily across the floor as she stood up. 'I can only window shop but they have some gorge stuff in TopShop.'

'Sure.' Charley shrugged in answer. Secretly, she wanted to sit here and chat to Alex through her phone. Or maybe go home and chat to him online. He'd mentioned something about FaceTime, or maybe they could Snapchat.

Later, as Charley waited while Sophie tried clothes on, she took out her phone and ran a finger over the image of Alex's smiling features. She clicked to make the photo larger, as she had on many occasions now. His hair was dark, black almost, and cut short. Teamed with a cheeky grin were the most amazing brown eyes, with a twinkle that made her stomach flip every time she saw them. He sat with his dog; a German shepherd she knew was called Murphy, on a wooden bench. It had been taken in his back garden.

Quickly, she thought of something witty to say and sent him a message back.

> 'Ha, ha. Very Funny. I am assuming that is you with Murphy and you're not actually a dog! xx'

Once the message had been delivered, she thought about that kiss again. Charley tapped the phone lightly on her lips and grinned. Maybe things might start to look up now and she could forget about those idiots at school.

'Happy Valentine's Day, ladies,' said Sam as she walked onto the stall just after ten o'clock the next day. She was late in after calling into the GP's surgery to see the nurse. She'd wanted to discuss a few options with her before booking an appointment to see the doctor about her inability to conceive.

She spotted a card shoved down by the side of the till and turned to Louise. 'Yours, I presume?' When Louise nodded, she continued. 'I wonder who it's from.'

'Hmm, I wonder.'

Sam grinned. Even though it wouldn't be signed, they knew it would be from Matt. He always sent Louise a card. As Louise shoved it back down the side of the till again, Sam wondered if she ever wished it was sent with feeling rather than in humour. She reached for it and put it on display.

'Hey!' Louise tried to take it down but her fingers were slapped away gently.

'True love needs to be acknowledged,' Sam teased.

'It would be, *if* it was true love.' Louise pointed at Nicci who was smiling brightly. Behind her were twelve red roses in a cellophane box and a red heart-shaped helium balloon. 'That's true love.'

Sam smiled, thinking about the secret wedding. What they were organising was about true love. She really hoped it all went to plan.

'You had anything from Reece?' Louise asked.

Sam shook her head. 'Just a card. We're far too married for that.'

Last week, Sam had deliberated about it for a while and then wondered why. Even though a card seemed false and a little over the top at the moment, it was a token gesture she was happy to go along with. So when a bouquet of flowers was delivered to the stall an hour later, she was left a little shamefaced. She smiled, feeling her skin flushing as customers cooed at her.

'I hope they're from Reece,' Louise muttered.

Goosebumps broke out over Sam's skin. Get a grip, she thought, chastising herself. Dan would have moved on by now. He'd probably be sending flowers to another woman today. She opened the accompanying envelope and sighed with relief, thankful that Reece had put his name to them rather than leave it a mystery.

'Aw, flowers for you, too,' Nicci said. 'Aren't we the Valentine honeys!'

'Speak for yourself,' said Louise. 'I might have a card but it doesn't mean anything.'

Sam raised her eyebrows as Louise stared over at Matt.

* * *

Charley was in a great mood. That morning, she'd opened an email from Alex to find a Valentine e-card and a message that she'd memorised since reading it again and again. '*I wish I could kiss my Valentine. One day I hope you will be mine.*' Even the boys at school continually asking her who would be her Valentine shag couldn't dampen her spirit. She was still beaming about it at lunchtime.

'I really wish I could meet him,' she told Sophie again as they sat in the bus stop eating their sandwiches. 'It was such a lovely card – with music and hearts and flowers.'

'I really wish you'd stop talking about it. I'm getting a bit sick of hearing about him, Charl.'

Charley frowned. 'That's not a nice thing to say.'

'Well,' Sophie picked at the corner of her bread, 'all I hear is Alex this and Alex that and Alex has done this.'

'But, you're the same about Owen and I listen to you,' Charley protested, stung by her friend's words.

'I'm not as bad as you. *All* you want to do is talk about him. I'm surprised you want to know me at all.'

'Oh, don't be stupid,' Charley said, brushing crumbs from her shirt. 'I talk to him because he doesn't know anything about me.'

'I thought he knew *everything* about you. You've told him so much.'

'I mean—'

'I know what you mean.' Sophie turned to her, raising her voice slightly as a lorry went rumbling past. 'But, don't you think you ought to be more careful? He's someone you met online.'

'So?'

'So he isn't really a friend. He's just someone you can talk to. I thought *I* was your best friend.'

'You are.' Charley paused. How could she explain to anyone how Alex made her feel? Just one look at his photograph made her go all squishy inside. She watched a group of boys from her year walk past. None of them were a patch on Alex, she mused, especially when they started pointing at her and laughing.

'He's just so ... so lovely,' she continued. 'He's always there for me—'

'No, he's not. He's on Facebook every now and then at the same time as you.'

Charley raised her eyebrows. 'We arrange times to be online, if you must know.'

'Like we used to,' Sophie said pointedly.

'Like we still do.'

'Yeah, whenever you aren't talking to him,' Sophie sulked.

Charley sighed. 'I like him. He never judges me and he makes me—'

'What's that supposed to mean?'

'You don't understand what it's like being me. People at school don't call you names.'

'You should ignore them.'

'That's easy for you to say. Who called me Charley Cock-head this morning? I heard someone shout it when we went to double maths.'

Sophie laughed. She couldn't help it.

But Charley didn't find it funny. She screwed up her silver foil and shoved it into the bin.

'For your information, I'm sick of you laughing at me too,' she said, glaring at her friend.

'I'm not laughing at you,' Sophie insisted.

'Yes, you are. And a true friend wouldn't do that. A true friend would support me.'

'I *do* support you.'

Charley ignored her. 'That's why I like talking to Alex.'

Sophie huffed. 'You really need to chill out, Charl. Stop getting your knickers in a twist. Not everyone is out to get you.'

'You're just as bad as the rest of them!' Charley stood up. 'I can't believe you'd turn on me too.' She began to walk away, shouting over her shoulder, 'Alex doesn't judge me. '

'Charley!' Sophie shouted. 'Charley, wait up!'

But Charley didn't stop. Ever since Sophie had got together with Owen, she had pushed her aside. Did she look down on her because she'd had sex with Owen now? She'd told Charley all about it and, even though she was still scared, she couldn't stop thinking about what it would be like.

No wonder she was always thinking about Alex. She had no one else to talk to. He was the only person who completely understood her – and was the guy she wanted to lose her virginity with.

But she wasn't going to tell anyone that.

* * *

After work, Jess had arranged to meet Ryan in the stock room. She'd bought him some aftershave for Valentine's Day. She knew he wouldn't be able to take it home, but that hadn't been her intention anyway. Instead, she planned to keep the aftershave in the stock room and bring it out whenever they met up illicitly there. It would be their secret – their code, in fact. She'd purposely bought him Armani Code as a joke between the two of them.

Ryan arrived in the stock room some ten minutes after her. It was nearly six as they'd had to wait until everyone had gone home. Even though there was a caretaker to lock up every night, all stallholders had front entrance keys. Ryan had told Mike he would set the alarms on the main doors once he'd finished stock taking. Now, they were all alone.

'Hey,' Ryan said, walking towards her. He was carrying a red gift bag.

'Hey, yourself,' she replied.

They kissed passionately. Jess pressed her body close to his and ran her hands over his back. They pulled apart and he thrust the gift bag into her hands.

'For you, my Valentine,' he smiled, raining kisses over her face.

Jess pulled out a box of perfume. DKNY Classic. She unwrapped it and sprayed it around liberally.

'It's gorgeous,' she smiled and kissed him again. As the scent of water lilies and white birch enveloped them, they slipped to the floor.

Jess laughed inwardly. This was a doddle. Mission accomplished.

Nicci couldn't wait to get home that evening after the text message she'd received from Jay earlier on.

'I have something waiting for you on the table.'

All the way home on the bus, she wondered what it could be. By the time she opened the front door, she was bursting with anticipation. She could smell something cooking. She sniffed. Ooh, curry! She hoped it was one of Jay's specials.

She took off her coat and almost ran through to the kitchen. But it was no different to how she'd left it this morning. The table wasn't set for a romantic meal for two. There were no flowers, no gift. Nothing.

Confused, Nicci went through to the living room, then smiled as she stood in the doorway. Jay was sitting on the floor, his back to the settee. His chest was bare, his legs covered with the duvet from upstairs. Next to him, the coffee table was piled high with food, a candle lit either end. There was wine chilling in an ice bucket, chocolates waiting to be opened.

Nicci giggled. 'You meant coffee table, didn't you?'

'Actually, I didn't,' said Jay. He stood up, the duvet dropping to reveal his nakedness. 'I intend to ravish you over the kitchen table.'

'What about Jess?'

'She's not coming home until ten. I bribed her …'

She giggled even more as she saw him getting aroused.

'But first.' He pointed down, raising his eyebrows.

Nicci rolled her eyes playfully. Despite what she'd done behind Jay's back, at least he wanted to make her happy. And he clearly still fancied the pants off her – as did she of him.

Who cared if she had to wait a couple of years to marry him? It would be worth it to become his wife.

CHAPTER SEVENTEEN

Over the next few days, Sam was kept so busy arranging the details for Nicci's secret wedding that she didn't have time to think about herself and the fact that Reece would soon be returning home. There was so much to organise before the date, set for the first Sunday in April, but at least now she had a list of definite things to show Louise and Jay, who were the only two people who knew for now.

They'd met up the night before to discuss things, Jay pretending he was working overtime. So far the hotel Nicci had already been in touch with regarding the reception had emailed back and offered a reduced rate as an incentive to rebook, but wouldn't do anything about giving a refund for the deposit she had paid. After discussing finances with Jay, she'd managed to negotiate a luxury room for the wedding night instead.

Sam had decided to call everyone together at the end of the week and announce it in one go. It would be far easier that way. And maybe she'd get some answers straight away. She studied her list again:

Venue – She'd tasked Jay with getting the registrar on board, and checking that everything needing to be done was set in place.

Dress – Jay had given her details of a particular one that Nicci had left notes about in her notebook. Helpfully, she'd also cut out a picture from a magazine, so Sam was going to see about getting it sewn up at a fraction of the cost.

Shoes – Clara had said she'd provide them for free. Melissa too had said she'd do all the make-up for the women in the bridal party. Charley, Louise and Ryan's twin girls, Amelia and Abigail, were going to be bridesmaids, as per Nicci's notebook. Mr Adams was making a cake like the one in the clipping Jay had brought for him from the wedding planning book. All that was left to organise was the flowers. Sam had given the florist notice of the wedding, and the colour scheme. All she needed to do was ask Jay if he knew Nicci's favourite flower.

Sam put the list away in her pocket. All in all, planning a wedding without letting the bride know was still possible but it would take a hell of a lot of organisation and co-ordination. Still, as queen-of-the-list-makers, she couldn't wait to get started. And at least it kept her mind from her own worries.

At five o'clock, Jay came to the market on the pretence that he'd knocked off work early after dropping off a delivery for his boss. Sam suggested that Nicci might as well finish now that he was here, rather than hang around for another half hour. Once they'd gone and the doors to the general public had been closed, everyone gathered around her stall. Sam stood at the front, Louise by her side.

'I won't keep you back for long,' she shouted, looking around at a sea of puzzled faces, 'but we have something we need your help with.'

She told everyone about Nicci and Jay's story. Not about the debt and the on-off wedding proposal. But about a hard-working couple who were struggling to plan their big day. She made out in the speech that it was their idea, that neither Nicci nor Jay knew it was planned and that she was after offers of help to make the day perfect for them.

Everyone began to pipe up with ideas. Sam held up a hand as they all spoke at once.

'I have to explain first that there isn't much money so I'll need you to offer your services for as cheap as possible. Maybe even,' she paused, 'for free?'

'I wouldn't want paying,' said Melissa.

'Me neither,' said Mr Adams. 'Nicci's like one of our own, we've known her for so long.'

'And Jay too,' added Nigel Beaconsfield, from the butcher's counter.

'Ooh, and I love picking out wedding shoes!' said Clara in an excited pitch. 'I already have some in mind that I've seen. I know Nicci will love them, depending on the dress, of course.'

Louise's eyes teared up. 'Thanks, you guys,' she spoke quietly.

Sam glanced around at everyone, still not quite believing what she'd heard. She caught Jess's eye, her face like thunder, but decided to ignore her. She wouldn't sabotage this wedding.

'Are you all sure you're happy to do this?' she asked again, just to clarify, but beaming with joy.

'Of course we are.'

'Yes, absolutely.'

'She's a good girl, is Nicci.'

'And Jay's a great guy too.'

'Well, it looks like we have a secret wedding to plan!' Sam shouted, amidst a few whoops and cheers.

Louise smiled at them. 'I can't thank you all enough. Nicci will be thrilled.'

Sam nodded, along with a few other people. Weddings were so good for the soul. Then she remembered something else.

'Just before we all disappear, Ryan?' she shouted. 'Are you still here?'

Although Ryan was back on his stall, he put up his hand. 'Yep, still here.'

'Jay wants you to be his best man. And you too, Matt.'

'Cool!' Matt grinned and shook hands with Ryan. 'Looks like we'll have to do a joint speech.'

'Yeah, we can be double funny,' Ryan replied.

'Or double naff,' Malcolm shouted. Everyone laughed, and headed back to pack up their stalls for the evening.

'I know which one I'd say is the best out of the two of you.' Jess licked her top lip and grinned at Ryan. 'I'd say that's definitely the right name for you, Ryan. The *best* man,' she purred.

A couple of heads turned abruptly and Ryan caught a few frowns and strange looks. He pretended he hadn't heard Jess and continued to banter with Matt.

But Louise and Sam had clearly caught what Jess had said.

'What did she mean by that?' Louise asked.

'I'm not sure,' Sam replied, not wanting to start an argument just as they were all on a high after soliciting help for the wedding.

Ryan watched as everyone around him dispersed, hoping he'd got away with it being no more than a throwaway remark. He'd scowled at Jess to let her know that he was mad at her, and she'd sidled off back to the sweet stall with a dramatic sigh.

But Matt didn't let it go unnoticed. 'Did you meet up with her?' he wanted to know.

'Just the once. I –'

'And did you screw her?'

Ryan didn't speak but his silence gave Matt his reply.

'You ... you ...' Matt pointed his finger in Ryan's face. 'You lowlife piece of shit. You said you'd never—'

'It was only the once!' he lied. 'I admit that batting too close to home wasn't such a clever idea but I haven't seen her since.'

'And you expect me to believe that?' Matt grabbed his coat. 'You can lock up tonight. I need some fresh air before I lamp you one.'

'Mate, it's not what you—'

But Matt was already gone.

At home, Jess thought about what she had done. Stupidly, she'd made some brash comment and now Ryan was angry with her. Things had been going so well after they'd met up in the store room on Valentine's Day, too.

Once most people had left the market that night, they'd had words about what she had said. He'd told her Matt had sussed what was going on. Jess had apologised but Ryan had stormed off regardless. Maybe she had pushed her luck a little too much.

She decided to bring her plan of action forward. She took a shower and sprayed herself liberally with the perfume Ryan had bought her. Sleeping with him again twice the week before would have worked out in her favour too. It would make everything seem more believable.

A few days later, Jess executed her fainting fit with precision. She knew that Matt and Ryan moved a lot of their electrical stock and locked it away in the stock room every evening in case anyone broke into the market. At the end of the day, while the traders were packing up for the day, she watched them leave their stall and followed them, carrying a plastic jar of sweets in the crook of each arm. She pushed open the door, saw them in front of her and suddenly dropped to the floor, letting the jars clatter to the ground.

Matt got to her first. 'Are you okay?' he asked, bending down to see.

Jess screwed up her eyes and frowned, as if she was trying to remember who they were.

Ryan waved a hand in front of her eyes. 'What happened?' he asked. 'Did you slip?'

'I'm not sure,' Jess lied. She tried to get up, pretending that she was dizzy.

'Whoa!' Ryan steadied her by the arm. 'Are you sure you're okay?'

'Here.' Matt pulled a plastic chair from a stack at the side of the room. 'Sit down here a minute and get your colour back.'

Once Jess had their undivided attention, she decided it was now or never. 'I'm fine,' she said quietly. 'It's just that I'm pregnant and–'

Ryan's hand moved from her arm. 'What?'

'I only found out yesterday. I was going to tell you.' Jess looked up at him, this time with tears in her eyes, hoping he didn't know too much about pregnancy.

'What's going on?' Matt glanced from one to the other. 'Oh no. Tell me you're not the father!'

'No!' Ryan coughed after his voice came out as a squeak.

'You are,' Jess said quietly. 'I haven't been with anyone else in months.'

Matt glanced at Jess with disgust. 'You planned this, didn't you?'

'No!' Jess lied again. 'I would never trap anyone.'

'In that case, get rid of it.'

'You can't tell me what to do!'

'Too right, I can't.' He poked Ryan's chest. 'But you can. And you'd better do it soon. You prick!'

'What am I going to do?' Ryan paced the stock room. 'Sarah will kill me.'

'What do you mean, what are *you* going to do?' Jess challenged, suddenly forgetting all her earlier fainting antics. 'This is our baby. We're in this together.'

'In what together, exactly? Christ, I only slept with you because you threw your tits into my face every day. What man in their right mind could refuse that?'

'I did,' said Matt.

'Shut up,' said Ryan. 'I'm in enough trouble without you going on at me.'

Jess stood up quickly. She rested her hand on Ryan's arm. '*We're* in this mess,' she told him. 'It'll be okay, you'll see.'

'A mess, that's right,' said Matt before walking away. 'You two deserve each other.'

'Wait!' Ryan shouted after him.

But Matt didn't stop. The door back into the public area slammed shut behind him. Jess stood silently, wondering if her plan had worked or not.

Ryan began to pace again.

'I'm still here, you know,' Jess said, annoyed at being ignored. 'Maybe we should meet somewhere to discuss things?'

'Yeah, I think we should,' Ryan agreed. 'I'll meet you after we finish tonight and we—'

'I can't – I have a doctor's appointment.' It was a complete fib but Jess wanted to keep him keen.

'Tomorrow night, then.'

Ryan had at least stopped pacing but the look of fear on his face made Jess feel secure. She had the upper hand for now. And once he got used to the idea, they could talk.

Charley wished she'd never come to meet her mum from work. While she waited for her to finish, Sam had asked her to fetch some paper bags from the stock room. She'd opened the door to the sound of raised voices and saw Matt, Ryan and Jess up ahead. She knew she should have walked away but natural curiosity got the better of her. Closing the door quietly, she'd sneaked across the room and hid at the side of a shelving unit in the distance.

From where she stood, she could hear some of the conversation. She held her breath as she watched first Matt, then her Uncle Ryan storm out of the stock room. A moment later, Jess followed and Charley was alone in the stock room.

Her heart beating wildly, she stood for a while trying to put together the different snippets she'd heard.

Jess was pregnant and Matt was going to become a father. Charley's eyes brimmed with tears. She thought he cared about her mum, and if she was honest, she thought he cared about her as well. What would happen if there was a baby too, and with Jess? How the hell was that going to work out? They would be out of the loop.

No, she shook her head, this wasn't happening. It couldn't happen. It would ruin everything.

The disagreement between Matt and Ryan continued when they were back on their stall.

'Is it yours?' Matt wanted to know.

'She got under my skin, okay!' Ryan wouldn't look him in the eye. 'I couldn't get enough of her. But I dropped it off because Sarah started to get suspicious.' He gulped nervously. 'I told Sarah I was with you.'

'I said I wouldn't cover for you!' Matt seethed, clenching and unclenching his fist.

'I'm sorry! But she collared me about being home late again and I – I just said the first thing that came into my mouth. That I was with you. I told her we'd started running to lose a bit of weight in time for the wedding. Best men, and all that.'

'But can't you see how awkward that is for me? I've known you both for years. I'm not going to lie to her. It makes me as devious as you.'

'Anyone would think I'd murdered someone and was asking you for an alibi! It's not such a big deal.'

'She's pregnant!' Matt cried, then lowered his voice, aware again of his surroundings. 'And you're not married to *Jess*.'

'Okay, okay! Keep your hair on!' Across the aisle, Ryan could see Sam glancing over. He could tell she was wondering what was going on. 'How about if I talk to her, finish things and –'

'You can't hide a baby, you stupid –'

'I can deny it's mine though.'

'What?'

'Everyone knows Jess is a dick tease. Of course she could make out it was mine, but she could just as easily have come back from London pregnant. I reckon she's trying to trap me.'

Matt was astounded at his friend's nerve. 'Sometimes I don't understand how we've stayed mates for so long.' He shook his head. 'You make me sick at times. It's all about how Ryan can get his end away and get away with it, isn't it? And this time it's come back to haunt you. This time, there's no getting away from it.' He pointed at Jess who was also watching them carefully. 'Because *she* won't let you. If you think you can walk away from her, then you're stupid.'

'She won't say anything,' Ryan said, shaking his head as if to make himself believe that. 'She won't – and I'm going to finish it anyway.'

'She's got you over a barrel, mate!'

'We'll see.'

Matt glared at him before he really did punch him. But Ryan was watching Jess.

'Look at her any more and everyone will know what you're up to,' Matt said. 'especially after that best man comment the other day.'

This time, Ryan looked away swiftly.

Sam had watched Matt tear into Ryan across on their stall.

'What's going on over there?' she asked Louise.

Louise stopped what she was doing and turned to look. 'Beats me,' she said. 'But Matt looks fit to burst. Oi, you two!' she shouted across to them. 'You sound like a pair of girls in a catfight. What's up?'

But the men ignored her. They were too busy arguing to respond.

'Charming,' said Louise. She spotted Charley coming back. 'Did you see anything going on with those two while you were in the stock room?'

'No, I didn't see them.'

Charley rushed through to the back room, for fear her reddening cheeks would give her away. What was she going to do? She wished she had someone to confide in. She couldn't tell her mum – she wouldn't be able to keep it a secret. And if she hadn't fallen out with Sophie, she could have rung her. Sam would be an obvious choice but it would be hard to get her alone. Or maybe she should just ask Matt? Or even have it out with Jess?

Charley couldn't decide. In the meantime, she'd have to act like nothing had happened.

'Good day at school, Charl?' Louise shouted through to her.

'Glad it's over,' came her reply.

'Sounds about right. I hated school too.' Louise grinned. She took off her apron and washed her hands.

'Louise?' Matt appeared suddenly. 'Do you want a lift home? I'm heading off soon. Hey, Charl, how goes it?'

Charley stiffened. Matt smiled, but she couldn't look at him. She couldn't pretend that nothing had happened. Pushing past him, she walked away down the aisle.

'Don't you want a lift home with us?' Matt shouted after her.

'What does it look like?'

'Charley?' She heard her mum shout but she ignored her. There was no way she was getting into Matt's car until she got to the bottom of this mess. If Sophie wasn't around she'd go and email Alex. Alex would tell her what to do.

'What's up with her?' Matt looked puzzled. What was it with people today?

'Beats me.' Louise grabbed her coat. 'Too many hormones, I reckon. She's been a right moody sod lately.'

'Takes after her mother,' said Sam from behind them.

Matt sniggered.

'Ha, ha.' Louise's voice was thick with sarcasm. 'Anyway, Matt – care to tell us what you and my brother were falling out about?'

'It's nothing.' Matt's shoulders drooped. 'Just boys' stuff.'

'That's worse than women's problems,' laughed Sam.

'If it wasn't for you women, we men wouldn't be falling out in the first place.'

'Why, you cheeky—'

'You little—'

Even though they were joking around, Matt turned abruptly and went back to the stall. He opened his mouth to speak to Ryan but decided better of it. Instead, he grabbed his coat and stormed off down the aisle.

He couldn't stand to be in the fool's company a minute longer.

CHAPTER EIGHTEEN

The following week, Matt was buying lunch for him and Ryan in Hedworth High Street. He'd just come out of a sandwich shop with two pies when someone tapped him on the shoulder.

'That's far too fattening for a best man to eat,' a voice rang out.

Matt turned to see Ryan's wife, Sarah, smiling at him.

'Not that there's an ounce of fat on you anyway,' she continued.

'Hi Sarah,' said Matt, returning the smile, but inside he was dying. Sarah was the last person he wanted to bump into. 'Haven't seen you in a while. How are you?'

Sarah sighed. 'Oh, you know, busy as usual. What with the wedding coming up and the girls so excited about being bridesmaids, I don't have time to think.'

Matt nodded. 'I'm really looking forward to it.'

Sarah laughed. 'But you're a man! You're supposed to hate that type of thing.'

Matt shrugged. 'I suppose I'm not your stereotypical man. I love a happy ending.'

'You soppy sod.' Sarah sighed. 'I wish Ryan was the romantic kind. He hasn't got an ounce of romance in him.'

At the mention of Ryan's name, Matt's guilt surfaced. Despite the goings on, it looked like Sarah hadn't got a clue about Jess and the baby. He desperately wanted to tell Sarah as a friend but knew it wasn't his place. Quickly, he changed the subject.

'I just hope we can keep it secret,' he said.

They walked side by side through the shoppers, chatting amicably. Soon they were at the entrance to the market.

'Are you coming in?' Matt asked as he held open the door, already dreading the scene if Jess caught sight of Ryan's wife.

Sarah shook her head. 'No, I'll see Ryan later. Tell him he'd better be on time tonight, though. I'm tired of him coming home late.' She smiled. 'It's no wonder there isn't any excess weight on you, with all those miles you clocked up last week.'

The smile slipped from Matt's face before he checked himself. So Ryan had been telling Sarah he'd been running with him, which meant that he'd probably been saying that for a while longer than he had admitted to. It could also mean that he was still saying it to hide the fact he was still seeing Jess. He would have to think of something to say to keep her from the truth.

But his silence spoke volumes, as did the blush creeping across his face. As the shoppers of Hedworth went about their daily business around them, Sarah stared at him.

Shit, thought Matt. *Think of something to say …*

Matt tried to laugh it off. 'I think he's taking this best man thing a little too seriously.'

Sarah's eyes dropped to the floor for a moment and when she lifted them again, they were watery.

'Matt, I've known you long enough now to know when you're lying,' she said. 'You're covering up for Ryan. What's going on?'

'I'd better get back.' Matt jerked a thumb over his shoulder. 'He'll be wondering where I've got to.'

Sarah held onto his arm with a firm grip. 'Is he playing around again?'

Matt gulped. 'I – I don't know what you mean.'

Sarah continued to stare at him, making him feel uncomfortable, as if she was trying to read his mind. All of a sudden, she let go of his arm.

'Sorry,' she said quietly. 'I shouldn't hassle you. It isn't you at fault.' Her eyes dropped to the floor for a moment. 'Just tell me one thing. Exactly how many times did you not go running with him?'

'I … I …'

'It's okay.' She nodded. 'I get the picture.'

While Matt was being grilled by Sarah and there was a lull in customers, Ryan took the opportunity to go and talk to his sisters. He wanted to know if either of them had any idea that he'd been messing around with Jess – Louise was such a gossip that Ryan knew if she was aware of it, everyone would know. He felt their fling had come to its natural conclusion – baby or no baby – and he was still planning on saying that the baby wasn't his if anyone found out. How did he know for sure it was his, anyway? He'd only slept with her a few times.

So far, his running excuse had been a godsend, but since she'd told him she was pregnant, he'd tried to keep his distance. It would only take Matt getting wind of what had really happened and he'd be in deep trouble for using him again. Still, Matt being Matt – boring and dependable – gave him the perfect alibi. Sarah wouldn't think anything of him coming home late if she thought he had been with Matt. It had been a stroke of genius.

'What's up with you?' Ryan asked Louise as she served a customer and then gave a heavy sigh.

Louise sighed again. 'Oh, I don't know. I'm just sick of everything at the moment. I feel like my life is so boring.'

'Tell me about it,' Ryan agreed.

'Don't you sometimes wish you could just up sticks and move away, where no one knows you? Maybe start again?'

'Yep, but it isn't that easy.'

'Oh, hark at you two, you're always the same,' Nicci butted in as she reached over for a bunch of bananas. 'It's enough to make me get out my violin. I wish you'd both cheer up.'

'We can't all be sunny and positive like you,' Louise retorted.

'Yeah,' Ryan joined in, nudging her arm and making her drop one of the potatoes she was now packing into a bag. 'Shut up, little Miss Sunshine.'

'You never change,' cried Nicci, retrieiving it as it rolled away. 'Even when we were younger, you pair were always moaning about something or other. You should be thankful for what you've got.'

'And you're our younger sister, we should be lecturing you!' said Louise. 'Although I do agree with you, for once. I don't know what's wrong with me half of the time. I think I need a man.'

'I thought you said you were through with men,' Nicci retorted.

'Oh, ha, ha. There's only so much time I can spend in my own company without going loopy.'

'Well, maybe Sam will start coming out with you again now Reece is back home permanently,' said Ryan.

'Permanently?' Louise frowned. 'I don't know what you mean.'

Ryan paused. 'She never told you they fell out?'

'No, she didn't!'

'Me neither,' added Nicci.

'He came home one Friday night and some fella turned up on the doorstep with flowers and that was that,' Ryan explained. 'He stayed in Sheffield for a while but now they've decided to give it another go. He moved back a couple of weeks ago. I can't believe she hasn't said anything.'

Louise was furious. All the time Sam was going on at her about getting a steady fella and Louise was feeling inferior because she couldn't find one … but Sam hadn't told her what had happened with Reece? And who had turned up with flowers – it must have been Dan Wilshaw. She'd wondered why his name had become off limits so quickly.

But what hurt the most was why the hell hadn't Sam confided in her? They were supposed to be best friends.

'And how do you know all this?' she asked her brother.

Ryan didn't have time to reply as he spotted Matt marching up the aisle towards them, his face like thunder.

'Don't tell me,' Ryan grinned. 'They've run out of vanilla slices.'

'I want a word with you.' Matt put down his food and for a moment, raised a clenched fist. Then he dropped it to his side quickly. Instead, he grabbed Ryan's arm.

'Let go of me!' said Ryan.

'Matt!' Louise gasped and turned to look at Nicci. She too, was standing open-mouthed. It had looked as if Matt was going to thump Ryan. What on earth had got into him? 'Matt,' she repeated.

'Keep an eye on the stall for a minute,' he told her before storming off with Ryan.

'What's eating him?' said Nicci. 'I don't think I've ever seen Matt lose his temper.'

In the staff room, Sam had heard all of Ryan's conversation. In fact, she'd cringed through every word of it. While she waited for Louise to come and speak to her, she rubbed at her neck. Squashed into the corner of the back room, she sat on a stool, trying to balance her laptop on her knee.

'Why didn't you tell me that you and Reece had split up?' Louise demanded as she barged in.

Sam closed her eyes momentarily and pinched the bridge of her nose. 'Because I didn't know if it was permanent,' she replied.

'So I'm not good enough to confide in now, is that it?'

'Don't be silly. I was just so ashamed over what happened with Dan Wilshaw and I didn't want to talk about it.'

Louise looked like she was going to burst. '*You* split up with your husband but you don't want to *talk to* me?'

'Don't make a big deal out of it,' Sam pleaded. 'It's just a little raw right now, okay?'

'No, it isn't okay.' Louise folded her arms. 'Were you even going to tell me at some point?'

'Of course.' But Sam wouldn't look at her.

'Before or after you'd shacked up with Dan Wilshaw?'

Sam shut the laptop lid. It was clear Louise wasn't going to let things drop. 'I keep telling you, nothing happened between me and Dan.'

'Did Reece find you in bed with him?'

'No!' Sam pushed the door closed with a kick. 'And do you mind not airing all my dirty laundry in public?'

Louise didn't seem to mind at all. 'So what happened?'

'Reece came home unannounced one Friday evening. The weekend before he'd told me he was planning on going to Germany for a few weeks.'

'Germany!'

'Yes, but he wasn't going really. He was testing me to see if I would make a fuss about it.'

'And you didn't?'

Sam shook her head. 'Because I was all messed up about Dan Wilshaw.'

'And how did he come to be there?'

'It's not what you think. Me and Reece were chatting, trying to work things out when Dan knocked on the door.'

'With a bouquet of flowers.'

'With a bouquet of flowers.' Sam looked annoyed that she knew so much. 'I had no idea Dan was going to turn up either. But when Reece saw him, and the flowers, well, he flipped. I can't say I blame him.'

'Me neither,' said Louise.

'You see?' Sam stood up. 'That's the reason I didn't tell you. He's back now, and we're going to make a go of it, so I was hoping not to have this conversation.'

'Why?'

'Because I didn't want to talk about how awful I felt, knowing I'd hurt Reece. I didn't want to explain how I thought I'd effectively thrown my marriage down the drain, even though I hadn't slept with Dan.'

Louise looked confused. 'You *didn't* sleep with Dan?'

'No.'

Louise was shamefaced. 'I just thought—'

'You just thought I'm like you? Sleep with the first man that comes along to get some attention? Well, I'm not.'

'Hey, that's not fair!'

'Isn't it? Ask yourself the real reason I didn't tell you about Reece leaving? It's because you don't care about anyone but yourself. You're so wrapped up in Louise's little world that you haven't noticed how upset your best friend's been.'

'I—'

'You're so wrapped up in Louise's little world that you also don't see that something is eating at Charley and needs to be sorted.'

'But–'

'And the worst of it all?' Sam found she couldn't stop now that she'd started. 'You're so wrapped up in Louise's little world that you wouldn't even *care* if anyone else had a problem that they might want to talk about. All you want to do is talk about yourself.'

Frozen in shock, Louise stood for a moment after Sam had finished. Then she grabbed her coat and handbag.

'I don't have to listen to this,' she said. 'I'm going home. Tell the boss I have a headache.'

'Yeah, right. Run away rather than face the music,' Sam snapped.

Louise stormed out of the room.

'Louise?' Nicci, who was on her way in after hearing raised voices, looked up as she flew past her.

'What's wrong?'

'Everything!" Louise turned back and glared at her sister. 'There seems to be an awful lot of secrets around here at the moment and that's without this bloody wedding!'

'What wedding?' Nicci frowned. 'Who's getting married?'

CHAPTER NINETEEN

It was Saturday evening, and Louise and Charley were having a standoff in Louise's bedroom. At that particular moment, it wasn't clear who had the upper hand.

'I don't want to be looked after by Matt, okay?' Charley snapped at her mum. 'I'm nearly sixteen. I'm old enough to look after myself.'

'I know that,' said Louise, running a comb through her wet hair, 'but I might be really late. Besides, the law says that—'

'You just want to go out. You're so selfish, thinking of yourself all the time. No wonder you can't find a man.'

'Oi!' Louise prodded Charley in the arm. 'Less of the cheek or else you're grounded.' What was it with everyone, just lately? That was the second person who had called her selfish that week!

'You won't ground me because you'd have to stay in then.'

'Oh, ha, ha. Anyway, there was a time a few weeks ago when you couldn't wait for me to go out.'

Charley flinched, recalling that Saturday and the rumours that followed. It was really strange how no one ever called Sophie a slag, even though she had gone all the way with Owen, whereas she was still a virgin. Charley wondered whether it was because Sophie's mum and dad were quite old-fashioned in comparison to Louise; they wouldn't be seen dead in a nightclub. Charley, however, was accused of all sorts – could it be because her mother was made out to sleep around? It wasn't fair.

But that had nothing to do with why Charley didn't want to see Matt. She loved hanging around with him usually. They'd order in a takeaway, play a few games on Xbox and generally have a good laugh. Charley could never understand how Matt got away with spending so much time with them. If she was his girlfriend, she wouldn't put up with him hanging around another woman's house to look after her child. Not that she needed looking after, of course.

'I'll just be in my room or in front of the telly,' Charley tried to reason with her mum again. 'I don't need Matt here.'

'Maybe not, but he's coming around nonetheless.'

'Oh, whatever!' Charley flung her legs off the bed and flounced out of the room and into her own.

'Arghhhhh!' She took her frustration out on the bed, beating down her fists as she hid her face in her pillow. Well, she'd just stay in her room and surf the net. She didn't have to sit with him, even if he was here.

First, she logged on to Facebook to see if Alex was around. But he wasn't. Neither was he answering her WhatsApp messages.

She closed the lid of her laptop with a sigh. It was going to be a long night.

Although it was a Saturday night and Jay and Nicci had gone out for a romantic meal, Jess was in her room. She lay curled up on her bed, squeezing her eyes tightly to stop tears from falling. There was silence all around her. The house felt as empty as she did. And her mind wouldn't let go of the conversation she'd overheard between Ryan and Matt. They'd thought they'd lowered their voices enough for no one to hear, but she had caught every word.

Ryan was going to deny the baby was his. He'd also denied having any feelings for her. He'd called her a slapper. Said she'd been gagging for it. Matt had surprised her by siding with her, saying that Ryan was the bigger slapper of the two. He'd walked off then, and she had pretended to be busy when Ryan had looked worriedly in her direction.

Jess knew she might be able to win Ryan over. He needed attention as much as she did. But she realised now that getting involved with him had been a silly thing to do, a gut reaction because Laurie hadn't wanted to know. She didn't want to be anyone's bit on the side anymore. And, let's face it, did she really think after they'd slept together a few times he would fall in love with her and leave his wife and children to be with her? More to the point, had she been thinking at all?

Why couldn't she find a man of her own? Would she always have to settle for someone else's?

Jess turned over onto her back and ran a hand over her stomach. She had two people to think about now. This little thing inside her deserved more from its mother.

'I won't let you down, bump,' she whispered.

* * *

As Jess contemplated her future that night, so too did Sam. She sat on the settee in her living room looking at, but not watching, some drivel on the television. Reece was over on the other settee, legs stretched out. He'd been asleep for over half an hour and it was only just gone eight o'clock.

It was strange to think that they'd only been back together for a couple of weeks. When he'd first got home, they'd been all lovey-dovey, spending time together and chatting over nice meals. But now they were sitting at either ends of the living room, with hardly a bit of conversation between them.

She wondered if they had made a mistake, or was it just taking her time to adjust to having Reece home full-time? Did they both want this to work but it was too damaged to fix – or perhaps things would settle down in time? It was bound to be awkward at first, but they could get through it, couldn't they?

Reece gave a loud snore, waking himself up momentarily. He opened his eyes, caught her looking at him and winked before closing them again.

Sam sighed. She felt as lonely now as she had been before Reece moved back for good. Except now she felt crowded too. Fighting for space to call her own. It just seemed so strange having him home again.

If this was what being part of Reece and Sam was, she wasn't sure if she'd ever get used to it again. Or if she even wanted to.

* * *

As soon as he got to Louise's house that evening, Matt wanted to know what was wrong with Charley. He'd noticed she'd been cold with him for a week or so but he hadn't got a clue what he'd done to upset her. Usually when he came to look after her arms round his neck in greeting and he would tease her affectionately. But tonight, she was in her room and even when he shouted up to her, she didn't reply.

'Where's Charley?' he asked Louise while he made himself a coffee.

Louise, who was busy finishing off her make-up at the kitchen table, shrugged. 'In her room, I suppose. I don't know what's wrong with her, but she's really annoying me lately. It's as if she doesn't want me to go out and enjoy myself.'

'Perhaps she *doesn't* want you to go out,' Matt replied. 'Have you ever thought that she might want to spend some time in with you?'

Louise stopped applying her mascara and glared at him through the enhanced eyelashes on one eye. 'I don't go out that often.'

'Come on, Louise. You go out most weekends.'

'I work all week too!'

'So do I but I don't feel the need to get off my trolley drunk every Saturday.'

'That's because you're a bore.'

'Thanks for that.'

'Well, I don't know another man who stays in as much as you, despite doing a favour for me. And what about Lorraine? What does she say about it?'

'About me being at your beck and call all the time? Or about me not wanting to get bladdered every Saturday night?'

'You know what I mean.' Louise pumped the mascara wand in and out of the container.

'If I did go out every weekend, then you wouldn't be able to, so I'd quit while you're ahead.' Matt's voice was cold as he stirred his drink. He took it into the living room.

Louise followed him, wondering if she'd been a little too hard on him.

'What's up?' she asked. 'You're not usually this grumpy. Have you fallen out with Lorraine?'

Matt sat down and grabbed the television remote control. 'If you must know,' he said, 'we've split up.'

'Oh, no.' Louise sat down next to him, her heart all of a flutter. 'When did this happen?'

'Last night.'

'Any particular reason why?' she pressed.

Matt shrugged. 'It wasn't really working for me.'

Louise paused. She wanted to say that he could spend as much time around here as he liked but she knew he didn't want to hear that. He'd probably think that she meant using him for even more babysitting.

'It didn't have anything to do with me and Charl, did it?' she asked.

'No. I won't let any woman dictate to me who I can and can't see.'

'That's good to hear,' Louise said, realising that actually it seemed that it did. 'I mean, for Charley. She really enjoys having you around.'

'Apart from this last week.'

'I know, I've seen the way she's been acting around you. Have you said something to upset her?'

'No. I don't know what's wrong but she's been really funny since I saw her in the market. I can't think—'

'What's the matter?' Louise prompted when Matt stopped.

'Nothing.' Matt frowned, remembering the last time he'd seen Charley. It was just after he'd been in the stock room with Ryan and Jess. Had she overheard them talking?

'Has Sam forgiven you yet?' he changed the subject.

When Louise had blurted out about the secret wedding, Sam had been furious. But Nicci had been delighted, hadn't stopped talking about it since. She'd rung Jay immediately and cooed down the phone at him. At least for now, she had no idea where the reception was being held. They had managed to keep that secret. And, said Nicci, now she had time to enjoy it too.

'I'm not getting the silent treatment any more,' said Louise. 'Me and my big mouth. At least Nicci doesn't know everything that's happening on the day.'

A horn peeped outside. Louise jumped to her feet, checked her appearance in the mirror above the fireplace and pouted. She turned back to Matt and planted a kiss on his cheek.

'Thanks for babysitting. I won't be too late,' she said. 'Are you stopping over or going home?'

'That depends on how late you are.'

But Louise was already gone.

Matt went to the window and once the taxi was out of view, he headed upstairs to see Charley. From the landing, he could see her through the half open door. She was lying on her bed, watching television. He knocked on the door and she glanced at him icily before returning her eyes to the screen.

'Can I come in?' Matt stood on the threshold.

Charley shrugged.

'What's wrong, Charl? It's not like you to ignore me.'

'It's because you hurt me.' Charley drew her knees up to her chest and hugged herself.

'I *hurt* you?' Matt raised his eyebrows. 'Have you heard something that you shouldn't have?'

'If it was a good thing to hear, you wouldn't be asking me that.'

'I don't follow.' Actually he did, but Matt needed to be sure.

'I always thought having no dad around was good because I got to spend time with you. You've always been like a dad to me, someone who I could have a laugh with.'

Matt noticed the subtle change from present to past tense. 'What is it, Charl?'

Charley had tears in her eyes, obviously struggling to keep in her emotions. 'I thought you cared for Lorraine. And my mum? I thought you cared for her too.'

'Well, I did care for Lorraine but that's over between us now.'

That threw Charley for a moment. 'Oh.'

'And I do care for your mum. You too.' Matt leaned forward to tilt up her chin. 'I hate to see you upset.'

'Well, you won't have time for me, or Mum now, will you?' Charley pulled her head back. 'Not now that you've got Jess pregnant.'

Matt closed his eyes for a moment. He knew it. Bloody Ryan Pellington!

'You got Jess pregnant and then you wouldn't stand by her,' Charley continued.

'I didn't get Jess pregnant.'

'Yes, you did. I heard you talking about it. You, Ryan and that – that bitch.'

Matt bit on his bottom lip as he wondered how to get out of this one. If he lied to Charley, he'd run the risk of losing her respect forever. But if he told Charley the truth, not only would he land Ryan in it too, but he'd then be in trouble with Louise for covering up for him – and not telling her that her own brother had cheated on his wife again. And if any of this got back to Ryan's wife, Sarah, then all hell would break loose and she might even take the twins away from their father. He couldn't have it on his conscience. There was too much at stake.

'If it wasn't you, who was it then?' Charley asked.

'I – I can't tell you,' he stuttered.

'It was you! You're just trying to deny it!'

'No, it wasn't me. It's …' Matt couldn't say Ryan's name.

But Charley wasn't stupid. 'Uncle Ryan?' she gasped. '*He* got Jess pregnant!'

Matt was still at a loss as to what to say. 'You need to let the grown-ups sort this out, Charl.'

'But Ryan is married to my auntie Sarah! How could he do that? And … oh, no. He was the one denying everything, wasn't he?'

Matt didn't answer that. 'Just think how Sarah would feel if you went over there blurting all this out? She won't want to believe you.'

'You're wrong. I'm her niece! And I know he's done it before. I might not be *grown up* but I do know these things.'

Matt stayed quiet then. He could only dream of the pain this would cause Sarah after the last time.

'I think you should talk to your mum about this in the morning,' he said.

'But you were covering for him.'

'No, I wasn't really. I didn't want Sarah to get hurt.'

'But he met Jess anyway, didn't he?' When Matt said nothing, Charley shouted, 'The sneaky bastard.'

Although Matt agreed, he tried to reason with her. 'I'll speak to your mum first and see what she wants to do. Maybe it'll sort itself out but we mustn't make things worse for Sarah, okay?'

Charley nodded. She felt stupid now that she'd jumped to conclusions.

'I'm sorry,' she told him, shame-faced. 'I guess I didn't want to lose you either. I like that you come round all the time and I was scared that you wouldn't.'

'Does that mean I have to suffer some dross on the television downstairs then?'

Charley grinned.

'It does, doesn't it?' Matt clicked his fingers with the wave of a hand. 'Damn. We should have had this conversation later on.'

Charley knew then how wrong she'd been. Matt had wanted to get this mess sorted out with her as soon as he could. How could she have doubted him?

'Shall I run to the shop and get us some goodies?' she suggested.

Matt nodded. 'It's a deal.' He held out his hand and she shook it. Then he gave her a hug. 'I'd never do anything to hurt you. I love you like you were my own daughter.'

Charley felt a lump in her throat. One day she hoped to find someone as lovely as Matt. But more importantly, she could clearly see that Matt loved her mum dearly.

She just wished her mum would see that she had someone special right underneath her nose.

Louise had been out for two hours, yet she was still sober. She'd gone into Hedworth to meet up with Melissa from work but couldn't relax into the night. For the first time in ages, she wanted to be at home. She wished she was sitting on the settee with Charley and Matt eating pizza and sharing a bottle of something chilled. She glanced at her watch. It was too early to admit defeat.

Melissa had spotted someone she knew as soon as they'd got to this particular pub and had been off once they'd bought drinks. It was someone Louise vaguely recognised but couldn't be bothered to go and chat to. She glanced around the bar, its clientele of mixed ages. In front of her were two women and two men out together as couples. To her right, two teenagers getting to know each other just a bit too much, considering they were out in public. To her left were a couple in their mid-forties laughing about something or other. She sighed.

Everyone seemed to be with someone.

For as long as she'd been going out in the pubs and clubs around Hedworth, Saturday nights had been known as couples' night. Friday nights were nights out with friends, so it never seemed as obvious that she was lonely. But Saturdays, when it was imperative to have a man or risk feeling out of place, Louise felt her loneliness. What did she have to do to find a decent man?

Tears welled in her eyes as she caught a glimpse of Melissa. It looked like she was exchanging phone numbers with the guy now.

And what did she have to look forward to? It would just be another boring week, working on the market stall and going home to sit on her own while Charley stayed in her room and chatted to her friends online. Louise would love to have someone show a bit of interest in her. She wasn't bad-looking for her age. She didn't dress slutty – well, not too obviously anyway. She was clean and tidy, and so was the house. She worked hard for what she had and had a good sense of humour.

She laughed inwardly at her thoughts. It sounded as if she was reading a profile on a dating site.

Melissa rejoined her after a few more minutes, a huge grin plastered on her face. 'That was Simon,' she shouted above the background noise. 'He's going to call me in the week and arrange a night we can meet.'

'How flipping wonderful,' Louise shouted back sarcastically.

'WHAT? I can't hear YOU!'

'I said, that's great.' As Melissa was pacified with this answer, Louise decided she'd had enough and called it a night.

Charley was asleep on the sofa when she arrived home just before eleven. Matt was watching a football match. He indicated his surprise with raised eyebrows.

'I know, I know.' Louise sighed. 'I must be getting old. I wanted to come home.'

'Do you have a thermometer?' Matt gasped comically. 'I think you must be coming down with something.'

Louise grinned. 'I'm making a cuppa. Want one?'

'Sure. Although I think you might need something stronger ... I have something to tell you.'

'Oh, that doesn't sound good.'

Matt followed Louise into the kitchen so as not to wake Charley.

'Let me guess.' She grinned. 'You've had a call from Lorraine and she's pregnant so you're stuck with her.' But then she turned away abruptly. Although she made a joke of it, inside she prayed it wasn't true. She didn't know what she'd do without Matt popping in as much as he did, plus helping her out with Charley, being there whenever she needed him.

'It isn't me who got someone pregnant,' said Matt. 'It's Ryan.'

Louise turned back quickly. 'What!'

'Look, I shouldn't be telling you but Charley overheard us talking. It's why she's been funny with me.' He sighed. 'It's Jess who Ryan has knocked up.'

Louise covered her mouth with her hand.

'That's not the worst of it. Sarah knows about the affair too.'

CHAPTER TWENTY

'You will never guess what I heard yesterday,' Louise said to Sam the minute she got into her car the next morning. 'I was going to text you, then I thought I'd ring you, but it's not my secret to tell and—'

'You mean you've *actually* kept a secret?' Sam sniggered. 'For a whole twenty-four hours?'

'Yes. Don't sound so surprised.'

'Well, you certainly didn't keep the one about the wedding to yourself!'

'I didn't blurt that out on purpose!' Louise leaned in close to Sam, ignoring her tone. She was dying to tell someone what she knew. 'Okay then, if you must know. That Jess has been sleeping with our Ryan and now she's pregnant.'

Sam was about to pull away from the kerb. She put a foot on the brake and turned back to Louise.

'What? I mean, are you sure?'

'Matt told me. Jess told him and Ryan.'

'Wow, I'm surprised you kept it to yourself at all, the way you revel in watching other people's downfalls.'

'That's really mean, Sam.' Louise looked hurt.

'It was a joke!'

'I may not be the best at keeping a man or holding down a relationship but I'd never harm anyone else's. I know how much that would hurt Sarah, especially as this isn't the first time. And I didn't say anything when you were having a fling with Dan Wilshaw.'

'That's not the same thing.'

'It's exactly the same thing. You were sleeping with Dan—'

'I was *not* sleeping with Dan!'

'—just like Ryan was shagging Jess. It *is* exactly the same. You were both cheating on other people. You're as bad as each other.'

'It's not ...' Sam's words tailed off because she knew Louise was right. How could she pass judgment on Ryan when she had behaved the same way herself? Just because she couldn't go through with the final act didn't mean that she hadn't had the intention of sleeping with another man. And was that the real reason she was being so nasty to Louise – because she felt so disgusted with herself?

'Oh, Louise.' She started to cry. 'I – I don't think things are working out as I wanted them to.'

The bickering forgotten, Louise pulled Sam awkwardly across the car and held her while she cried.

Jeez, what was happening to them all lately, she thought? They used to all be friends. Now they were all falling out. Ryan and Matt, Sam and Reece, Charley and Sophie. Thank goodness she and Sam never let an argument fester. That Jess had a lot to answer for.

And, after seeing how upset Sam was, she couldn't risk her sister-in-law, Sarah, getting hurt too. Louise would bide her time but she would tackle Jess and tell her to back off her brother.

On the stall, Nicci was a happy girl. She couldn't believe everyone around her would do all that for her and Jay. And although she loved the idea of a secret wedding – once Sam had got over the fact that Louise had let slip their plans – she also cherished the fact that she could now join in with the excitement.

'I'm getting married in four weeks, can you believe that?' she said again, with a contented sigh. 'I never thought it would happen. Oh, it's going to be so magical!'

'It would be if it wasn't April Fool's Day,' said Louise.

Nicci nudged her. She quite liked the idea of getting married on April 1st. It would be something to tell the grandchildren about. She grinned: blimey, she was even thinking of grandchildren!

'Can I help it if I want to get married on a Sunday and the only one available is that date?' she said. 'I'm so glad that our registry office opens every day now.'

'I think it's quite good, actually.' Louise nodded. 'You're both fools anyway.'

'Oh, ha ha.' Nicci nudged her sister.

Sam smiled. Last night, they'd had a girlie get together and discussed where they were at with the arrangements. Nicci was blown away with the organising. So too with the generosity of the stall holders, most of whom she'd grown up beside.

'Everyone loves a wedding, don't they?' Nicci sighed contentedly again.

Sam rolled her eyes at Louise. Even though she was looking forward to Nicci and Jay's, weddings were the furthest thing from her mind at the moment.

Having now had time to think things through, Jess had made her mind up about what to do next. Tears welled in her eyes as she pressed a hand to her stomach, feeling the delicate bulge, knowing that it would soon be visible to everyone else, wondering what people would say when she was the talk of the market. Apart from Ryan and Matt, she hadn't told anyone about the baby yet.

At lunchtime, while she was in the stock room, she texted Ryan, letting him know where she was. When he didn't appear in five minutes, she rang him.

'I'm waiting for you in—'

'Yeah, I know. I'll be there.' The phone went dead.

Jess hugged herself against the cold of the room. It was the first week in March and although it was fairly mild outside, sometimes the stock room could be as cold as the middle of winter. She sat down on a pile of boxes and waited.

A few minutes passed before the door opened. She looked up to see Ryan approaching.

'What do you want?' His tone was sharp.

'You,' Jess said quietly. 'It wasn't long ago that I gave you a blowjob behind these boxes. Or have you forgotten that?'

'I haven't forgotten.' Ryan was silenced for now.

Jess took a step towards him and pushed him out of sight behind the boxes. 'Good. Because I didn't want you to come to the stock room to talk.' She pushed him back some more. 'I wanted to be somewhere that no one can see us. Somewhere we can be private. Do things in private, if you catch my meaning.'

Ryan's back was against the wall now. Jess placed a hand on his crotch and leaned forward to kiss him. He groaned as her tongue searched the inside of his mouth, his hands moving to clasp her breast. She left it there for a moment, then pushed him away roughly.

'Just as I'd suspected,' she said, wiping her mouth as if in disgust.

Ryan looked baffled.

'You're more of a slapper than me, Ryan Pellington.' Jess prodded him in the chest sharply. 'You only think of yourself. I heard you the other night, talking to Matt. "Everyone knows Jess is a dick tease," you said. "I reckon she's trying to trap me," you said.'

Ryan stood motionless, appearing to have lost the ability to string a sentence together.

'I was ... I didn't ...'

She held up a hand. 'But you were right about one thing.' Jess paused and with a sigh continued. 'The baby isn't yours.'

'If you'd only just listen to me ... I— what?'

'This little squirt.' Jess placed her hand protectively over her bump. 'This is my mistake.'

'But why did you tell me that it was mine?'

'Because I am a selfish bitch, and I could see you were easy to manipulate.'

'You – you –'

'Lost for words?' Jess laughed snidely. 'I thought you wanted to finish things with me. That's what you told Matt. That I was just a sleep around.'

For a moment, Ryan was quiet. Then he glared at Jess with such venom that tears pricked her eyes.

'As much as I'm glad to be out of this situation and as much as I am equally to blame,' he said, 'that is still some fucking low trick to play.'

'I know.' Jess fought to hold in the tears as she nodded slightly. 'That's why I have to tell you. I want to finish this mess and walk away with my head held high. What I did was wrong but what *we* did was wrong too. You're so lucky to have what you have. Go back to your wife,' she pointed to his crotch, 'keep that in your pants and just – just be grateful for what you have before you screw it up completely.'

'I wish I'd never met you.' Ryan pushed past her and out of the stock room.

Jess covered her hand with her mouth and squeezed shut her eyes. But it didn't stop the tears from falling when she realised she was on her own again. What was it with her? It was one thing for her to choose the wrong men but to pull a trick like that, when there was no purpose except to make trouble for Ryan? Could she really blame that on hormones?

One thing was certain. Jess knew she needed to sort herself out. She owed her baby that much.

At the end of the day, Louise watched as Jess closed up the sweet stall. Since she'd started to work there, Jess always stayed behind for the last couple of hours of the day, allowing Malcolm to finish early or catch up on his paperwork in the café. Or so they'd all thought. It was obvious now that she'd been hanging around waiting for Ryan so they could sneak off for a secret rendezvous.

Louise couldn't contain herself a minute longer. 'Oi!' she shouted to Jess. 'I want a word with you, Miss can't-keep-her-knickers-on!'

Jess cursed inwardly as Louise came towards her. Still upset by her conversation with Ryan earlier, she'd tried to keep her emotions in check, at least until she got home and she could cry in private. Jess hated anyone to see her upset.

'Leave me alone,' Jess said, keeping her back to her. 'It's nothing to do with you.'

Louise grabbed hold of her shoulder and twirled her around. 'It has everything to do with me,' she said. 'I know you're pregnant and I know that you're trying to pass it off as Ryan's, but it can't be.'

'And why's that?' Jess tried to look bored, but inwardly she was shocked that Louise had found out.

'I've always been good at maths, funnily enough. That bump.' She pointed to Jess's stomach. 'How long is it is since you've been back? Unless you've been eating like a horse, that's more like four months gone than a few weeks.'

'How would you know?'

'Dur – I have a daughter, remember?'

'Oh, I remember.' Jess realised that she could use this to her advantage. 'But no one knows who her father is, right?'

'That's none of your business!'

'And this is none of yours. So keep your nose out.'

'Why, you little—' Louise's hand went up to strike Jess but just in the nick of time, Sam, who had followed her over when she heard raised voices, stopped her. She held onto her hand in mid-air.

'That's enough, you two. You're not kids anymore.'

'She acts like one,' cried Louise. 'She's nothing but a slag.'

'Takes one to know one,' Jess spat back at her. 'And anyway, you need to get your facts right. I *am* pregnant but it has nothing to do with your brother, so back off.'

Louise lunged for Jess again but still Sam held her back.

'I said that's enough!' She turned to Jess. 'You. Go home and think yourself lucky that I'm not the one having this conversation with you. Because if I was, baby or no baby, I'd be telling Ryan's wife what was going on. I wouldn't be keeping any of this secret.'

'It's all secrets on this market, isn't it?' Jess raised her voice purposely. She pointed at Louise. 'With your reputation, I wouldn't be surprised if her husband,' she gestured to Sam, 'was Charley's father. I wouldn't put it past you not to screw your best friend's husband, the rumours I've heard about you.'

'Why, you nasty little bitch!'

Sam intervened just in time, pulling Louise away. As they went past Matt's stall, Sam spotted Ryan trying to blend in with the shelves at the back.

'This is your fault,' she told him.

'Yes,' agreed Louise. 'You and Jess, it stops right now or I'll spread some rumours of my own. Do you hear?'

'I hear you. And it's over.' Ryan nodded curtly. 'But the words kettle and pot spring to mind.'

Louise glared at him before following Sam back to their stall.

'Men!' She shrugged on her coat, ready to declare the day well and truly done with. 'All they do is make you argue. Are you sure you want to get married, Nic? It could all go wrong once that ring is on your finger.'

'You won't put me off, big sis,' Nicci shook her head. 'It's taken me years to get to this stage.'

Louise sighed. Why couldn't she find someone who wanted to marry her and for keeps this time, not like stupid Brian Thompson? Idiot that he was, she had loved being married. Belonging to someone, going home to someone, not having to do everything on her own, make her own decisions, good or bad.

And anyone that could help with Charley and her teenage strops and tantrums would be extremely welcome right now!

CHAPTER TWENTY-ONE

When she got home from work that evening, Louise found a letter in the post from Charley's school. She ripped it open. What a perfect ending to a crappy day, she sighed. Charley's form teacher was asking to see her.

She shouted to Charley to let her know she was home, but ten minutes later, Charley hadn't surfaced.

She went upstairs to see why. The door was ajar. Charley was sitting at her desk on her laptop.

Louise tapped on the door and went in. 'Hey, Charl,' she smiled. 'Good day at school?'

Charley closed the lid. 'The usual stuff,' she replied.

'Have you made up with Sophie yet?'

Charley shook her head.

'Bit strange for you two not to be speaking for this long.' Louise paused. 'Want to talk about it?'

Charley shook her head again.

'Look, if there's anything that –'

'Mum, I'm fine!'

'Okay, okay.' Louise turned to go but stopped. 'It's just, if you ever want someone to talk to, I'm here for you. You do know that?'

'Whatever.'

Louise sighed and left the room. Not wanting to say anything about the letter until she knew the reason why she'd been called into the school, she let the matter drop for now.

Once her mum had gone, Charley grabbed her phone and sent a message to Alex.

> CP: Are you there? I need to talk.

She waited for a moment, hoping he would be able to reply. His response came back in seconds:

> AL: Yeah, here. What's up?
>
> CP: I really hate going to school right now.
>
> AL: Still bad?
>
> CP: Yeah. If it wasn't for those stupid rumours, me and Sophie would still be friends. Now she's gone off with Angela Wilson, I have no one to talk to except you…

Charley paused. She was going to type *and you're not always there when I need you*, but realised that wasn't his fault.

> CP: That's why I haven't been going to school, she said instead. I don't feel like I belong there anymore.
>
> AL: Don't say that.
>
> CP: It's true. I don't feel like I belong anywhere really. Mum doesn't care about me. Everyone at school just wants to spread rumours about me or laugh at me and call me names. It's horrible being on my own. At least when Sophie was around, I had someone to stick up for me. Now I have no one.

AL: You have me to talk to. I know it's not the same but I
   thought we were friends.

CP: We are!

AL: I have to go. Mum is calling me. Speak later, yeah? And
   remember, Charl, I like you. I like you a lot!

Charley's smile was faint as she typed goodbye.

As soon as Sam arrived at work the next morning, shortly
after ten, Louise followed her through to the back room to
speak to her.

'I've had a letter from the school,' she said, 'I have to go
and see Charley's form teacher. I've just rung up and he can
see me this afternoon. Is it okay if I finish early tonight?'

'Of course,' nodded Sam. 'Any idea what it's about?'

'Apparently she hasn't turned up for a full week since Janu-
ary. Honestly, it's like looking after a mini-me. How can I tell
her off for something I used to do all the time?'

'I remember it well,' said Nicci. 'I was jealous because you
hardly ever went to school during your last year.'

Louise grinned as she remembered too. 'Mum was always
having a go at me.'

'But she only did it because she cared. Don't you want Charley to get on in life and have a good education?' asked Sam.

'I suppose so.' Louise sighed dramatically. 'She's clever
enough to go to university if she put her mind to it. Not that
I'd ever be able to afford the fees.'

'She's working here, though,' said Sam. Charley had been working on the stall for the past three Saturdays. 'That shows initiative, so I reckon she'll provide for herself. I've enjoyed having her here, too. She's quite the little worker.'

'Then why isn't she going to school?' said Louise.

'Have you asked her?'

'I tried speaking to her last night but she said she was okay. And I didn't want to push it until I've spoken to her teacher.'

'I bet she misses Sophie,' said Nicci. She was putting together an order for a woman who had left her a list while she did her shopping. She ran her pen through red pepper and mushrooms. 'It seems strange not to see them together anymore. Charley looks lost without her. Did you ever find out what they'd rowed about?'

'Nope.'

'Do you *ever* talk to Charley and ask her stuff?' asked Sam, holding a bag out for Nicci as she weighed out potatoes and slid them in. 'You sound as if you don't really know each other.'

'We don't.' Louise sat down on a stool. 'I just can't seem to get through to her anymore. One minute, she was a sweet kid; the next a stroppy teenager. And now I have to go into school and face the teachers. Just the thought of that makes me feel like *I'm* the one in trouble.' She shuddered. 'Brings back bad memories.'

'Oh, it'll be something and nothing, you'll see,' Sam tried to soothe her fears. 'There might be a valid explanation once you get there. Don't be too quick to think it's Charley.'

'There you go again, trying to put the blame on me!' Louise retorted. She got up to serve a new customer.

'I wasn't.' Sam shook her head. 'I'm just saying wait until you've been to see her teacher before ranting and raving about it.'

'Yeah, right.'

'Look, if it helps, I can call in on my way home from work. Give you a bit of moral support if you need it?' *Anything to stop me going home to be with Reece*, Sam thought to herself.

'Would you?' Louise nodded. 'Ta. It riles me to say, but she always listens to you.'

'That's because I'm not her mum.'

Louise pouted. 'I just think it's because she can't stand me.'

'Well, there is that.' Sam grinned. She ducked when Louise threw a satsuma at her.

At the end of the day, Sam locked up the stall and made her way over to Louise's house. After all the recent fallings out, she was looking forward to a couple of hours with Louise. They hadn't had a good chat in ages, despite seeing each other every day on the stall. Maybe if Charley wasn't sulking too much after Louise had spoken to her, they could all sit down together and have a laugh. And if it meant a couple of hours away from Reece and the tension in their home, she was all for it.

'How did it go at the school?' Sam asked as she shrugged off her coat in Louise's hallway.

'Flipping awful,' Louise replied.

'Oh dear. Where is she?'

'In her room.' Louise pointed to the ceiling. 'And she can stay there as far as I'm concerned. I've just about had enough of her lip.'

Sam sat down at the kitchen table as Louise banged crockery around while she made coffee. Then she turned back to Sam, fury etched across her face.

'That teacher of hers accused me of neglecting her, can you believe that?'

Sam could actually, but didn't want to inflame Louise any further by saying so. 'Did he give any reason why she was skipping days?'

'*He* reckons she's been unhappy for a couple of months now. That if *I* spent more time talking to her, and encouraging her to talk to me, then *we* might be able to get to the bottom of things. Patronising git.' Louise added sugar to one mug and slammed down the lid of the container.

'Did you tell him that she'd fallen out with Sophie?'

'I didn't get the chance. He told me! He said Charley has become withdrawn, not wanting to join in with any discussions, sitting in the class on her own – when she can be bothered to turn up – walking around on her own.'

'That doesn't sound like Charley,' Sam commented, as a mug of coffee was put down in front of her with another bang.

'He reckons she's been the victim of a smear campaign. You know, a little ribbing and something called cyber bullying.'

'You mean on Facebook and such?'

Louise nodded. 'And kids sending texts and these Snap-Chat things, and emails about her to everyone in her year.' She sat down opposite Sam with a scrape of her chair across the flooring.

Sam was shocked. 'Do you know what it's all about?'

Louise shuffled in her seat. 'He thinks it something to do with the boys teasing her about being a sleep around.'

'But that's absurd.' Sam frowned. 'Isn't it?'

'He thinks everyone is teasing her because – because of me.'

'He said that?' Sam was outraged for her friend. 'I'd complain about it if I were you. He shouldn't –'

'Okay, he didn't exactly say that but I knew what he was getting at.'

'Well,' Sam chose her words carefully, 'in a way, I probably agree.'

'That's not fair!'

Sam raised her eyebrows. 'What did you say in response?'

'I told him that kids can be nasty when they want to be. And latching onto a clever girl at school is what they do. They try to bring them down to their level. It seems to me that someone was threatened by Charley and wanted to take her out of the equation.'

'What did she say when you spoke to her?'

'She called me a stupid tart.'

'And what did you say to that?'

'I didn't say anything.'

'You never addressed the fact that Charley was getting bullied at school?' Sam shook her head.

'No, I just grounded her.' Louise folded her arms.

'She'll never confide in you if you lash out every time she gets upset!'

'She shouldn't have said that to me!' Louise snapped. 'I'm her mother.'

'Louise! What kind of mother doesn't have sympathy for a child who is getting bullied?'

'She isn't getting bullied. It's just name calling. Besides, she should have some respect for me.'

'Like you had for your mum, no doubt. She's fifteen, not twenty-five.'

'I knew you'd side with her.' Louise put down her mug and folded her arms. 'You always think you know better than me.'

'Don't be ridiculous. I don't think that at all. I just see things from a different perspective. You and Charley are so alike, you're bound to argue. But,' Sam shrugged a shoulder, 'she's your daughter.'

'Yes, she's MY daughter,' said Louise. 'Mine – nothing at all to do with you.'

Sam recoiled from the bitter edge of Louise's voice. How had they come to be arguing already?

'I wish I'd never come around tonight,' Sam said, tired of hearing about other people's problems.

'So do I! You're as bad as that teacher, practically accusing me of neglecting Charley and—'

'I've done nothing of the sort. I merely said I think you should try and talk to her, get her to tell you what's wrong and if you can't get through to her, then I'll try. She's crying out for help by not going to school.'

'She won't get any help at all if she gets me into trouble.'

'Oh, Louise.' Sam wanted to reach across the table and slap some sense into her. 'Why is everything about you?'

'If you think you'd be so good at parenting, why don't you take Charley for a couple of months and see how you get on with her then? See how cheeky she is, how rude she is.'

'It's part of being a teenager!'

'Some of it is,' Louise agreed. 'But some of it is downright cheek. If I ask her to wear a blue T-shirt, she'll wear a red one. If I ask her to come downstairs, she'll sit in her room. If I ask her to run the hoover round or peg the washing out, she's having a go before I've even finished the sentence. It's not—'

'You're back to feeling sorry for yourself again,' Sam interrupted, her patience being tested to the limit. 'Why can't you admit for once that you think you've failed Charley?'

'What?'

'Firstly, you never told her who her father was.' Sam looked directly at Louise. 'Then, when you married Brian, she looked on him as a father figure but you couldn't keep him. And now there's Matt looking out for you, *loving* you, but you don't appreciate him either.'

Sam knew that some of her words had sunk in when Louise stood up, her face contorted with rage. But she knew she hadn't heard the ones about Matt. She was too wound up by being criticised to hear her point.

'You're no better than me,' Louise sneered. 'Your husband left because you were messing around with another man.'

'I told you that wasn't true. And he's back now so I don't see your point.'

'But you don't want to be with him anymore.' Louise thought back to their last conversation where she'd been comforting Sam after she'd burst into tears. 'You *must* have slept with Dan. Reece would never leave you unless it was true; he worshipped the ground you walked on.' She paused. 'Lucky bitch.'

Angry beyond words, Sam stood up too and they faced each other over the table.

'Oh, I'm a lucky bitch, am I?' she spat. 'You have Charley. You have the only thing I've ever wanted, a child of my own. I've had to sit back and watch you ruin her life while I – we – while me and Reece watched on from the sidelines. It literally tore us apart because I couldn't get pregnant.'

Louise sat open-mouthed while Sam continued.

'You had your chance at happiness but you blew it.'

'I didn't ask to get pregnant with Charley,' Louise protested. 'I was only eighteen. I had my whole life ahead of me until she came along and spoilt everything.'

'I doubt that very much. You were quite capable of making a hash of it before you became pregnant. And I still can't believe you wouldn't tell me who her father is. Me! Of all people. I'm supposed to be your best friend.'

'I haven't told anyone. Ever.'

'That's because it was probably one of your Saturday night conquests. Everyone thinks it's Rob Masters anyway.'

'You really want to know who Charley's father is?' In temper, Louise opened a drawer, rummaged round in it until her hand clasped onto a small mirror. She thrust it into Sam's hands.

'Look at it!'

'Why?'

'Look at it and tell me what you see.'

'Nothing but my own reflection.'

'Exactly! Which is what I see every time I look at Charley.'

Sam frowned. Why would Louise see her face whenever she looked at Charley? Suddenly the realisation dawned on her. Her hand covered her mouth and her eyes widened in disbelief.

Martin.

'Your dad was Charley's father!' said Louise, her voice breaking as she burst into tears.

CHAPTER TWENTY-TWO

'You slept with my dad?' Sam whispered.

Louise nodded slightly, still afraid to admit the truth. 'Can't you see? I've never told you before because I knew it would hurt you too much to find out the truth.'

Sam didn't know what to say. Could it be true? That Charley was in fact her half-sister? Quickly, she did the sums. Charley was sixteen soon. Louise was thirty-four, which meant that her dad would have been thirty-four too when they had slept together. It would have been a couple of months before he died.

'Sit down, Sam,' said Louise. 'And I'll explain it all.'

Before she could, they heard a cry from the hall.

'I HATE YOU!'

'Charley!' Louise and Sam spoke in unison, rushing out of the kitchen. When they reached the hall, they found Charley sitting at the top of the stairs, clutching her knees, looking very young, and very vulnerable.

'I heard you!' she yelled. 'I heard every word.'

Louise rushed up the stairs towards her but Charley ran to her room and slammed the door shut.

'Please, let me explain!' Louise went straight in and saw that Charley had thrown herself onto the bed.

'You should have told me!' Charley screamed.

'You should have told me, too.'

Louise turned round. Sam was standing in the doorway.

'I couldn't tell you.' Louise began to cry as she looked from one to the other. 'I thought I was doing the right thing – by both of you! I thought I was protecting you!'

'No, you were protecting yourself,' Sam said quietly.

'I wasn't!'

'Yes, you were. By not telling me, you played on our friendship for years. You knew if I ever found out I wouldn't want to know you anymore. You had no right to deceive me like that.'

'I didn't deceive you!'

'It was all about you, once again. You never think about anyone but yourself.'

Louise shook her head. 'You're so wrong.'

Sam pointed at Charley who was crying into her pillow. 'No wonder that poor girl feels like she's not wanted.' Then she turned and walked away.

'Sam! Wait!' Louise rushed to the bedroom door.

'You've never got close to her because you've always blamed her for your mistake!' Sam took a few steps down. 'She's there as a constant reminder of what you did!'

'It *was* a mistake!' Louise covered her ears with her hands. 'I didn't mean for it to happen.'

'Like I believe that.' Sam glared up at her. 'She'll never forgive you for this, and neither will I.'

'Sam!' Louise shouted down, unsure whether to follow her friend or comfort her daughter. 'Sam, please!'

Sam retrieved her bag from the kitchen, swiped her coat from the banister and left the house with the slam of a door.

At the top of the stairs, Louise dropped to her knees. 'I was eighteen!' She sobbed, bitterly. 'I was eighteen.' But no one was listening to her.

As soon as Louise left her room, Charley logged into Facebook to see if Alex was online to chat. Luckily, he was.

> CP: 'I hate her. She says I was a mistake. How can she say that? So hurtful.'
>
> AL: 'She doesn't deserve you. I think you should teach her a lesson.'
>
> CP: 'How?'
>
> AL: 'Maybe you should go somewhere for the night, not tell her and let her worry.'
>
> CP: 'I'm not sure what good that would do.'
>
> AL: 'If she really cared about you, she would be concerned.'
>
> CP: 'Maybe. But I don't have anywhere to go.'
>
> AL: 'My mum and dad have a static caravan near to the sea at Rhyl.'
>
> Euw, a caravan. Charley paused. That was her worst nightmare.
>
> AL: 'Think about it. Just for one night.'
>
> CP: 'I don't know how to get to Rhyl. I don't even know where it is.'
>
> AL: 'I could show you. I could stay with you, if you like.'

Charley stopped typing. She knew what Alex really meant was that they could sleep together in the caravan. A little tingle ran through her. She was ready, wasn't she? This is what she wanted.

> CP: 'Do you think we could do it?'
>
> AL: 'Yes. Make her worry about you for a change. See how
>   she likes it.'

Even though Alex couldn't see her, Charley nodded through her tears. Oh, how she wanted to make her mum worry. She wanted to make her hurt, like she was hurting. Someone had to pay for all those lies.

But, more importantly, she wanted to be held by Alex. Comforted in his arms. Be loved by him, feel wanted by him. Alex would make everything better. She couldn't wait to see him.

She pulled out her secret diary from her shoe box at the bottom of her wardrobe. Inside it was the money she'd saved from her Saturday job. She checked the notes. There was thirty pounds there now, plus twenty pounds of her own she'd saved from birthday money. Was it enough? She decided to chance it.

> CP: 'When?'
>
> AL: Tomorrow?
>
> CP: Okay. Let's do it.
>
> AL: 'Really?'
>
> CP: 'Yes, really.'
>
> AL: 'Cool!'

The screen went blank as they each gathered their thoughts. Then the cursor flashed so that she knew Alex was writing something.

AL: 'I can't wait to meet you properly.'

Charley gave an excited squeal.

CP: 'I can't wait to meet you too.'

AL: 'I'll check train times and figure out somewhere we can meet and then I'll email you. Laters. x'

As Charley planned her escape, Louise sat in the living room, a wet tissue screwed up in her hand. The television was on but she couldn't see through the tears that kept flowing. All she could see were Sam's angry eyes glaring at her and Charley's face all screwed up with hurt. Two of the people she cared most about and she'd hurt them both in a matter of minutes.

She shouldn't have taken her anger out on Sam. It wasn't her fault that Charley's teacher had wanted to see her. And why had she let things escalate so that she hadn't kept her mouth shut about Martin? Or, more to the point – why hadn't she come clean to Sam all those years ago? If she'd just said something to her straight away, none of this would be happening. She'd wanted to, ever since she'd first found out she was pregnant, but in the end it had gone on too long.

You silly cow, Louise chastised herself.

She shouldn't have told either of them. Not even if Martin was still alive. It would have been spiteful and no matter what Sam thought, she hadn't kept the secret to save her own skin. She'd done it because she cared. She knew how much losing Martin had devastated Sam and she didn't want to do anything that would taint him in her eyes.

No wonder she had never found the right words. There had never been any.

'You're home early,' Reece shouted as Sam came through the door.

'I don't feel well,' she replied.

'What's wrong?'

'Oh, just a headache.' Sam flopped into the armchair. She wasn't quite sure why, but she didn't want to tell Reece what she'd found out. 'I'm not in the mood for Louise harping on about herself.'

Reece stood up. 'I'll make a coffee.'

He ruffled her hair as he walked past and Sam smiled faintly. She thought back to her last words with Louise. She knew the truth would come out eventually but she hadn't realised it would have something to do with her. Tears filled her eyes. She longed to let them out but knew she had to keep them hidden for now.

She tried to put herself in her friend's position. Had Louise been wrong to sleep with her dad, way back then? Louise had been wild at eighteen. That's what Sam loved about her. Opinionated, daring, extrovert and quite the opposite of her. She'd loved hanging around with Louise because of it. Would that have changed if she knew she was after her dad?

She wondered how long it had been going on, and how hadn't she noticed that Louise had fallen for him? She tried to think back but it was too far. There were no memories she could recall that would make her think about anything in particular. Louise always seemed to be round at her house because her own was too noisy. She had to share a room with Nicci so being here with Sam was more private.

Had Louise used Sam all that time and she'd never known? And why hadn't she told her? Was it because she'd known that she'd lose her? After Martin's death, would Sam have been excited about a baby he'd fathered? She very much doubted that.

She held in a sob. Had Louise chosen her as a godmother to Charley because of her father? Had Louise stayed friendly with Sam all that time just because of the connection between them? She had to admit they didn't always get along. But she'd always thought of them as best friends.

Reece came in. He handed her a glass of water and two painkillers, then brought in their drinks before lounging out on the settee. With a quick smile in her direction, he went back to watching the television.

Sam drank her coffee and excused herself as quickly as she could. At least in the shower, she could cry in solitude. Once under the water, she let the tears fall. For her; for Charley; and most of all, for her dad.

Bringing this up now made her wonder what it would be like if he was still alive. Sadly, she would never find out.

And that's what hurt the most.

* * *

The next morning, Charley had been awake since five a.m. She'd stayed in her bedroom the evening before, gathering together the things she needed. A night away would be enough to teach her mum a lesson. Then maybe she could come back and move in with Sam – or even Matt.

Charley glanced around the room she'd always loved so much. Just lately, it had become her prison as well as her sanctuary. The walls had never felt like they were closing in on her until now. She'd always loved this room. She and Sophie had hung around in it, had a laugh together so many times over the years.

Tears glistened in her eyes as she thought of the last time she'd seen her best friend. Sophie had been with Angela Wilson again. She couldn't understand why she didn't want to hang around with her anymore. They'd been friends for years. She thought they'd be friends for life. She thought Sophie would stick with her through thick and thin. All of a sudden, she realised she had no one to depend on but Alex. He would look after her.

She logged onto her laptop and checked her emails. There was one from him, giving details of the train times and where he'd meet her at the station. She pressed print. Then she logged onto Facebook to see if he was around. When there was no reply, she remembered what time it was; Alex would still be asleep.

Instead, she sent him a quick text message to say she'd received his email. She'd try again later if she had time before she left for the train.

It was nearing seven fifteen when he replied:

'Really can't wait to see you. x'

She texted back a reply:

'Me too. Am excited. x'

Her bag packed, she lay underneath her duvet, fully clothed, just in case her mum tried to talk to her before she left for work and spotted she was dressed. It was Wednesday and Louise usually took the bus into Hedworth as Sam caught up on her paperwork and came to the stall a little later. Not that Sam was likely to pick her mum up after what had happened.

Charley still couldn't believe what she'd learned last night. Ever since she could remember, she'd dreamt of meeting her dad one day. She'd dreamt about him holding her in his arms, saying he'd never stopped thinking of her. She'd daydreamed about him saying he was sorry and that it was Louise who'd told him not to stay in touch. That it was Louise who'd told him to stay away. And now she knew she would never get to meet him. Charley would never forgive her mum for keeping this secret.

A knock on her door just before half past seven made her jump.

'Charley?' said Louise, quietly.

'Leave me alone,' Charley shouted, glad that her mum hadn't barged in like she normally did.

'I'm not coming in and I'm not going to try and talk to you right now. And even though I really shouldn't do this,

I'm going to ring the school and tell them you're sick and won't be coming in today. Okay?'

Charley had an idea. 'Thanks,' she replied.

'Okay. Ring me if you need anything … or just, you know, if you want to talk.' A pause. 'I'll see you later then, yeah?'

No, you won't. Charley said nothing, knowing that she'd given herself a bit of time to get away. If her mum thought she was at home, she could travel to see Alex, safe in the knowledge that no one would find her until she was ready to come home.

She smiled. See how Louise coped with worrying about someone other than herself for a change.

CHAPTER TWENTY-THREE

While Charley made her way to the train station that morning, things were decidedly icy on the fruit stall.

Although they kept up a front, Sam and Louise were pussyfooting round each other. Nicci was the first to comment.

'What is it with you two?' she asked. 'You've obviously fallen out over something.'

'No, we haven't,' said Sam.

'It's nothing,' said Louise.

'Yeah right, and I'm not getting married in two weeks,' Nicci said sarcastically. Then she gasped. 'Ohmigod. Can you believe it? I'm getting married in TWO WEEKS!'

Pleased to discuss the wedding and throw themselves into something that didn't involve much personal conversation, Louise and Sam went over some of the finer details with her between serving customers.

'Jay needs to collect the suits for the boys and I have my last dress fitting this weekend,' she said finally. 'And you two need to come as well.'

'You know they've forecasted snow for that week,' Louise teased.

'For Easter?'

'It's been known to happen before.'

Nicci slapped her arm playfully. 'There will be no snow on my wedding day, thank you very much.'

'But just think how magical it will make it.'

'Just think how cold my feet would be!'

'We could get you some wedding wellies!' laughed Sam.

Louise picked up her phone and rang Charley but there was no answer. She slid the cover back up with a snap.

'Did you speak to Charley last night?' Sam gave her a warning look that she took to mean not to say too much in front of Nicci.

Louise shook her head. 'I tried again this morning and she said she wasn't going in.'

'What's up?' Nicci asked.

Louise filled her in on some of the happenings of the previous night. She watched as Sam squirmed, wondering just how much she would tell. But she wasn't going to let on about their row. She'd never told anyone about Martin until last night and she certainly wasn't going to announce it to the world now.

'What do you think I should do?'

'How would I know? She's your daughter,' Sam said pointedly. Then she relented. 'Charley's a bright kid. She'll work it out for herself.'

'Who's for coffee?' Nicci said. 'I think it's my turn to make it.'

As Nicci collected their empty mugs, Louise gave Sam a half smile. One less than that was returned. She really hoped in time Sam would come to understand that she'd been young and stupid. Then again, she still was stupid. Not even getting older had made her wiser. Or wise up to herself.

Louise sighed again. What the hell was she going to do about Charley? Like every parent, Louise wanted the best for her child. She didn't want her making the same mistakes she had. Shame rushed through her as she thought how much her life had impacted on Charley. Louise had always put herself first, never her child. Charley was living with a mother who had no ambition, with no father figure to look up to. Apart from Matt, she supposed. Matt doted on Charley. Something else she was jealous of. Why couldn't he dote on her too?

She tried Charley's phone to see if she would answer. When there was no reply, she left a voicemail.

'Hi, Charl, it's only me. Listen, when you get this message, give me a quick call, yeah? Speak soon.

Love you. Bye.'

'Any luck?' Sam asked, passing her a mug from Nicci.

Louise shook her head. 'The stubborn little minx isn't answering.'

Nicci laughed. 'Like mother, like daughter.'

Neither Louise nor Sam joined in.

Although she was nervous about catching – or rather missing – two trains to Rhyl, Charley was bubbling with excitement. She'd spent so much time recently day dreaming about meeting Alex. She gazed through the window at the passing scenery, wondering if he would be as nice in real life as he was online. Was his profile picture really him, all sexy eyes and dark, spiky hair and sleek like a racehorse or would he be a spotty boy with greasy hair and a weedy frame? She smiled to herself. Soon, she would find out. And at least she'd bought a return ticket home. She wasn't that stupid.

Twenty minutes later, the train pulled into the station. Charley reached for her holdall from the luggage rail above her head and stepped down onto the platform. Her eyes searched through the people milling about but she couldn't see anyone that looked like Alex. Unsure what to do, she moved to the side by the coffee stall where she'd arranged to meet him.

No one came towards her. She checked her watch: the train was on time. Where was he?

Fear gripped her as she wondered if it had all been a big joke. That Alex wasn't really going to turn up. Had it been someone from school winding her up, pretending to be her friend? Tears brimmed in her eyes.

Then she noticed someone waving. She looked across the platform. An old man in his fifties, with greasy grey hair and a scruffy jumper over disgusting looking corduroy trousers walked towards her. He was smiling at her. Oh no, she didn't know what to do. She'd heard stuff about men who lured young women away, pretending to be someone younger than they were. Please, no.

She turned towards the coffee stall as he came closer, anxiety starting to flood through her, then sighed with relief as the man moved past and said hello to a lady behind her. Then she heard her name and a hand on her shoulder. She turned and this time she knew it was Alex.

'I'm sorry,' he said, struggling to get his breath. 'I missed the bus and had to wait an age for another one. I see you got here on time.'

Charley was sure her heart stopped beating for a moment as she stared at him. Close up, he really was all sexy eyes, dark, spiky hair and body sleek like a racehorse. He wore a thick fleece jacket over a zipped up jumper, a scarf thrown around it casually, dark jeans and thick soled boots. And his smile. There was no mistaking him.

'Hi,' she said shyly.

'Hi yourself,' Alex replied.

They stood for a moment in the chaos around them and then they laughed.

'Well, this is weird,' he said eventually. And then he kissed her. Right there at the side of the platform, right next to the coffee stall. It wasn't a long kiss, but it was a good kiss. A warm welcoming and tender first kiss; she hoped it would be the first of many. He reached for her hand and they walked away, suddenly unable to stop talking.

Charley felt so happy, she thought she might faint. She was actually here with Alex!

'What am I going to do with her, Matt?' Louise asked as they shared a quick break together over coffee in the café. 'I can't seem to get through to her no matter what I say.'

'I'm not sure, really.' Matt added sugar to his coffee. 'Ordinarily, I'd tell you to wait until she's calmed down and try to talk to her again. But she's skipping school. You have to do something or you'll both get into trouble.'

Louise glanced out into the aisle, watching the passing shoppers. Matt was right but he hadn't come up with any practical advice. What she wanted to know was how to handle the situation. How to get Charley to go to school. Or more to the point, find out why she *wasn't* going.

What she couldn't tell Matt was the reason Charley hadn't gone to school today was not the reason he thought it was. She frowned, annoyed with herself. Even now, after all that had gone on, she was still keeping secrets!

'Penny for them,' Matt interrupted her thoughts.

'Hmm?' She glanced back at him. 'Sorry, I was just thinking.'

'How about I have a word with her?' Matt suggested. 'Maybe she might tell me something that she wouldn't tell you.'

'You mean you want to be a negotiator?' Louise teased. 'You've been watching too much TV. Charley's fifteen – a teenager, remember. She won't spill anything, unless it's to Sophie.' Louise sighed then. 'I wish those two would hurry up and get together again. I miss the laughter they bring to the house. It's like a morgue in there at the moment.'

'Well, the offer is on the table.' Matt squeezed her hand before knocking back the dregs of his drink and standing up. 'A man's perception might do the trick.'

'Ha, ha. Any idea where I might find one?'

Louise planted a smile on her face. Joking aside, she was worried that she had really messed everything up. Because that wasn't the offer she was interested in.

Had she missed her chance with Matt?

Charley and Alex were getting off the bus they'd caught outside the railway station when Charley's phone rang again. She pulled it from her pocket to see who it was.

'Is it your mum?' Alex looked at her.

Charley nodded.

'Are you going to answer it?'

'Nope.'

'Nice one.'

Charley felt like a rebel as Alex grabbed her hand again and they walked together along the pavement.

There was a long, straight main road in front of them. On one side, there were terraced rows of guest houses and hotels for as far as the eye could see and on the other, a three foot hop over the wall lead to the beach. The sea was choppy, sand flailing about with the wind but Charley didn't mind. She caught the smell of fish and chips wafting in front of her nose and checked her watch to see it was lunchtime.

'I'm starving,' she said. Apart from a piece of toast this morning, she hadn't eaten anything substantial since yesterday lunch. 'Fancy some chips?'

They each had a cone and walked on for a good twenty minutes before Alex pointed to his right.

Charley saw a gate and a sign announcing Sun Valley Caravan Park.

'That's the entrance.' He pulled a key from his pocket. 'We should be safe here tonight. It's quite empty at this time of year, apart from people coming to air out their vans. The season starts at Easter.'

'Aren't your parents going to worry about you?' Charley asked as he let them in.

'Naw. I told them I was stopping at my friend's house tonight. They won't be looking for me any time soon.' Alex took out his phone and waggled it about. 'Aren't these things amazing? I can speak to them or text them from anywhere and they wouldn't have a clue if I was in the next room or had caught a plane to America. Unless they wanted to check up, of course.'

Charley giggled. 'I've never been to America. We could go there tomorrow,' she joked.

'Or maybe Australia.'

'Or to the moon.'

Alex laughed too, as he closed the gate behind them. 'You're so cool, Charley Pellington.'

Charley felt herself blushing as he kissed her again. This time there was no one around to bother them. She wanted to stay there forever but soon after, Alex grabbed her hand and they ran to the caravan.

From first impressions, it seemed okay. It wasn't one of those tiny four berth nightmares that she remembered loving when she was younger but didn't want to go near now she was older. This caravan was more like a small flat; she reckoned it could sleep about eight people. It had two separate bedrooms, one with a fixed double bed, not something that had to be made up with cushions every night. The living area had a table with four chairs, a settee and armchair, a small flat-screen television and a gas fire, which they were going to need as it was freezing.

Alex pointed to the large bedroom with the double bed. 'Put your bag down in there and we can go for a walk and get some food. There's plenty of stuff like soup and pasta in the cupboards. And there's always coffee and teabags so all we need is bread and milk and something to drink.'

Charley could hardly contain herself. Alex was so grown-up compared to most of her friends, as well as being gorgeous. If only Sophie could see her now, she would be green with envy!

As soon as she got home that evening, Louise shouted out to Charley. When there was no reply, she listened for music but couldn't hear that either. She stomped up the stairs, expecting to find Charley with her earphones in, but the room was empty. She glanced around. Nothing seemed to be out of place – there was still lots of teenage detritus around the room and on the floor.

She went back downstairs and tried Charley's phone again. Still no answer and there were no missed calls from her. Unsure what to do, she started to prepare something to eat. Charley would turn up soon, no doubt, and then she'd be in for it.

But when it came to half past seven and several phone calls were still unanswered, Louise decided she'd clock-watched enough and rang Sam in a panic.

'I'm sorry,' she said quickly, realising that they were hardly on the best of terms, 'but Charley hasn't come home yet and I don't know want to do.' She felt a lump in her throat. 'Sam, I don't know where she is.'

'It's probably something and nothing. Maybe she's still annoyed about what happened yesterday. Have you contacted Sophie?'

'No, they're not speaking, remember?'

'But all the same, she might be able to tell you what's been going on with Charley lately. Do you have her number?'

'Yes, it's stored on my phone.'

'Is Charley's phone switched off?'

'No, but it's been ringing out for hours.' Louise began to cry.

'I'm on my way over. You try to reach Sophie and see if she can shed any light on it.'

'What if anything's happened to her? She's all I've got, Sam.'

'I'll ring Matt. Don't worry. We'll find her.'

Sam was round at Louise's house within fifteen minutes. Reece had joined her too. Neither of them were surprised when Matt answered the door.

'She's in bits,' he told them. 'Reckons it's all her fault for being a bad mother. I can't get any sense out of her.'

Sam went through to find Louise sunk in the settee, clutching her phone. Forgetting their recent argument, she rushed across to sit next to her.

'She's run away with a boy!' Louise cried.

'How do you know?'

'Sophie told me. His name is Alex.'

Sam wrapped her arms around her. 'Is he someone from school?'

'No, much worse than that. It's some boy she's met on Facebook.'

Sam felt goosebumps break out all over her.

'Sophie said Charley was obsessed with him. She was always emailing, texting him, messaging him through Facebook and something called WhatsApp, and that's what they'd fallen out about. I had no idea.'

'And she's sure she's with him?'

Louise shook her head. 'She says they haven't spoken to each other in a while. They used to be such good friends. But she says Charley might have gone to meet him.'

'Do you think we should call the police?' said Matt, who had stayed in the background with Reece, unsure what to do.

Sam didn't know what to suggest. On the one hand, no one had seen or spoken to Charley since this morning – she could be anywhere by now. But she was a fifteen-year-old girl; she could easily be sulking, trying to teach Louise a lesson. They'd all look silly if she came rolling in as they were reporting her missing. But it was hard to know where to draw the line. And more so now that there was a boy involved. For all they knew, he could be someone older than he was making out to be. He could be a paedophile.

What would Sam do if it was her child that was missing? Charley was, after all, only fifteen.

'Maybe we should leave it for another hour or so?' Reece suggested. 'I know it isn't ideal but I think you can trust Charley. If she's safe, she'll let you know.'

'But what if she isn't safe?' said Louise. 'She could have been kidnapped and tortured. She could be in danger right now. I'd be responsible for that.'

'I know it's a risk but Reece is right, Louise.' Sam got out her phone. 'And I bet if the police know you and her were arguing yesterday, they'd tell you to wait a while longer too.'

'You had a row?' said Matt.

Louise said nothing.

Sam began to type out a message. 'Let me send a text asking her to contact me, just to let us know she's okay. Hopefully, she'll text me back. At least if she does that, we'll know she's all right.'

'But I need to know where she is *now* so that I can go and fetch her!' Louise started to cry again. 'I want her home with me, where I can see her.'

Sam held her while she cried. 'She'll be okay, Louise,' she stroked her hair. 'She'll be okay.'

She looked up to see both Matt and Reece staring back at her. They wore the same worried expression that she did.

It was evening when Charley and Alex arrived back at the caravan, each carrying a shopping bag. After hanging around the centre of town for most of the afternoon, drinking coffee and window shopping, they'd bought a pizza to share and a bag of salad. They also had fresh bread and butter, and chocolate trifle for afterwards. Charley had added sweets and chocolate into their basket: Alex, a bottle of coke and a few cans of lager.

But Charley was getting increasingly more worried every time she looked at her phone. She was getting more and more phone calls. Oh, no, she was in so much trouble.

Seeing her apprehension as she checked it once more, after he'd put the bags down onto the table Alex stopped to give her a hug.

'It'll be okay,' he reassured her. 'You can go home tomorrow but you must make her worry about you. Do you want to check out what's in the cupboards while I switch on the gas? It's just outside.'

Charley watched him disappear out of the door. She could have made a run for it quite a few times during the day. Even now, she'd only have to go back to the main road and flag down a taxi or something.

But she didn't want to. She felt safe with Alex. She had nothing to prove to him: he liked her for who she was. It was just what she needed right now.

She opened kitchen cupboards and put away their little bit of shopping. Then she emptied her bag, placing things down on top of the fitted dressing table. Glancing at the double bed, she wondered about what would happen later. Would she be able to go all the way this time?

She picked up her phone. There were lots of missed calls from her mum – voice messages too. And text messages – including one from Sam.

> 'Hi Charl. Wherever you are and whatever you are doing,
> it's okay. But you need to let your mum know you're
> safe. Text me back. S x'

Charley typed a reply. She supposed she was okay with letting her mum know she was safe. Then she heard the caravan door open and Alex bounding up the steps, so she pressed send quickly, switched off the phone and shoved it back inside her bag.

Sam wasn't sure what to think when she read the text message. Nor what she should tell Louise standing in front of her.

'What does it say?' asked Louise, apprehension clear in her voice.

'She's okay, for starters.' Sam decided to tell her the good news first.

Louise cried with relief. 'Oh, thank goodness.' But then she panicked. 'That text might have been sent by anyone! Someone could have her phone! Let me read it. What exactly does it say?' Before Sam could stop her, she snatched the phone from her hand. The message from Charley read:

'Tell Mum I'm ok but not coming home. Cx'.

'She's not coming home?' Louise frowned as she looked up at everyone. 'Do you think she's with that Alex? Alex might not even be Alex, for all we know. He could be some sex fiend acting as a boy called Alex. I can't stand around anymore. I'm calling the police.'

Sam shivered, her eyes filling with tears as she listened to Louise reporting Charley as a missing person.

CHAPTER TWENTY-FOUR

Although Charley and Alex chatted quite amicably for most of the evening, by half past nine their conversation had more or less dried up. They'd enjoyed the pizza and Charley had had a can of lager but she didn't want to get drunk. She needed to keep her head clear for what was about to happen.

If they had been on a first date, she'd be dying to go home now so that she could recall their first kiss in detail, think about what had happened, analyse everything Alex had said to her. She'd go to bed with a big grin as she looked forward to their next date. Now she was so nervous that her left leg kept shaking involuntarily.

She was worried about the night to come even more than she wished she'd never run away. The caravan was cold, despite the gas fire being on full so Alex fetched the double duvet from the bedroom, she made coffee and they settled down underneath it and watched television. It would have been great if there wasn't an atmosphere. For her, it was an atmosphere of dread.

She wondered if Alex was nervous. He was only just sixteen. Was this the first time he'd slept with anyone? She wanted to ask him but didn't dare. What if he'd been with lots of girls and she wasn't good enough? She glanced over at him. He was checking his phone again. He'd been doing that regularly for the past couple of hours. Was he regretting letting things go so far, too?

She drifted off to sleep for a while and when she woke up, she and Alex began to fool around. She tried to enjoy it, hoping it would be over soon. There had been a bit of kissing and fumbling earlier but neither of them seemed to want more. And now Alex had stopped again.

'I'm tired,' he said, pulling back the duvet. 'I'm going to brush my teeth and call it a night.'

Charley fought back tears. What was wrong with her? First Aaron and Connor made up rumours and now Alex didn't want to sleep with her? Was she – what was the word they used at school – frigid? Did she give off 'keep away' signals?

Then she gasped, all of a sudden understanding that he wanted to get into bed with her. Maybe he felt it would be more comfortable, or more romantic? Either way, it sent her into a complete panic. How would she take off her clothes?

Charley cleaned her teeth after Alex. With dread, she came out of the bathroom. Alex stood in the kitchen area waiting for her.

'I don't know about you,' he said, hardly able to look at her, 'but I think it's too cold to get undressed. I'm going to sleep in my clothes.'

The relief must have shown on Charley's face, because Alex grinned.

'You obviously don't mind then?' he asked.

'I – I'm not sure.' Charley gulped. 'Don't you want to sleep with me?'

'Of course I do!' Alex looked sheepish. 'I mean – well, I think you're gorgeous but it's just that ... I've never done it before.' He smiled awkwardly. 'I think I'm more scared than you are.'

'I'm not scared,' retorted Charley.

'It was *your* leg that shook every time I came near you.'

It was Charley's turn to grin. There really was no point in getting mad at Alex. She didn't want to sleep with him either.

'You can take the double bed,' he told her as they stood there awkwardly. 'I'll have one of the smaller beds.'

A few minutes later, Charley lay in the dark, fully clothed underneath the double duvet. Even though Alex was only a few feet away, part of her wished he was here with her. He could warm her up and cuddle into her, even if they didn't want to do anything else. She pulled the duvet closer around her neck and tried to get to sleep. The quicker she did, the quicker the morning would arrive and she could go home.

Alex knocked on the bedroom door a minute later. He got into the bed beside her.

'Don't panic,' he said. 'I'm not going to do anything. It's just warmer under the duvet.'

It was so quiet that Charley could hear the silence ringing in her ears. She could feel her heart beating wildly inside her chest. She didn't dare move a muscle and she knew she wouldn't be able to sleep.

Again, she wished she was at home. She couldn't wait for the morning.

* * *

Louise never went to bed that night. Reece went home about ten and, despite Matt sleeping over in the spare room, Sam had insisted on staying downstairs with her – a fact that she was grateful for.

It was five a.m. Both she and Sam had stayed awake until the early hours but she was the only one awake again now. While Sam dozed, Louise thought about Charley. She prayed she'd be okay and that this was some kind of schoolgirl prank that she'd thought up to wound her mum. If it was, it had definitely done the trick. Louise was hurting so much there were no words to describe her pain.

She thought back to the first time she'd seen her daughter. She'd been at the hospital with her mum and Sam, trying to make out that she was brave at eighteen when really she didn't have a clue what to do and when. The nurse had put Charley into her arms and she'd fallen in love with her, forgetting all the pain of the birth. A few days later, she'd taken her home to her parents as a six pound bundle of screams and baby powder. If it wasn't for her mum and dad helping out, she wouldn't have coped as well as she did. But despite her downfalls, Louise always did the best she could for her daughter.

She remembered Charley's first steps, her first day at school. When she learned how to tell the time. The first width she swam in the pool, after she'd seemed to swim but get nowhere for ages. The time she'd dressed up as a rat in the

school play, *The Pied Piper of Hamlyn*. When she won a prize
from the school for the best written essay.

She recalled what a stubborn minx she'd always been but
what a lovely warm character Charley was too. And over the
years, she'd turned into a beautiful young lady, one Louise
was proud to call her daughter. She felt so ashamed that she
hadn't let Charley know that, because she'd been too wrapped
up in herself.

If she came home – no, *when* she came home – Louise was
going to put that right. She'd start by telling her all the things
she should have said. She'd stop messing around and act like
a parent should. And she would make it known that she had
the best daughter in the world.

She started to cry again. Please don't let memories be all
that I have left of her. Please let her be okay.

Despite her anxiousness, Charley managed to get a little
sleep, but she still woke up early. In the dark, she could just
about make out the shape of Alex sleeping next to her. She
couldn't see his features, just his shadow, but she knew he had
his back towards her. She turned on her side and squeezed her
eyes shut to stem the tears threatening to fall.

Last night had been one of the worst nights of her life. She
remembered tossing and turning, thinking about how mad
her mum would be when she finally got home. She remembered scooting across to the other side of the bed when Alex

turned over. More than anything, she remembered wishing she was back in her own bed the whole night through.

'Morning,' Alex said, making her jump. She hadn't realised he was awake.

'Morning,' she replied.

'What time is it?'

She shrugged then realised he couldn't see her. She reached over for her phone and illuminated the screen.

'It's quarter past six.' Charley saw an icon indicating another voice message. She hoped it was from her mum. She went through to the kitchen and called it up.

'Charley, it's Mum. I know you might not be able to hear this message or even respond to it in any way but I just want you to know that I've called the police and they'll find you soon. And if this isn't Charley answering this phone … if this is Alex I'm talking to and you hurt my little girl, I … I … I'll fucking kill you!'

There were a few sobs and then the call ended.

Oh, no!' Charley was horrified. Everyone knew about Alex! Her mum must have contacted Sophie. She was the only one who Charley had spoken to about him.

'What's up?' asked Alex.

Charley turned to see a light on in the room. Alex was sitting up now, his spiky hair in a definite bed head style. Somehow his good looks of yesterday had gone and she saw him for what he was. A sixteen-year-old boy who'd befriended a fifteen-year-old girl. And now both of them were in big trouble.

'It's all gone wrong!' Charley burst into tears. 'My mum's rung the police and reported me missing. I can't go home now. She'll—'

'Whoa!' Alex interrupted. 'Wait a minute! She's contacted the police?'

'Yes! She rang them last night.'

'And are they looking for you?' Alex was pulling on his shoes.

'They must be! What am I going to do? I can't go home now. She'll kill me.'

'They'll kill us both if they find us here.' Alex was up now and running a hand through his hair. 'I'm in so much trouble.'

No, you're not.' Charley was going to learn by her mum's mistakes and admit the truth. 'This is my fault.'

'But, can't you see? I'm sixteen and I – I suppose I'm responsible for you. If I get caught with you and they think we – we've – *you know*, then I could be in trouble.'

'But we didn't – you know.'

'You have to ring her. Tell her you're okay. It might not be too late.'

'I can't!'

'But you might get away with it if you talk to her.' He came to her then. 'Think about it. She'll be so pleased to hear from you, the police will stop looking for you and we – we can grab a coffee before you catch a train back.'

Charley paused. Was it really that easy? Alex went outside the caravan to switch off the gas. She flew down the steps beside him, the chilly sea air catching her breath. 'Alex!'

'Ring her!' he shouted above the noise of the wind. 'We have to go. Get your things.'

Charley didn't understand. What was all the big rush?

'What's going on?' she asked him once they were back inside. 'Why are you so afraid of the police?'

'I'm not.'

'Yes, you are. It should be me who's scared. I have to go back and face the music. You can just disappear into thin air, can't you?'

'Do you want me to do that?'

'No!'

Alex paused for a moment. 'My old man's a copper,' he admitted. 'He'll go mad if he finds out what I've done.'

'Ohmigod!' Charley gasped. 'You idiot!'

Alex grinned nervously. 'I know.'

There was nothing for it but to admit defeat. Charley dialled a number on her phone.

'Where can she be?' Louise asked Sam for the umpteenth time that morning. They were in Louise's kitchen and it was half past six. Although Reece had gone home at ten after the police had been alerted, Sam and Matt had stayed over. Sam wouldn't have left Louise, the state she was in, but neither had she wanted to. Charley was such a huge part of her life; she needed to know that she was safe too. Louise had finally gone to sleep, with exhaustion, about two a.m. Sam had stayed downstairs with her, urging Matt to go on up to bed.

They were both sitting in silence when they heard Matt coming down the stairs. Louise's heart lurched when she saw him barefoot in hastily pulled on clothes. Because he was smiling.

'Guess who I've just been woken up by?' he asked, waggling his mobile phone in the air. 'I got a call from Charley. She's okay!'

'Oh, thank God.' Louise stood up and hugged him. 'Where is she?'

'She's safe and she's sorry and I'm going to pick her up.'

'Yes, but where *is* she?'

'She's in Rhyl.'

'Rhyl!' Louise and Sam said in unison.

'What the hell is she doing there?' Louise added.

'Apparently, she got a train,' Matt explained, 'went to the seaside, hung around a bit and then was scared to come home.'

'And what about this Alex? Was he with her?'

'I didn't ask. I thought it best not to. She's probably scared enough about what you're going to say anyway.'

'Too right she should be scared,' Louise said. Then she laughed with relief. 'I'll kill her when I see her! How long will it take to get there?'

'About three hours I reckon. I'll have a quick cuppa and then I'll go to fetch her.'

'Are you sure? I know she can catch the train and I could meet her at the station here but I want her with me. I could get the train to Rhyl and then travel back with her?'

'No,' said Matt, shaking his head. 'It's fine. I've checked the trains and they're don't start for another couple of hours anyway. I'd rather have her in my car safe and sound.'

Louise's heart went out to him.

'Well,' Sam hurried them along, 'don't you think you should get on your way then?'

'I'll get my coat.' Louise smiled again.

'Wait!' Matt touched her forearm. 'Do you think that's wise?'

Louise looked at him as if he had three heads. 'Of course I do.'

'But what happens if she's frightened and she—'

'Frightened of me?' Louise looked appalled at the thought. 'That's ridiculous.'

'Matt's right,' said Sam. 'Charley was upset enough to stay out overnight. Shall I go instead? She always speaks to me and—'

'Oh, that's right, get another dig in,' snapped Louise. 'You always think you'd be better at playing mother than me.'

'No,' Sam reassured her. 'Maybe the reason she ran away could have been sparked by me as much as you, so she might want to chat it through first.'

'What reason's this?' Matt wanted to know but Sam shook her head.

'Just women's talk,' said Louise.

'We can be home in a few hours,' Sam said. 'Why not go and do some shopping and treat her? Buy her something nice to eat for later, just the two of you. Get her that chocolate cake she likes and stay in with her. Talk to her. Try to find out what's wrong rather than ...' Sam stopped, realising she'd said too much.

'Rather than storm in and have a full-blown row before she's even got her feet through the front door,' Louise finished off for her.

Sam said nothing.

Matt jangled his car keys up in the air. 'I can't wait around for you two all day. Which one of you is coming or am I going alone?'

'Sam's right,' said Louise with a sigh. 'The last person Charley will want to see is me. You two go and bring her home and I'll have a chat to her afterwards.'

'And you'd better ring the police. Let them know she's safe.'

Louise baulked. 'How stupid am I going to look?'

'You did what any responsible parent would do,' said Matt. 'They're probably used to these kinds of things resolving themselves overnight anyway.'

Once they were ready, Louise followed them to the front door. 'Ring me when you have her, won't you?' she asked.

Despite the unresolved argument hanging over them, Sam gave her friend a hug. 'This will sort itself out, you'll see,' she smiled.

Louise watched them drive off in Matt's car before closing the door. It was only then that she sunk to the floor, collapsed in a heap and sobbed.

Her little girl was safe.

CHAPTER TWENTY-FIVE

In ten minutes flat, Charley and Alex headed out into the cold and dark morning and off the camp site. Twenty minutes later, they were walking along the sea front when Alex pointed to a café that was just opening its doors.

'Good morning,' a loud voice boomed out. A man with a round face and stomach smiled at them from behind the counter. 'You're my first early birds today. What can I get you?'

They ordered tea and toast and scrambled eggs and Charley went to sit down as Alex waited for their drinks. The café was a typical seaside establishment. Plastic gingham tablecloths on square tables, hard-backed chairs with seats made of raffia. Charley sat down at a table and ran a hand across the steam on the window so she could see outside. The day was just beginning but already she could sigh with relief.

Lucky. That's what she'd been, Charley realised. Lucky to find someone as kind as Alex to look after her when she'd been so stupid. He could have turned out to be anyone. And even if he wasn't some weirdo in real life, he could have forced himself on her last night – but instead, he was as scared as she was. Neither of them were grown up enough to deal with the situation, despite both of them thinking they were.

What a fool she'd been, over-reacting like that. Fortunately she'd be home soon, once Matt arrived. She was pleased he was coming to fetch her with Sam, although she'd yet to talk to her mum. But deep down, she knew she'd be able to sort things out. Her mum had only acted in everyone's best interests, even though it had turned out wrong.

She wondered, was she ever going to tell her who her real dad was? It still hurt that she had been so secretive about it, but it wasn't as if she had stopped her from seeing him. He hadn't been alive. And she realised that Sam was actually her half-sister. Now, that definitely wasn't a bad thing.

She'd been surprised to get a couple of text messages from Sophie too, asking if she was okay. Quickly, she sent a reply while she waited for Alex to join her.

> 'Hey. Just letting you know that I did stay out all night but I'm going home now. Matt's coming to pick me up. Cx.'

A message came back almost immediately.

> 'So glad you're safe. Do you fancy hooking up in the market café later? Can't really stand Angela Wilson. You can tell me all about Alex. Sx.'

Charley grinned.

> 'Sure. Catch you later. Cx.'

She gazed out at nothing in particular. When Alex sat down opposite her, she grinned at him. He grinned too, waiting for her to share the joke.

'What?' he asked when she didn't come forward with an explanation.

'Your dad is a copper?' she giggled.

Alex laughed then. 'I know. I can't get away with anything.'

'No, you're just too sweet to get into trouble. You're a decent boy, Alex. There's not many like you.'

Alex leaned forward and kissed her lightly on the lips. 'Will I get to see you again or is this it?'

Shy again now, Charley shrugged. 'I'm not sure. What do you think?'

'I think we should stay in touch online and see what happens.'

'Cool.'

The man from behind the counter whistled a tune as he popped down their breakfast. 'There you are, my love's young dream,' he beamed. 'Enjoy.'

'Anyone would think we're having smoked salmon with these eggs,' Alex said.

Charley tucked into her breakfast.

'There is something you need to do for me,' she said after she'd eaten some of it.

Alex looked up with a forkful of egg in mid-air.

'Leave, before Matt gets here. I don't want to scrape you off the floor.'

'Don't worry,' said Alex, 'I shall be *eggstra* careful and leave soon.'

Charley groaned, grinning. Yes, she really was lucky.

'So tell me what Charley really told you,' Sam said to Matt, as soon as they were out of Louise's driveway.

'She spent the night in a caravan with Alex.' Matt was deadpan. 'Then she found out that Louise had called the police and decided to ring me. She and Alex should now be having breakfast somewhere on the seafront.'

'Do you know if they – if he touched her?'

'No, but I hope he kept it curled up in his pants or else I'll search him down. He had no fucking right to do that.'

'We don't know he did do anything yet, so let's keep calm.' Sam spotted the tears in his eyes. 'She means so much to all of us, doesn't she?'

Matt nodded, swiping away a rogue teardrop that fell.

'And what about Louise? When are you two ever going to get together?'

'What?'

'Oh, come on, Matt.' Sam glanced out of the window at the passing scenery. 'We all know you love her.'

Matt coughed.

'Why don't you tell her?' She turned back to him.

'Because she doesn't love me.'

'Yes, she does. She's mad about you.'

'No, she isn't!'

'I think you'll find that she is.'

Matt grinned. 'You're going to make me crash the car!'

Sam smiled. At last the penny had dropped for one of them.

'Has she said something to you?' Matt enquired after a moment.

'She doesn't have to. I can see it when you're together.'

'When we're together, she treats me like her best mate.'

'Oi, I'm her best mate.' But even though Sam made a joke about it, she didn't feel like laughing. Best friends didn't keep secrets from each other.

'I know that,' Matt sighed. 'I just think she sees me as someone to look out for her and Charley.'

'And you do it so well that she takes you for granted,' Sam pointed out. 'Have you ever tried telling her how you feel?'

'No!'

'Why not?'

'Because I'm a man, and men don't do things like that.'

The sat-nav informed Matt that he needed to come off at the next junction.

'Come on, you know her better than that now. Do you want me to ask her if she'll have a date with you?' Sam laughed. 'Like we did when we were at school?'

Matt grinned too. He checked in his mirror before indicating to change lanes.

'Do you love her?' Sam asked when she'd read the sign to see they were three miles from Rhyl and would soon be with Charley.

'*What's love got to do with it?*' Matt teased, channelling Tina Turner.

Sam shook her head. 'Seriously, just tell her, before it's too late.' She reached for her phone. 'I'll text Charley to let her know we're nearly there.'

* * *

After sitting in the café for as long as they could without over-staying their welcome, Charley and Alex had been sitting in a shelter on the sea front for the last hour while they waited for Matt to arrive. When the text message beeped, Charley opened it eagerly.

'They're here, aren't they?' said Alex.

Charley nodded.

'How long have I got?'

'About ten minutes, I reckon.'

'Do I have to go?'

'If you value your life.' Charley grinned to ensure Alex knew she was joking. Still, she wished it didn't have to be like this. They'd already decided to arrange to meet up again, once they'd got to know each other a bit better first.

'I wish you didn't have to go.'

'Me too.'

Now that the problem of them sleeping together had been lifted, Charley found they'd both relaxed enough to enjoy each other's company again. She'd been so grateful that Alex had waited with her. Sitting alone for three hours, she'd have worried herself silly about the trouble she was in and she knew she would have been crying by now. Being with Alex had made it bearable.

'You will keep in touch online?' she asked, almost timidly.

He put his arm round her. 'Of course.' Then he kissed her.

Charley didn't want it to end. She knew it was the last kiss they'd be able to share.

'Bye, Charl,' Alex said. With a wave, he walked off. 'See you online.'

'Bye, Alex.' Charley watched until he was out of sight. She was still thinking about him when her phone rang a few minutes later.

Then she began to panic.

While Matt and Sam went to fetch Charley, Louise did indeed go shopping. She came back with a bag full of Charley's favourite things to eat, trying to convince herself that she hadn't bought them because she felt guilty. She also treated her to some new clothes. They were all she could afford but she knew Charley would like them – a pair of skinny jeans, a short jumper and a longer cardigan to wear with leggings. She also bought her a nice set of underwear to show she knew she was growing up.

She'd decided not to ring Charley, knowing it would put added pressure on her. She wanted to chat to her face to face. Instead, she asked Sam to send texts every now and then, updating her of their progress.

By the time she got home from the shops, Louise was desperate to see her daughter.

'We're driving along the promenade,' Sam told Charley. 'Whereabouts are you? Yes, come out near to the kerbside. What's opposite you? Look out for the clock tower,' she told Matt. 'No, don't cry, Charl. Everything's fine. Look, she's there! Pull in, Matt.'

Sam got out of the car and Charley rushed into her arms.

'I'm sorry.' Charley started to cry. 'I'm so sorry.'

'It's okay.' Sam hugged her fiercely. 'You're safe, that's the main thing.'

Matt beeped his horn behind them. 'Stay here. I'll find somewhere to park and then come back to you.'

Sam took Charley back to the shelter and they sat down together. There still weren't many people about, the cold wind obviously keeping people away from the beach. The sea was quite calm, even though the gusts were swirling rubbish around. The seagulls looked on eagerly, waiting for scraps of anything to eat.

Sam passed Charley a tissue. 'Want to tell me about it?'

'I was – I was just so mad with Mum when I found out about . . . ' Charley didn't know what to say then, so she stopped.

Sam put an arm round the girl's shoulder and drew her near again.

'So was I,' she acknowledged. 'I can't believe she kept it from both of us for so long.'

'Were you really upset?'

'Yes.' Sam recalled how she'd cried the night she'd found out. 'But I suppose I can't blame your mum. She was only young. I think my dad should have known better though.'

'Did he know about me?'

'No. Louise didn't want to tell him but a few weeks later he died anyway. Lord knows what she thought I would have said about it. I think that's what hurt the most. That she kept it from me. But I can see why, I suppose.'

'She really is a silly cow, isn't she?'

Sam could hear the affection in Charley's tone.

'Yes, she is. But her heart's in the right place.'

'I don't think she has a heart.'

'Of course she has a heart.'

Charley's face creased up again. 'Then why is she always fooling around with everyone?'

'She's just afraid of getting hurt again. Sometimes it's easier to deny yourself happiness than dare to have another go at things.'

'You mean with Matt, don't you?'

Sam grinned. 'It's obvious to you, too?'

'I think it's obvious to everyone *but* Mum and Matt. I wish he was my dad.' Charley pulled away from her. 'Oh, I didn't mean –'

Sam smiled. 'I know what you meant.'

They sat in silence for a moment. In front of them, two seagulls fought over the remains of someone's bacon butty. The noise became deafening. Time to go.

Sam spotted Matt walking towards them, carrying three cartons of coffee with both hands. He held a small paper bag between his teeth. She turned to Charley.

'I think you should text your mum to say that we'll be on our way home soon.'

Charley took out her phone. 'She's going to be so mad, isn't she?'

'Yes, but only because she cares about you.'

'Do you think so?'

'Of course I think so! She just has a funny way of showing it sometimes.'

They smiled at each other.

'Hey,' Sam whispered just before Matt reached them. She leaned in close to Charley again. 'It's great to have a little sister.'

Charley's face lit up.

By the time she saw Matt's car pull up outside her home, Louise felt like a yo-yo. She'd been up and down to the window that many times. She opened the front door, flew out of the house and ran towards the car.

Charley got out and fell straight into her mum's arms. 'I'm sorry,' she cried, holding onto her. 'I didn't mean to hurt you.'

Louise was crying too. 'I'm just glad you're back and in one piece. We were all so worried.'

Through her tears, she mouthed a thank you to Sam and Matt before tightly holding onto Charley as she ushered her into the house.

'Should we go in or leave them to it?' Matt asked Sam.

'I think we should leave them to it.'

'I'm glad it's a happy ending.'

'Me too.'

'I suppose we'd better check out what's happened at the market without us there.' Matt started the engine up again. 'I bet all hell's let loose without us.'

'Speak for yourself,' said Sam. 'I have Nicci manning my stall. She might be rushed off her feet but she's capable. Whereas you have Ryan.' She smirked. 'I know who my money is on.'

'It's a good job all this happened when it did. It's going to be manic setting everything up for the wedding.'

'Maybe, but it might be good practice for someone sitting not so far away from me.'

Matt grinned. 'Oh, I reckon there'll be at least one more family fall out before the big day. It's part of the fun, isn't it?'

'You know that's not what I meant.'

'Sorry.' Matt turned up the radio. 'I can't hear you. La, la, la, LA!'

Sam grinned back at him but the smile swiftly dropped from her face. If only the wedding was all she had to concentrate on right now.

CHAPTER TWENTY-SIX

It was Sunday evening and a week to go before the wedding. Sam was curled up on the settee with a glass of wine. Thankfully, Reece had gone to have a couple of pints with Ryan and Matt so she had the house to herself. It was something that she was beginning to miss.

She sighed. All this wedding talk was making her think of her own marriage. How the hell was she going to tell Reece that things weren't working between them anymore? She couldn't stay with someone that she loved like a brother. Yes, the sex was still there but even that was beginning to get complacent again. A case of *if we must* rather than *I'd love to, darling*.

Jay and Nicci's wedding was going to be so stressful for her. She'd be surprised if she got through the day without bursting into tears. Despite what had happened over the past few weeks, she missed Louise. She needed her support now more than ever but since she'd made up with Charley, she was spending more time with her. Rightly so, in Sam's opinion, but it left her with no one to confide in.

So she wasn't expecting to open the door shortly after seven o'clock and find an embarrassed looking Louise on the doorstep.

'I was just thinking about you,' Sam said once they'd gone through to the living room and sat down.

'Oh?' said Louise, sounding a little shocked.

'Yes. I was wondering how Charley was doing.'

'She's great.' Louise was unable to stop the grin spreading across her face. 'We've had a few long chats now. We also talked about the bullying. I told her how sorry I was that it was down to me. She's gone back to school.'

'Good. I'm pleased.'

'Yeah, me too. Which is why I came round to see you.' Louise paused for a second. 'I'd like to talk to you, see if we can smooth things out now.'

'And what makes you think you can make peace with me that easily?'

Sam left the room, leaving Louise to stew, until she returned with another wine glass and poured her a drink.

'Well, go on then,' she said after she'd sat down. 'Tell me what you want me to know.'

And so the whole story finally came tumbling out of Louise.

'When I was seventeen, you know that I was round at your house so much because mine was always so noisy.' Louise smiled shyly at the memories. 'I used to love nothing more than spending time with you here because your dad was out at work a lot and we had the house to ourselves. It was like having our own pad.' She laughed, a little awkwardly.

Sam remained straight-faced.

'I – I never told you, but I always had a crush on Martin. He was so good-looking and so, well, grown up compared to the boys we knew. There weren't weeks or months of flirting on his side. In fact, he never took any notice of me in that way at all, if I'm honest, because I remember feeling upset about it. But then I caught him on a rare occasion when he'd had too much to drink.

'I'd come over to see you one Sunday afternoon after I'd had a row with my mum and dad but you weren't in. Martin had been to the pub and was a little worse for wear. He said I should come in and wait for you. He offered me a glass of wine and for every sip I had, he took in more of the whisky he'd poured himself.

'He suggested putting on a video and picked out *Dirty Dancing*. And just before the I-carried-a-watermelon scene came on, he pulled me to my feet and we had a laugh trying to dance. He was so drunk he kept falling over and well, you can imagine the rest.'

Louise paused to catch her breath. Sam was staring at the floor.

'Afterwards, I was so embarrassed,' Louise continued. 'I went upstairs to your bathroom and sat for a while to gather my thoughts. It felt so wrong – yet so right at the same time. But when I finally went back downstairs, Martin was fast asleep on the settee. I prodded him a couple of times but,' she looked at Sam, 'I couldn't wake him so after about ten minutes I went home.

'When I next saw him, either he remembered and didn't want to admit it or he didn't remember a thing, because he never mentioned it to me ever again. There wasn't any awkward moments either as he wondered if I'd bring it up. I don't think he even knew what he'd done.

'I was upset but relieved at the same time. I can remember imagining what would have happened if he really did have feelings for me. How terrible would that be – the old cliché, my best friend's father? And despite what you think of me now, I would never want to hurt you, so I never told you. And I never told him.

'Two months later he died, and a week later I found out I was pregnant.' Louise paused to see if Sam would speak. When she didn't, she carried on.

'I'm not proud of what I did but you must see that I did it to protect you. Martin was your rock. You'd always looked up to him and I didn't want to change that over one stupid, childish moment of mine. He was drunk and even at eighteen, I took advantage of him. I'm sorry.'

Sam still didn't speak but there were tears pouring down her face. Louise started to cry too.

'I know I'm a selfish bitch,' she cried, 'but I only did what I thought was best. Maybe if Martin had been alive, I might have told him. Maybe I would always have kept it secret … I don't know.'

'And my dad was definitely Charley's father?'

'Yes. I wasn't sleeping with anyone else then.'

'I …' Sam struggled to speak. 'I think you should leave.'

Louise shook her head. 'Not until this is sorted. You're my best friend and I want—'

'But, don't you see? You've ruined everything! Every good memory I had has been tarnished.'

'No!'

'You took advantage of him and betrayed me because you were jealous of the relationship I had with Reece.'

'You're wrong. I didn't take advantage of Martin because I was jealous. I was eighteen, unlucky in love and just wanted a bit of fun. Unfortunately for me, I got a reminder of that one night of fun for the rest of my life.' Louise swallowed. 'Still, I have Charley and, despite our ups and downs, I love her so much.'

When it was clear that Sam wasn't going to say anything else, Louise stood up. 'I'll see you tomorrow then. That is, if I still have a job?'

'Of course you have a job!' Sam raised her voice. 'What do you take me for?'

'Well I wouldn't blame you if you never wanted to see me again, so . . .'

Louise left, closing the door quietly behind her, hoping her tears wouldn't fall until she was away from the house. But by the time she got to the bottom of the drive, she could hardly see.

She hoped that Sam would forgive her eventually. Because although she had her daughter back, she might have lost her best friend now. And that hurt more than she'd ever thought possible.

* * *

Sam burst into tears again as soon as Louise left. For years, she had thought Charley was the mistake of a drunken one night stand. She'd thought the father would be someone that Louise couldn't remember. Even when she'd caught Charley smiling, or laughing in a way that seemed familiar, never once had she imagined she and Charley would share the same father – and that her face resembled Sam's own.

After so many years, the news was bound to come as a shock, a double shock in actual fact. But deep down, she realised why Louise had never told her; why she'd never told Charley either. It was to protect them all. Louise didn't want Sam to bear any malice towards Martin. She didn't want Charley to know because it would have made things awkward. And she didn't want Martin to be ostracised by people – even though, drunk or not drunk, at thirty-four he should have known better than to take advantage of an eighteen-year-old girl.

Some of the things she'd talked over with Charley the other day came back to her. People make mistakes, she'd told her. And maybe it wasn't fair for anyone to judge someone who was so young and found herself pregnant by her best friend's father who died shortly afterwards.

How would she have felt if Louise had told her then? Hell, Sam wondered if she would have even believed her. Would she have accused her of vying for attention, like Louise was always prone to doing? Either way, she knew their friendship would probably have been over. She wouldn't have wanted to see Charley growing up as her father's child. Now, knowing Charley for so long, she realised she was glad of that.

She also wondered if Louise would ever have told them the truth if she hadn't blurted it out that evening. Maybe – maybe not. But it was out now and they'd all just have to make the best of it.

All of them.

Louise got home to find a note from Charley to say she'd slipped over to Sophie's house and would be home for half past eight. Her heart lurched as she thought back to last week and the night her daughter had spent away from her. But since she'd been home, Charley and Sophie had become thick as thieves again and for the past two days, it was as if they'd never fallen out. It was great to hear their laughter around the house once more and it eased the tension as she and Charley both learned to forget the argument and move forward. At least that way Louise could settle, knowing that giving her daughter the freedom to grow, despite wanting to have her close all the time, was good for both of them. She and Charley had had a good chat about Martin too. When Charley had asked why she had never told her the truth, she'd felt selfish all over again.

Shivering, she switched on the gas fire and flopped into the settee. Tears poured from her eyes but she wiped angrily at them. There was no time for self-pity. Louise had known for a long time that she needed to change. It was just so hard to do when she felt she was stuck in a rut.

But she realised lately there was more to life than putting Louise Pellington first. She cared for Charley. She cared for Sam. And she cared for Matt. Three important people in her life – and she had walked all over them to get her own way. Well, not anymore.

From now on, things were going to change. She might not ever be the best mother and she would never make the greatest best-friend-forever but she could improve on what she was and try to make amends.

After all, it was her mistake that had caused the heartache.

Two nights before the wedding, most of the women involved in the big day were round at Sam's house for a girlie night in. Nicci hadn't wanted to have a hen party; she hadn't fancied trawling around the pubs of Hedworth or going out for a meal. Louise hadn't even been able to persuade her to have a night out down at the local pub. But she'd finally succumbed to pressure when Sam suggested getting together at her house. She asked everyone to bring a plate of food and a bottle of something to drink, and the table in the kitchen looked fit to collapse under the weight of cupcakes, sandwiches, mini quiches and pizzas, and numerous nibbles, as well as every type of drink concoction possible.

Despite it being laid out in the kitchen, most of the women were in the living room. Reece, Matt and Ryan had gone

CHAPTER TWENTY-SIX

315

into town to meet Jay and his mates for a low key stag do. Charley had brought a Wii console with her and a dancing game. She'd been teaching her Nan to Zumba for the past half hour.

'Oh, my back is going to be killing me in the morning,' said Sandra, 'and I'm mother of the bride ... I'm supposed to be sophisticated. At this rate, I'll be walking like John Wayne!'

'Me too!' Louise's auntie Marilyn held onto her stomach as she laughed again. 'Oh, I haven't had so much fun in ages. I've got a stitch.'

As the games were swapped over, Nicci decided to join in. She grabbed Ryan's wife, Sarah, and pulled her up too.

'Come on,' she said, a little unsteady on her feet. 'Let's show the young ones how to do it.'

They stood behind Charley and Sophie, poised and ready to start. The music kicked in and they were off. Louise looked on, laughing as Charley and Sophie did a perfect routine to one of Little Mix's songs while Nicci and Sarah bumbled along in hysterics, thrusting hips and waving arms around.

A few minutes later, Louise noticed Sam sidle out of the room. They still weren't speaking properly and despite her intentions to change, she didn't really know what to do to make things better.

When she'd been gone for a while, Louise went to find her. She wasn't anywhere downstairs so she had a look upstairs. From the landing, she noticed Sam's bedroom door slightly ajar. Louise peeped around it.

Sam was sitting on the corner of the bed. There were photos spread over the duvet cover. She guessed they must be of Martin. Louise ached to go to her, to put her arms round her and hug her tightly, but she didn't feel able to intrude. She heard Sam sniff and realised she was crying as she held one of the photos to her chest.

Louise turned to go back downstairs quietly, but a squeaky floorboard gave her away.

Sam looked up, quickly wiping at her eyes.

'I came to see where you were,' Louise said. 'I'm sorry. I was just leaving.'

Sam gathered the photos together and shoved them back in the drawer they'd come from.

'I was just coming,' she said, waltzing past Louise and down the stairs without another word.

Now it was Louise's turn to wipe away tears. After keeping her secret for so long, she had to realise that she might have blown it altogether now it was out. And it made her feel desperately sad.

While the women enjoyed themselves over at Sam's house, Jess sat curled up on the settee. With Nicci and Jay out, it gave her time to sit and think without anyone interrupting her – or making her feel like she was in the way.

But she didn't really want time to think. Because time to think made her realise how much she was dreading the wedding that weekend. She'd give anything not to be a part of it but it was too late to back out. And it was her brother getting married, not someone who she could lie to by faking illness.

She wasn't sure how she was going to get through the day seeing Ryan playing happy families with his wife and daughters when all she wanted was to be happy too. Didn't she deserve a little happiness after all she'd been through? Left holding a baby at the age of twenty-eight, with no father to support them, not even financially as much as emotionally. No man to rely on, to be there for her.

If only she hadn't been asked to be part of the wedding party. It was another adage that the bridesmaid got off with the best man but this time it would be true. How could she have started an affair with Ryan? Talk about bringing it to your own doorstep. She was so ashamed of herself. She'd been looking for someone to blame her baby on and realised that he would be open to persuasion as soon as she saw him again.

Crying now, Jess hugged a cushion to her chest and tried not to think about it anymore. Instead, she looked forward to the day that she would get married and have her own big day like Jay and Nicci, surrounded by family and friends. One day, she would find a man who would love her bump as much as her, maybe even have more kids.

More importantly, she needed to ensure that she found her own man this time rather than think it was okay to steal someone else's.

CHAPTER TWENTY-SEVEN

'Ohmigod!' Louise cried as she opened the curtains the next morning. 'The weather forecast was right. It's been snowing. There must be at least six inches. We're going –'

'It can't be – not today!' Nicci jumped out of bed and joined her sister at the window.

'April Fool!'

Nicci thumped her arm, hard.

'Ow!'

'You nearly gave me a heart attack.'

'Well, that'll teach you to get married on April 1st, you daft mare.' Louise grinned. 'And I can get my own back on you for last night. You snored like a pig.'

Nicci grinned. They stood silent for a moment and then she threw herself back on the bed, laughing.

'I'm getting married today. Can you believe it?'

'Believe it? I can't forget it. It's the only thing I've heard about in weeks since I let it slip.' Louise sat on the edge of the bed as Nicci pulled down the zip to the cover of her dress; smiled as she watched her sister run a hand down the material afterwards.

'I'm so proud of you,' she told her. 'I hope you have a fantastic day today.'

Nicci shuffled back across the bed and gave her a hug.

'Don't worry, big sis,' she soothed. 'You'll find your Prince Charming one day.'

'Now's the time *you* shout April Fool.'

Nicci sighed. 'It wasn't meant as a joke. You never know.'

'Yeah, right. And my bum is blue.'

'It will be if it snows!'

Louise grinned, not really knowing where that saying had come from. Then she sniffed long and hard. Her eyes lit up with anticipation. 'Can you smell that?'

Nicci smiled. 'Bacon!'

'Race you for the first sarnie.'

As if they were teenagers again, they flew down the stairs and into the kitchen. Their dad, Terry, was the one frying the bacon; while their mum was busy buttering toast and making tea.

'Just in time, girls,' she smiled. 'Nicci, you can set the table and—'

Nicci looked puzzled. 'Since when have we set the table for breakfast?'

'Since my youngest daughter decided to get married.' With a warm smile, Sandra slapped her hand away as Nicci tried to grab a piece of toast. 'Do as you're told, Missy, or else ... Louise, go and see where Charley is.'

'It's seven thirty, Mum. She'll still be asleep.'

'Well, get her up then. We have a busy day ahead.'

'Yes, because,' Terry broke out into song, 'you're getting married in five ho-urs. Ding dong the bells are going to CHIME!'

Nicci laughed and then her face was etched in worry. 'Oh, I hope everything goes all right today. I've waited so long for this moment.'

'Everything will be fine.' Sandra placed a pot of tea onto the table. 'And besides, something has to go wrong on the day – it's tradition.'

'It's also a tradition that the bride eats a lovely big fry up.' Terry slid the bacon and eggs on to plates and handed one to Nicci. 'Get that down you, my lovely.'

Later that morning over at the market, Sam stood mentally ticking off her list, scrutinising everything to make sure nothing was out of place or hadn't been done. She removed a rogue piece of cotton from the tablecloth at the wedding table and smiled. It all looked so special. The wedding party wouldn't know but they would be sitting at several trestle tables covered in cream material, gold tassles hanging from a runner that ran the whole length and down the sides, almost touching the floor. Two chairs at its middle had been covered too, for the bride and groom.

She sat down on Nicci's seat and surveyed what everyone had worked hard to create. Gone was the market hall and in its place was a spectacular wedding room. All the junk had been moved to the stock room, leaving them ample space for eight circular tables set out for guests. Each table had mini chocolate wedding fancies for the women, miniature bottles

of whisky for the men. Gold and cream helium balloon deco-
rations graced the centres. The places were set and she was
waiting on Mr Adams bringing in the food. The wine glasses
shined and awaited the drink. There was a space left in the
middle of the floor which would do as a makeshift dance
floor and a local DJ had set up in readiness at the far end of
the room. The only noise at the moment was coming from
the clink of glassware as the bar was set up to her right.

Sam prayed it would all go well for Nicci and Jay. They
were a lovely couple and doted on each other. She realised
she and Reece must have been the same all those years ago,
imagining they'd be together forever. She wished she knew
the secret to keeping it that way. But for her, there was no
going back.

Taking one last look around, with great satisfaction and
anticipation of what was to come, Sam left to get changed for
the wedding ceremony. Things might not have gone to plan
for Nicci but everyone had certainly done her proud today.
She couldn't wait to see her face.

It was half past eleven. Upstairs in Nicci's old bedroom, the
chatter was loud and the champagne was flowing. The wom-
en were adding the final preparations to ensure everything
was just perfect for the big day.

Louise and Sam helped Nicci step into her wedding dress
and then fasten it up. The off-white dress was understated

perfection; long and sleeveless satin with a v-neckline pleated bodice. The skirt was A-line and cut on the bias.

'At least you don't have to breathe in to fit in your dress,' sighed Louise, zipping it up easily and fastening the hook and eye.

'That's because I've been on the wedding nerves diet,' Nicci laughed.

'Oh, don't worry,' said Sarah, running a brush through her daughter Abigail's hair as Amelia, her other daughter, tried to do her own. 'Besides you've got the old traditional good luck charms, haven't you? Something old, something new, something borrowed and something blue?'

'Have I?' Nicci turned round with a worried look on her face.

'Sure you have,' said Louise. 'Something old is Jay.'

Nicci's mouth dropped open before she grinned.

'Something new is your dress,' said Sam, running a hand down the front of it to smooth it out.

'Something borrowed is your necklace,' said Sandra, doing the same to the back. 'Borrowed from your mum.' Nicci fingered the thin gold chain with its diamond pendant.

'And something blue is this.' Nicci lifted up the skirt of her dress, much to the annoyance of Sam and Sandra, and snapped the elastic on her lacy garter. 'Perfect!'

Charley's hair was piled up in a bun, tendrils hanging down by her ears to frame her face; tiny white flowers weaved in here and there. In her pale pink dress, she looked angelic.

'You look like a magical princess,' Louise smiled affectionately.

Charley grinned at her. 'I look more like a fairy. I can't wait to wear the new dress you bought me this evening.'

Sarah was helping the twins into their clothes, tying ballet shoe ribbons round two pairs of fidgety legs. They each wore halos of flowers matching their three-quarter length dresses with a huge bow at the centre of the back. Cream tights and fluffy angora cardigans finished their outfits off completely. She gave them both a hug before showing them off to everyone.

'Now, that's what fairies look like,' muttered Charley. Louise giggled.

Over in the corner of the room, Jess stood quietly, trying to get ready alone. She didn't want to join in even if they had let her; she wanted to blend into the background. It was hurtful to see Sarah and the twins.

She stepped into a simple pink dress that stopped at her ankles. A month ago, it would have fitted perfectly but due to the baby bump she was now showing, the dress had to be let out at the last minute and was stretched to its maximum. Still, it was only for one day.

Jess put her hand around her back to pull up the zip. But it was a struggle to do it by herself.

'Here, let me help,' Sarah offered, coming over to her.

Oh no, not her of all people, thought Jess.

'Oh, it's fine,' she said blushing crimson.

'It won't take me a minute.' Sarah pulled up the zip and turned Jess round to face her. She stared at her for a moment, eyes brimming with tears. Then she smiled.

'You look gorgeous,' she said.

'I look fat and pregnant,' said Jess.

'No. You look radiant because you're pregnant.' Sarah paused for a moment and then spoke quietly. 'Was it you?'

Jess decided she didn't want to lie again. Besides, she'd been deceitful and Sarah deserved to know the truth. She nodded.

Sarah's eyes dropped and then met Jess's again. 'Is it his baby?'

'No.' Jess shook her head this time. 'It was only the once or twice.'

'Was it once or twice?'

'Well, I—'

'Oh, what does it matter anyway? It's another once or twice too much again as far as I'm concerned. Ryan is good-looking and he has the gift of the gab. You weren't the first woman to fall for his charms.'

The two women looked at each other. There was no need for any more words, even though Jess knew that Ryan wasn't the only one to blame.

'Mummy, Abby needs a wee and my ribbon has come undone,' Amelia shouted from the other side of the room.

Sarah took a deep breath and held her head high. With one last look at Jess, she gave her a faint smile before reaching down for her daughter's hands.

'Come on then, poppet,' she said. 'Let's get you sorted. We can't have any mishaps, today of all days.'

Before she moved away, Jess reached for Sarah's arm. 'I'm so sorry,' she said. 'And, for what's it worth, I've learned my lesson. I just never saw what this would do to you, and your family.'

'I don't blame you,' Sarah replied. 'I blame Ryan.' She paused. 'Still, that won't be my problem soon. Okay, okay. I'm coming!'

As Sarah was dragged away by an impatient Amelia, Jess stood alone again. She wanted to cry but knew she needed to stay strong. This wasn't the time or the place for self-pity. Besides, she didn't want to stress herself out. She knew it wouldn't be good for the baby.

She cradled her bump and looked around the room – grandmother, mother, sister, niece, auntie, all intent on making this day special. And she would be Nicci's sister-in-law, despite trying to scupper the wedding when she'd come back to Hedworth.

If she changed, she had a loving family to bring her baby into. And she needed them. Bringing up a child on her own would be hard enough, she could do far worse than settle in Hedworth again, surrounded by family – and maybe even make some friends. She could make a fresh start.

She glanced at her own mother, Maureen, who was laughing at something Sandra had said to her. Maureen caught her eye, smiled and beckoned her over. Jess paused for a moment. She had two choices. Either she joined in and enjoyed the day or she sat back and sulked, causing an atmosphere.

She decided to choose the former.

CHAPTER TWENTY-EIGHT

An hour later, the cars arrived to take them to the wedding. Amidst lots of chatter and laughter, they all took their places and set off. At the registry office, Nicci waited for Jay to arrive, nervously playing with the diamond pendant on the chain at her neck. But he was early, much to her surprise.

Terry Pellington walked his youngest daughter down the tiny aisle to where Jay was waiting to receive her. Matt and Ryan stood by Jay's side, Ryan keeping his eyes ahead but Matt kept glancing over at Louise. Sam smiled when he caught her eyes and he grinned back at her.

Neither Nicci nor Jay fluffed up their lines, Louise and Sam failed to keep their tears in, laughing at each other when they spotted they were both crying. Both sets of parents smiled and cried too.

In what seemed to be no longer than a blink of an eye, Nicci became Mrs Worthington. Photo after photo was taken – Jay joked that his jaw was aching from posing for pictures. Then, with the formalities over, the bride and groom climbed into their wedding car and headed off to the reception. There was only Nicci who didn't know where they were going.

'Can't you tell me, Jay?' she pleaded as they sat in the back of the car, sharing a bottle of champagne. She giggled as the bubbles went up her nose. 'I promise I won't tell anyone and I can wear a surprised look.'

'Certainly not,' he admonished, sliding a hand up her leg. 'I hear brides wear garters, let me see.'

'Stop changing the subject.' Nicci snapped his hand away playfully.

Jay grinned. Leaning in close to her, he kissed her on the nose. 'I love you, Mrs Worthington,' he said. 'But I don't know where we're going either. All I know is that it will be very special. But first, we have to call in at the market.'

'The market?' Nicci wrinkled up her nose. 'What on earth for?'

'Sam has something for you but she doesn't want everyone at the reception to see.'

'You'd better not be planning me a party down the aisle,' she cried, 'or else I'll be very cross.'

'Don't be daft.' Jay held his nerve, trying not to give the game away. 'Only the best for my wife.'

Nicci beamed and then her hand moved to cover her mouth. 'I think I'm going to be sick.'

'Thanks a bunch!'

'No, it's nothing to do with that. My stomach is churning over and over.'

'You're not actually going to be sick, are you?' Jay looked a little concerned. 'Because if you are, you'll start me off too.'

'I'm fine. Just a little nervous.' Nicci glanced at him shyly.

'What about me?' said Jay. 'What if I have a fit of giggles when I'm saying my speech or some squeaky voice comes out? Or worse than that, faint like they do on those clips on *You've Been Framed.*'

'Which reminds me, I need to make sure I remember how to record a video on my phone, just in case,' Nicci teased. 'I can't miss an opportunity to make £250.'

Jay's eyes widened in disbelief. 'Seriously?' he asked.

'Of course ... not!' Nicci gave him a kiss this time. 'It will all turn out okay,' she reassured him.

'They're here!' cried Ryan as he ran into the hall where everyone had rushed to after the service. 'Take your places, and, remember kids, be quiet!'

'You need to be quiet!' Louise whispered loudly as she punched him in his arm. 'She'll be able to hear you shouting.'

'Sorry!'

Louise turned to Sam and rolled her eyes. Then she frowned when she saw her friend's worried face. 'What's wrong?'

'I'm so nervous,' said Sam. 'What if Nicci hates it?'

'She won't.' Louise shook her head, her straightened hair in curls shaking about. 'How could you not like it? You have the place looking beautiful. No one would recognise it.'

Sam turned back to see that it was indeed a sight to behold. All in all, everyone had made a tremendous effort. And now they were lined up either side of the doors. Family, and friends from the market stalls, who had given their time and their wares for free to make Nicci and Jay's big day perfect.

Sam felt herself welling up again. But as the door handle went down, everyone in the room froze.

The door opened and there was a squeal.

'Congratulations!' rang out around the room.

'This is amazing!' Nicci turned to Jay wide-eyed, and when she saw him grinning, she clicked in. 'You *did* know, didn't you?'

Jay shrugged and she flew into his arms. Afterwards, she turned round and round in circles taking everything in, before running over to greet her family.

When she got to Sam and Nicci, she pulled them both close. 'I can't believe you did all this for us. Thank you, thank you, thank you!'

'It is amazing,' said Louise, giving Nicci's hand a quick squeeze.

Once the wedding meal was served, and everyone's glass had been filled, Sam realised she could finally relax. Only the evening to go and it had indeed all worked out perfectly on the day.

As usual, Matt and Ryan were like a double act with their pre-rehearsed routine as best men. They had the bride and groom's family and friends roaring with laughter in no time as they relayed anecdote after anecdote about Jay – luckily, keeping them all clean. They even managed to remember to thank the bridesmaids as tradition expected them to. Ryan then went on to have the last word.

'And finally, may I say a special thank you to *my* wife.' He raised his glass in salute to Sarah. 'Not only does she do a fantastic job of raising our daughters, she also looks after me – and that's a hell of a thing to ask anyone to do.'

Everyone laughed.

'To Sarah Pellington.'

As family and guests toasted her health, Sarah smiled, but inside she was fuming.

'And what about you, Matt?' Jay shouted up. 'Any special lady in your life?'

'Sure there is.' Matt looked at the other end of the table to where Louise was sitting.

As all eyes in the room followed his gaze, Louise looked on in bewilderment. What did Matt mean by that?

When everyone had finished, and Nicci and Jay were doing the rounds chatting to their guests, Ryan joined Sarah at the end of the table where she'd sat with the twins. Sandra had taken them off her hands for a while, no doubt enjoying the opportunity to show the guests what beautiful grandchildren she had.

'Was I good or was I good?' Ryan asked with a smirk as he sat down next to her.

'Oh, you're always good, aren't you?' Sarah spoke quietly, not wanting to bring attention to them.

Ryan sat down with a frown. 'What's up?'

'I've just had enough of you.'

'Give me a break.' Ryan reached for a half full glass of wine that had been left on the table and took a sip. 'I've only just sat down.'

'I mean it, Ryan,' Sarah hissed. 'I want you to leave. I want you out of the house.'

Ryan was about to take another sip, but stopped, glass in mid-air.

'I know about Jess.' Sarah watched the colour drain from his face. 'I know that it isn't your baby – thank the lord – but it still doesn't excuse the fact that you slept with her.'

'I—'

'Don't you dare think of lying!' She held up her hand.

Ryan gulped. 'But it was only the once or twice!'

Sarah laughed inwardly at his choice of words, exactly the same as Jess had chosen earlier. She still didn't want to know exactly how many times it had been. Because, sitting here with him, Sarah realised that she wasn't actually concerned.

'It's over now anyway,' Ryan added.

'I don't care!' Sarah took the glass from him and knocked back the rest of the wine. She placed the glass down onto the table and stood up. Not wanting to make a scene, her tone was quiet but forceful. 'I want you out of the house by next weekend.'

'Wait!' Ryan grabbed her hand as she began to walk away. 'Please. I can explain.'

'No!' Sarah snatched it away. 'I don't want to play happy families anymore. It's too late.'

'Sarah!'

But Sarah didn't stop.

Around seven thirty, the music started up and as evening guests began to filter in, Nicci and Jay took to the floor for their first dance as a married couple. To the sounds of 'Thinking out Loud', by Ed Sheeran, people clapped, oohed and aahed and took more photos. It was a magical moment for everyone involved in the day.

Over at her table, Sam sat with Reece, grinning like a madwoman. She glanced around the room to see all the people she worked with, the ones who had made this day possible. Geoff Adams was chatting to Malcolm. Melissa was over at the bar with Clara, laughing at something that Duncan, the delivery man, was telling them. Marilyn stood with Sally from Cupcake Delights, waiting to dance. All in all, it had been perfect.

Louise came over and sat down.

'Why can't I have that?' She sighed, pointing at the bride and groom as they smooched in the middle of the floor with their friends and family surrounding them. By this point, several other couples had taken to the floor too.

'Marriage isn't all it's cracked up to be,' said Reece. Then he glanced at Sam guiltily. 'I didn't mean to say that out loud.'

Despite his insinuation, Sam grinned. Before she had time to come back with something jokey, Matt raced over, grabbed Louise's hand and led her onto the dance floor. Sam realised this might be the right time to let Reece know how she felt.

'It's not working for you, is it?' she asked.

Reece shook his head. 'I'm sorry.'

'Don't be. It's not working for me either.' She smiled, for the first time ever feeling shy around her husband. They sat in silence why they each digested the other's words.

Reece reached for her hand finally and gave it a quick squeeze.

'Will you be going back to Sheffield?' Sam asked.

'Is that all right with you?'

She nodded. 'When were you planning on leaving?'

'In the morning. Is it okay if I stay one more night?'

'Well, I'm hardly likely to kick you out right now.'

Reece leant across and ever so tenderly kissed her on the lips. 'I'll miss you,' he said.

'No,' Sam smiled through her tears. 'No, you won't.'

Matt twirled Louise around in his arms as they made their way to the makeshift dance floor.

Louise threw her head back and laughed. 'I take it you want to dance, Mister.'

'Mmm – hmm.'

'Just the one dance?'

Matt shook his head.

'Two?'

He shook his head again.

'More than two?'

A nod this time.

'I'm not sure my feet will take much more. These heels are killing me.'

'Then let me sweep you off your feet.'

'Ooh, get you, you smooth talker,' she teased.

With a nod of his head at the DJ, the music changed to a slower pace and Matt cleared his throat. 'Maybe it's time I just came out with what I really want to say.'

Louise frowned. 'I thought you just did.'

'I want to ask you something.'

'I'm not covering for you on the stall while you swan off somewhere on holiday, if that's what you're after. You know I need to stay in Sam's good books. I've caused her enough trouble lately and –'

'Can you just shut up for one minute?' he whispered into her ear. Before she could protest, Matt silenced her with a kiss. Louise resisted at first, mainly out of surprise, and then melted into his embrace.

Once they stopped, Matt reached into his waistcoat pocket and pulled out a small, black box.

Louise's eyes widened as she flipped it open to reveal a band of gold with a collection of stones.

'Louise Pellington, I think I've wasted far too much time just being your friend when I really want more. And I know there'd normally be a long time while we went out with each other before getting into a serious relationship. But I want to be a permanent part of your life right now. I love you so much. I want to wake up with you. I want to fall asleep with you. Hell, you need someone to keep you on the straight and narrow. And I want – I want … Louise, will you marry me?'

Louise's mouth gaped open. Did Matt just …?

The music went lower still and everyone's eyes were on her. Matt dropped to his knees, right there in the middle of the dance floor.

'Will you marry me?' he repeated.

'Ohmigod!' Louise squealed.

'That's not the answer I was looking for.' But Matt was smiling.

'Yes!' Louise pulled him to standing and flung her arms around his neck. 'Yes! Yes! One hundred billion trillion times, yes, I will marry you!'

The room broke out into applause. Louise and Matt grinned at each other like two five year olds sharing a secret. Then there was no time for grinning as Matt kissed her again. She vaguely recalled someone shouting 'get a room' before they stopped.

Giddy by the euphoria of her proposal, Louise searched Charley out with her eyes. She was by the side of the dance floor with Sophie, waving at them. Louise beckoned her over and she ran into her arms.

'I was waiting for you to finish with the necking first,' Charley shrieked, hugging her tightly. 'I can't believe it! After all this time, you're getting married.'

Louise feigned hurt. 'Didn't you think anyone would have your old mum?'

'I mean that I can't believe after all this time you two have finally got together.' Charley gave Matt a hug too.

'You knew how I felt about him?' said Louise.

'Mum, *everyone* knew how you felt about him and *everyone* knew how he felt about you.'

'Really?'

Charley nodded fervently. 'Does this mean that I get to be bridesmaid again? Because if it does, please let me pick my own dress. I don't want to look like an overgrown fairy at your wedding.'

Louise grinned and they hugged. Behind Charley, she spotted Sam. She was holding out her arms. Louise rushed into them. They hugged each other tightly, tears pouring down their faces.

'Can you believe he proposed to me?' Louise spoke finally, wiping at her eyes.

'He should have done it years ago,' Sam told her. 'I've always thought you were made for each other. But you wouldn't listen to anyone.'

'I know, I know, I'm a bolshie cow. It's definitely where Charley gets her stubborn streak from.'

'Oh, I don't know so much. I think she takes after her father for that.'

Louise grinned. Sam wouldn't have brought Martin into the conversation unless she had forgiven her.

They embraced again.

'So that's the last time I have to save you from the clutches of Rob Masters, then?' Sam added.

'Oi, you cheeky cat.'

'You're supposed to say thank you!'

Louise glanced over her shoulder to where Matt was being congratulated by her mum and dad. 'Thank you,' she smiled. 'Not just for that, but for everything. For being here for me, for putting up with me, for standing by me through thick and thin. I don't know what I would have done without you.'

'It's been a pleasure – well, most of it.' Sam grinned too. 'And, anyway, that's what friends are for.'

A LETTER FROM MARCIE

First of all, I want to say a huge thank you for choosing to read *That's What Friends Are For*. I hope you enjoyed getting to know the characters as well as I did. I had so much fun writing it. In my next book, *Broken Heels,* you'll hear from more characters who live in the fictional city of Hedworth. I hope you'll continue to enjoy getting to know them too.

Many thanks to anyone who has emailed me, messaged me, chatted to me on Facebook or Twitter and told me how much you've enjoyed reading my books. I've been genuinely blown away with all kinds of niceness and support from you all. A writer's job is a lonely one but I feel I truly have friends everywhere.

If you did enjoy *That's What Friends Are For*, I would be forever grateful if you'd write a review. I'd love to hear what you think, and it can also help other readers discover one of my books for the first time. Or maybe you can recommend it to your friends and family …

You can sign up to receive an email whenever I have a new book out here:

www.bookouture.com/marcie-steele

love, Mel Sherratt (Marcie) x

Keep in touch!
www.facebook.com/MarcieSteeleauthor
www.twitter.com/marcie_steele

Lightning Source UK Ltd.
Milton Keynes UK
UKOW06f2313110116

266228UK00019B/778/P